BLUE RIDGE
CALLING

OLIVIA NEAL

Blue Ridge Calling
Text copyright © 2025 Olivia Neal
Edited by Aimee Hardy

Published in North America, Australia, and Europe by RIZE.
Visit Running Wild Press at www.runningwildpublishing.com/
rize, Educators, librarians, book clubs (as well as the eternally
curious), go to www.runningwildpublishing.com/rize.

ISBN (pbk) 978-1-963869-32-3
ISBN (ebook) 978-1-963869-31-6

To
my fellow Southern queers.
We're here,
and
we're not going anywhere.

CONTENTS

PROLOGUE

S am looked up at the stars through the treetops. Usually, he could tell which direction he was going from the sky. The sun, the moon, the stars. He had spent so much time in these woods—sometimes he could just close his eyes and feel which way to go.

But now, he was lost.

The stars seemed to blink in and out of the sky like a flickering candle. The howling wind swept through the trees, but he couldn't tell which way the sound was coming from. When he stuck his finger in the air, he felt nothing.

When he stopped to listen, he could hear voices on the wind. Some were baleful and almost human, some were malevolent and impossible to understand. Sam kept walking, hoping the sound would die down.

He stepped between two trees, hoping desperately that a trail would appear in front of him. No such luck. But now, the sky seemed to brighten, like it was almost dawn. Only seconds ago it had been dark as midnight. He looked down at his wrist before he remembered that he'd lost his watch. For some reason, he doubted it would work here anyway.

These woods had been such a comfort to him. In the last two years, he had spent more time wandering the Appalachian Trail than he had in his own home. But now, they felt alien to him. Not like he was in a different place, but like the woods themselves had changed overnight.

His sister would be worried. He always came home when he said he would. Always. The night their mom died, the worst part was the waiting. They both had a feeling something was wrong, but they just kept waiting for her to come home. The minutes felt like hours. He would never put Sage through that again. If he needed to be gone longer than he said, he would call.

Sam patted the back of his jeans for his cell. Nothing was there. He tried to remember how long he had been out here. He had promised Sage he would be home by Sunday, but he couldn't remember what day it was. Where had he started? What trails had he taken? He couldn't even say which park he was in.

Suddenly, it was night again. He looked up at the sky and saw a different set of stars than before.

All his reading and research had only gotten him so far. These woods seemed to sense that he knew too much and had turned him around on purpose.

They were old. The Appalachian mountains were ancient; older than the Rockies, older than the Alps. They had seen species come and go like phases of the moon. Humans were only the latest creature to wander through their trees. Sam imagined they did not take kindly to being mapped and carved and separated by highways. Their anger pulsed through the trees and seeped up through the mossy dirt.

This time of night, he could usually hear animals for miles, but for once, they were quiet. The voices had faded and the only sound was the wind blowing through the branches. He couldn't even hear his own footsteps. He looked down and only saw fog around his ankles.

After years of reading ghost stories that took place in these mountains, he was finally starting to feel like he could understand them. This place was magical and unknown. It waited and watched. Spirits joined the trees and started watching, too. Even without the sound of the forest creatures, Sam could feel eyes on him.

He stopped walking. Every direction looked the same. His pockets were empty; no compass. Wandering was only getting him more lost. He wanted to call for someone, but he knew no one would hear him. And who would he call? Sage was fifty miles away. His dad couldn't be counted on anymore. And his mom was gone. He was all alone out there.

From the wind in the trees, he thought he heard a voice—clearer and sharper than the cacophony that had thundered through the valley before. It sounded familiar, but he couldn't quite place it. Sam took a deep breath and stepped further into the woods.

CHAPTER 1

The summer started—like every summer before it—with a party.

Each year, the senior class of Oakcrest Academy threw a bonfire at an abandoned overlook to celebrate graduation. Embers flickered into the sky above a sprawling view of the valley below, including the small collection of lights that made up their town of Pinebrook, North Carolina. The mountains stretched on for miles in the distance, but in the dark, all they could see was the line where the glowing windows of houses turned into the bright pinpricks of stars.

Kora had been to three of these bonfires already, one for each year that she had completed at Oakcrest, but this time, she was the one being celebrated. It seemed like her entire graduating class of forty-four students—as well as a hefty number of underclassmen—were gathered around the giant, roaring fire.

Someone had set up a foldable table with bottles of cheap vodka and chasers. There were sleeves of plastic cups, but Oakcrest taught their students that wasting single-use plastic was a cardinal sin. Most of the people around the fire were drinking rudimentary cocktails out of reusable water bottles, camping thermoses, and canteens.

Kora sipped on her vodka cranberry. She had brought cranberry juice from home and contributed it to the table, and she was very glad, because the only other option besides flavored liquor was a suspiciously sugary-smelling Jungle Juice.

While her classmates played games and drank and celebrated, Kora sat alone on a log by the fire. During the day, it was already warm enough for shorts, so her knees were exposed to the heat of the flame.

Across the fire from her, two juniors she only sort of knew were sitting in the same camping chair making out. She looked down at her shoes to avoid accidentally making eye contact.

Her secondhand Doc Martens—her prized possessions, a miracle thrift store find—were dusted with red clay dirt. She tried wiping them off, but it was only smearing the dirt into the creases. She gave up, pulled her long, unruly curls over one shoulder and began to braid them. It was a habit when she didn't know what else to do with her hands. When she finished, she pulled the braid out and started again.

Kora's best friend Sage, who would be going into her senior year in the fall, was already well acquainted with the mysterious Jungle Juice and plopped down unsteadily onto the log next to her. Sage said something, but between the crowd, the crackling of the bonfire, and music coming from a small, scratchy speaker, Kora couldn't hear her. She cupped her hand over her ear.

"I said," shouted Sage, her cheeks flushed, "where's Connor?"

Kora leaned forward and rested her chin on her hand. She did know where Connor was—he was standing about twenty feet away, talking to some other senior about how their economics final went—but she wished she didn't. Ever since Kora had broken up with Connor, her boyfriend of two years, seeing him opened up a pit in her stomach that was starting to feel like an ulcer. Guilt and nostalgia combined to make her feel faint and nauseous whenever they were near each other.

"Don't know," she yelled back. They could talk about it when Sage was sober.

Kora nursed her drink and stared into the fire. It was so hot and bright that it hurt to look directly at it, like a miniature sun embedded into the cliffside. Flames consumed the easy kindling of empty beer boxes and small branches while the large logs were reduced to coals.

When Kora looked away, Sage was off dancing with one of the other juniors. A few years ago, this would have been unimaginable. Being on the school's championship-winning swim team meant that she was on a strict diet and woke up at 5 a.m. almost every morning. Sage used to say she thought teenagers who drank were losing valuable brain cells that they could be using to pass their chem tests.

But then her mom died. It had been almost two years, and it was becoming increasingly clear that the Sage who had existed before was gone forever. The new Sage got drunk with seniors, slept through swim practice, and nearly flunked Honors History.

To most people, she was the same—still wicked smart, studious, and more disciplined than Kora could ever hope to be. Same pencil-straight blonde hair, same swimmer's build, same icy gray-blue eyes that drove fear into the hearts of her Academic Decathlon competitors. She was several inches shorter than Kora, but if she didn't know her as well as she did, Kora would be afraid of her, too.

But this Sage just didn't care as much, seemingly about anything. School, swimming, college applications—she was just doing those things out of habit. Her heart wasn't in it anymore.

At least she was having fun. Kora watched as Sage twirled around and laughed, spilling most of her drink and licking it from her arm.

Kora smiled, until she remembered she would be the one taking care of her friend later that night.

Usually, the seniors were the ones to overdo it, seeing as how it was their celebration, but Kora didn't really feel like partying, and she didn't want to lose control with Connor around. It was bad enough that she had dumped her high school sweetheart two weeks before the end of their senior year. She didn't want to rub it in by getting drunk and making out with a cheerleader in front of him.

She also didn't want to get drunk and try to make out with Connor. That would make things much, much messier.

Without Sage as a buffer, the crowd felt uncomfortably close, and she started to get too warm by the fire. Kora finished off her drink and headed for the table. A large jug labeled "Earth Sauce" was filled with water, and she poured it into her mug. Somebody had brought marshmallows to make s'mores, and she popped one into her mouth without bothering to roast it.

In the distance, Kora heard the roar of a motorcycle. She shuddered. Driving on these twisting mountain roads at night was already a risk, but on a motorcycle, it was asking to drive over a cliff.

Kora felt a familiar twinge of grief as she remembered the car accident that had killed Sage's mother. It was just starting to hurt a little less whenever Kora thought of her. She and Sage had known each other their whole lives because their moms had been friends before they were born. Losing Sage's mother had been like losing her own.

From this far away, the fire just warmed the small of her back while the cool late-spring air raised the hair on her arms. She shuddered again, this time from the breeze.

"I'd offer you my jacket," said a familiar voice from behind her, "but I know you don't like this one."

Kora smiled without turning around. "Is it the windbreaker?"

Connor stepped up to the table next to her, the nylon of his jacket crinkling as his sleeve brushed her arm. She elbowed him gently. Even facing away from the fire, his hazel eyes lit up as he poured himself a screwdriver.

"Still worrying about your vitamin C levels?" Kora said, smirking.

"You know my mom," he said. "Imparting her anxieties onto her children is like a sport to her."

Kora's heart squeezed in her chest. She had spent nearly every day with Connor's family for the last two years, and the weight of everything she'd lost through this breakup kept piling up.

"How is your mom?" she asked, trying to keep the hurt out of her voice.

"She misses you," said Connor, clearly not trying as hard. "We all do."

He looked up at her as he took a sip of his drink. Kora suddenly wasn't cold anymore, and the back of her neck was starting to sweat.

"I miss her too," said Kora, before looking down at the table.

"Kora—" he said, his voice melancholy. Before he could finish, Sage crashed into the table between them.

"Connor," she said, sloppily grabbing each of his shoulders with her hands. "We're playing flip cup, and I need your mad flipping skills. Melanie's getting on my nerves, and she needs to be taken down a peg."

He started to object, but Sage pushed him toward a group of friends who sat in a circle and used a tree stump as a makeshift table. When Connor acquiesced and sat down, Sage turned back, and Kora mouthed *Thank you*. Sage winked with obvious difficulty and took her place in the circle.

Kora turned back to her water and noticed that her hands were shaking. She couldn't remember the last time Connor made her that nervous. When they were first dating maybe, but even then, they were so comfortable together. Everything was so easy with him. Now, things were decidedly not. She wondered again if she had made a mistake throwing away the only thing in her life that felt natural.

As she tried to steady herself, her mug slipped off the edge of the table and rolled into the dirt, the water turning the ground beneath it into mud. She was about to turn on her phone's flashlight to look for it when someone emerged from the woods to pick it up.

"Had a few too many?" said the stranger. It was a girl, a little older than Kora, with straight black hair down to her chin and several tattoos on her bare arms. A muscle tee exposed a good stretch of her torso and revealed another tattoo on her ribs.

"No, actually," said Kora. "Just one, so I have no excuse."

The girl wiped the dirty mug on her dark jeans and placed it back on the table. "In that case, why don't I pour you another?" she asked, picking up the vodka and holding it over the mug as a question. Kora nodded.

After four years at a tiny school in a small town, Kora could name every single person at the party. She knew their siblings' names, their summer jobs, what years they had braces. But this girl was new. The fire made her skin glow like it was lit from underneath, and her smile was a little bit crooked.

"Who's your date?" Kora asked. While the girl poured her another vodka cranberry, the lean contour of her bicep revealed the most prominent of her tattoos, some kind of long animal skull with flowers and mushrooms sprouting from it. The artwork was beautiful, like something from an old book.

"Who says I have a date?" There was that crooked smile again, like it was flickering between a smirk and a genuine grin.

"Well, I don't know you, which means you don't go to Oakcrest," said Kora, taking a sip of the drink. "And I don't know how you would have found out about this if you weren't someone's date."

"I'm a tattoo apprentice. A client I worked on today told me about it." She pointed behind her at Amber Summers, who had her forearm wrapped in a plastic bandage.

Kora made a face, remembering her brief and humiliating fling with Amber in the 10th grade. "I'm guessing the invitation came with a lot of batted eyelashes."

The new girl laughed. "It's hard to flirt with someone while they're stabbing you with needles, but she managed."

Kora took another sip of her drink. "So I guess that answers my question about your date."

"I wouldn't say that. I just like a good fire." As she said this, the new girl's eyes flashed with the reflection of the flames, and even from this distance, Kora could feel the warmth spreading up her bare legs.

"I'm Kora," she said.

"Hunter."

Behind her, Kora could hear the sound of Connor and Sage cheering while the rest of the group groaned. She didn't turn around to see what had happened.

"Where are you apprenticing?" Kora asked, her eyes poring over the dark linework on Hunter's shoulder and the strip of her side that peeked through her shirt.

"Cabin Fever on Main."

"Oh, I went there last summer. Is Jeb still there?"

"Yep, he's my boss. What did you get?"

Kora turned around and pulled her denim jacket far enough off her shoulders to show Hunter the bouquet of delicate flowers just below the base of her neck. Hunter stepped closer to see them in the dim light of the fire.

"Nice linework," she said. She held out her hand so that Kora could see it and said, "May I?" Kora nodded.

Hunter traced the flowers with her fingers, starting from the top and moving down the spine. Kora shivered, and Hunter pulled her fingers away.

She turned back around and pulled her jacket back over her shoulders, silently wishing she could have controlled her reaction to Hunter's cold fingers. They left a tingling sensation where they had touched her skin.

"I haven't seen a lot of single needle tattoos yet," said Hunter, still thinking over the process.

"Maybe you can do my next one," Kora said. Her voice came out softer and more hopeful than she intended it.

"Come by the shop sometime," Hunter said, grinning. "I'm sure I could squeeze you in."

Before Kora could answer, Sage's arms wrapped around her from behind, leaning her whole weight onto Kora's back.

"Okay, I'm ready to go home," she moaned. "We won, but Melanie is even more annoying when she's trashed."

Kora spun around, careful to keep Sage from falling as she shifted her weight. When she had steadied them both, she saw Connor watching them from the circle, his eyes moving between Kora and Hunter, assessing the new girl with the same curiosity Kora had. When he saw how close they were standing together, his curiosity turned sullen. Kora looked away.

"Come on," said Kora, pulling Sage's arm around her to prop her up as she moved them toward the car. "You're sleeping on the couch tonight. With a bucket." Sage laughed and stumbled over a tree branch.

"Need help with that?" Hunter asked, already taking Sage's other arm over her shoulder.

"Thanks," said Kora.

Together, they managed to walk back to the car and pour Sage into the backseat. Kora rolled the window down and turned around to see Hunter already walking back toward the party. Her stride was confident and sturdy, no hesitation. Kora watched her walk up to a small, beat-up motorcycle and climb onto it.

The drive home was a familiar route on the parkway through the mountains. Tall, black pine trees towered on either side, but occasionally the trees would break, and Kora could catch a glimpse of the edge of distant peaks carved out by moonlight.

Her senior year was officially over. With finals, graduation, and the bonfire done, Kora's summer stretched before her. Soon she would be leaving for a college that was far away in a big city, abandoning the sweeping valleys and high-altitude air that had raised her. Her beautiful Blue Ridge Mountains and all their sweet, earthy memories flooded her. She saw lightning bugs and blackberries and Sage's ash blonde hair knotted by the wind.

There was nothing particularly interesting about Pinebrook. No one could place it on a map who didn't grow up there. She'd always assumed she would leave someday. When she got into a big arts school in New York, she had slept with the acceptance letter under her pillow for a week, convinced it was a dream. But now that she was faced with actually leaving, she was certain nothing would feel quite like the languid haze of Southern summers.

But she couldn't think about that yet. As she pulled into the driveway of Sage's creaky old house and half-carried her drunk best friend toward the door, she remembered she had all summer to make her last memories in their little mountain town.

Behind her, cicadas hummed and the crickets chirped. An owl called out from the trees. Kora closed her eyes for a moment and listened. She didn't want to forget what home sounded like.

CHAPTER 2

S age had made studying into an art, a science. Those were the same thing to her.

It was the final week of exams, and the pages of her textbook seemed to get heavier each time she flipped them. Kora had managed to drag her out to the bonfire the other night, which was inconveniently planned for the weekend after graduation. Since the finals for their classes were over, most students had nothing left to study for, but Sage still had AP exams to worry about.

She reorganized her desk before she started working, as she did every time she was stressed about a test. Then she lay out her textbook in the middle of her desk with her pencil case to her left and a stack of notecards to her right. She kept her coffee in a thermos between her legs where she could easily reach it and went downstairs to top it off every time she finished a chapter.

The medication she took for her ADHD had long worn off, and she kept finding herself re-reading the same paragraphs without comprehending them. Coffee helped a little, but it made her head hurt and left a bitter taste in her mouth. She pinched the sections she had left to cover with two fingers, trying to calculate if she had time to brush her teeth before bed.

While she played with the corner of the page, there was a knock on her door. She said, "Come in," without looking up. The door opened and closed again with no sound. Knowing her father usually just stuck his head in, she turned around.

Her brother Sam was standing by her dresser, looking at all of the knick-knacks she had arranged on top of it. He was supposed to be out of town for a few more days, but here he was.

This was something he did often: coming home unannounced. He would pick up the things in her room one by one and look at them, flip through her magazines and textbooks, and play with her stuffed animals. It was like he was cataloging everything in her room.

"I thought you weren't coming home until Friday," she said.

"I ran out of supplies," he said. He was examining her Bill Nye bobblehead. "I'm leaving again tomorrow."

He paused to put down the toy and pick something else up. Sage couldn't see what it was.

"Test tomorrow?" he asked, nodding his head toward the desk.

"Physics," said Sage.

"With Mr. O'Connell?" Sam had graduated from Oakcrest just a couple years before, when Sage was a freshman.

"No, he teaches Honors. I'm in AP with Ms. Bickman."

Sam smirked, playing with a Jacob's ladder toy. "Right," he said. "Nerd."

She wanted to retort, but his tone was half-hearted and distracted. She watched as his eyes wandered to the pillow and blanket carefully folded and placed on the end of her little couch. This was her ritual to prepare for a sleepover.

"Kora?" he asked.

She nodded and then realized he wasn't looking at her, still staring absentmindedly at the blanket. "Tomorrow night, once the AP exams are over."

Sam didn't respond. Sage examined his profile while he was still turned away from her. Right after their mother died, Sam had spent all the money he saved up from graduation on trips into the depths of the mountains, tracking some of North Carolina's most famous ghost stories. Sage figured his obsession with death was wrapped up in understanding what had happened to their mother, but she never asked. She didn't believe in ghosts, but she thought he would eventually find an answer that satisfied him. It had been two years.

"You're taking physics as a junior?" he asked.

Sage took a moment before she answered. It was the kind of question that, coming from anyone else, she would take as a compliment. But it was also the kind of question a brother shouldn't have to ask.

"If you were around more, you would know that," she said. She turned back to her desk and picked up a pencil as if to illustrate her point. It hovered over her notecard at the ready, but she couldn't think of anything to write. Behind her, she couldn't detect a change in Sam's silence.

"I know," he said after a while, his voice sounding a little less distant. "I'm sorry."

Sage wanted to turn around and see his face, but she rarely let her anger with him rise up above her sternum, and she didn't want to let it go just yet.

"I'm in physics because I'm really smart," she said, still looking down at her notecard. "In case you haven't noticed."

She'd stopped in the middle of a chapter, and she couldn't pick back up where she'd left off. As she looked at the page, her eyes glazed over, and the anger roiled in her stomach.

He sat down on her bed and didn't say anything. She wouldn't turn around to look at him again, but she heard his head hit her pillow. Her ceiling fan made a calming noise as it spun around; it was all the background music she needed when she studied. She tried to focus on it.

"Did you find anything?" she asked.

She didn't usually ask this. She knew the answer; there was nothing to be found. But she liked that he still hoped that something was out there. As much as it bothered her that he was never around, she wished one day he would come through the door with the childish grin she could only remember on a rounder version of his face. He would tell her about the magic he had found, something impossible and big. A picture of a ghost, maybe. Or possibly their mother following behind him, flesh and bone again. Sage assumed that was the point: to accomplish the impossible. To bring back the dead.

"Not yet," he said. "I still have some leads to follow."

"What leads?" Sage asked, unable to keep the skepticism out of her voice.

"You know," he said. "Just picking up where I left off."

That wasn't really an answer to her question. She put down her pencil and finally turned around to face him. He was lying on his back on her bed, looking at the ceiling fan.

"Do you really think you'll find anything?" she asked. She didn't let him answer before asking her next question. "Do you really believe in ghosts?"

"It's not about belief," he said, closing his eyes. "I just have to do it." He took a deep breath through his nose and covered his eyes with his arm. He used to do that when he was little and he was about to cry, but when he put his arm back behind his head, his eyes were dry. "Do you think about her a lot?"

"Yeah," she said. Her voice didn't sound like it belonged to her, like it was dull and lifeless. She felt a little guilty. They didn't talk like this very often. Sage preferred not to. She didn't go into her parents' room—unoccupied since their father had moved into the guest room. She did care, she just couldn't care out loud too much. "When will you be back?"

He sat up on the bed. "Few days," he said. "Friday at the latest." He mussed her hair on his way out of her room, and she shoved his hand away.

Once she heard the door close, she took another sip of coffee and went back to studying.

───◆───

Sage spent the next several days in a blur of studying and taking exams. She almost regretted the decision to take three A.P. classes as a junior, but she felt confident she'd done well.

When she got home after her last exam, she hung her backpack on its hook on the back of the door and flopped onto her bed with a sigh. That feeling was exactly why she made her bed every morning—because it felt good to sink into when she was finally done with school.

She spent the next hour flipping through magazines and blasting her music so loud that she didn't hear the front door open. She didn't have to worry about it; Kora never knocked, and the garage door was always unlocked. Kora opened the door to Sage's room and dropped an overnight bag on the floor.

"Um, you may have forgotten the rules around here," said Sage in a mocking voice, "but your stuff remains in a neat pile on the couch, not thrown around the room."

"Such a neat freak," said Kora with a laugh. "I got it. No mess."

Sage was pretty sure that Sam had also inherited the ADHD gene from their eccentric, academic father, but he had never been formally diagnosed. His room was constantly in a state of unrepentant chaos, and Sage avoided it at all costs. It manifested differently for Sage. She found that she couldn't focus at all if her space was cluttered. The meds helped her maintain her careful routine of tidying. She refused to let Kora, who seemed to be messy simply because she was an artist with an absentee parent and an undisciplined childhood, disrupt that delicate balance.

Kora sat down on the bed next to Sage, who handed her an old issue of *Seventeen*. They each flipped through one, pointing out looks they liked and outfits they thought were hideous.

It had been a while since they had done this. When Kora and Connor had been together, they were inseparable, and her regular Friday night sleepovers with Sage disappeared, instead turning into dinner dates and making out in his car, Sage assumed. But as they fell back into the rhythm of turning glossy pages and insulting celebrity haircuts, it felt like no time had passed.

They had been this way since they were kids, their friendship predestined—the second generation of Rivera-Mason best friends. Their moms had met in their mid-20s when they had both recently become mothers. Sage's mom Liz was in graduate school for English, while Kora's mom Ronnie was working for a landscaping business. Both of them were terrified of failing at motherhood and they soothed and exacerbated each other's fears in equal parts. As a result of their friendship, Kora had been a permanent installation in the Rivera family since babyhood. She was more like a sister than a friend.

As Kora pointed to something in the magazine, Sage studied the splotches of acrylic paint that coated her fingers. It was common to see Kora with colorful hands in between art classes at Oakcrest, but outside the context of school, it seemed like a strange adornment, like a peacock's feathers. She used her paint-covered hands to pull her thick chestnut curls over one shoulder, half-heartedly braiding them with swift fingers. It was a habit of hers, and it amazed Sage how fast she could do it. Sage rarely did anything with her hair besides brush it, and the little practice she had with braiding it had proved fruitless.

"Working on anything good lately?" she asked, pointing at the colorful marks. Kora looked down and smiled, just noticing the mess.

"Not really," she said. "Ever since I finished my portfolio, I haven't had much inspiration." With obviously fake nonchalance, Kora said, "I'm actually thinking about getting into tattoo designs."

"Oh yeah?" said Sage. It was a departure from her typical work but not too much of a stretch. Kora was looking at her weird.

"How much do you remember from the bonfire?"

Sage recalled blurry, warm bits and pieces: the smell of wood smoke, loud shouts during flip cup, threatening to beat Melanie Hammond with a stick. Her memories were embarrassing and vaguely nauseating, but unfortunately, nothing out of the ordinary. Before her mom died, Sage had never had more than a glass of champagne at New Year's. After, things were different.

"Not much," Sage shrugged. "Why?"

"I kind of met a girl," Kora said in a dramatic voice. Sage raised an eyebrow.

"Spill," she said.

"Her name is Hunter. She's a tattoo apprentice at Cabin Fever."

"Ooh," said Sage. "Could she get you a discount?"

"Not the point," said Kora, shoving Sage lightly.

"Right, continue."

"There was definite flirting."

"And then?"

Kora made a face. "And then she helped me carry you to the car."

Sage looked down at her hands and pretended to focus on her collage. That wasn't ideal. Her whole life was constructed around being in control, but lately she was losing some of her drive. She didn't like the idea of Kora cleaning up after her messes.

"Well, did you get her number?" asked Sage, filing her guilt away to think about later.

"No," Kora frowned. "But I can always stop by Cabin Fever."

Sage smiled. "Go get her, tiger." Kora groaned and covered her face with a magazine.

Sage picked up a pair of scissors and began cutting out a picture of a pair of Adidas sneakers. Sometimes they took all their cut-outs and glued them onto paper for outfit inspiration. Kora smiled and joined in, grabbing the scissors. She eyed a picture of a girl with cheeks coated in bright purple glitter before cutting along her jawline. Sage glanced up at Kora's own face to confirm that she was already wearing a more subtle, but still excessive, dusting of white glitter. Kora's cheeks were almost always sparkly in some way.

As they worked, something occurred to Sage.

"Wasn't Connor at the party?" she asked. She vaguely recalled seeing him choke back some hard cider before failing spectacularly to land a cup flip.

Kora's bashfulness turned to guilt. "Yeah," she said. "I think he noticed me talking to her."

Sage wanted to be on Kora's side. She *was* on Kora's side, and she always had been. But Connor had been a part of her life via Kora for two years. She considered herself his friend, too. She didn't like the idea of hurting him.

"I didn't mean to be so obvious about it," said Kora. Sage's thoughts must have been obvious on her face. She turned back to the magazine. "It just sort of happened."

"Well, school's over," said Sage. "Now there's no reason to see him again."

"Yeah," said Kora, focusing her attention on a picture of a pink skateboard. Sage couldn't be sure, but she thought Kora looked disappointed. She decided not to push.

◆◆◆

After ordering takeout from the Chinese place down the street, they settled on the couch for a movie.

"It's my turn," said Kora. They alternated who got to pick the movie.

"No, it's my turn," said Sage. "Remember? You picked that gladiator movie."

"Oh yeah," said Kora, deflating. "What a waste of a turn, that movie sucked."

"Lucky for you, I have excellent taste."

Sage picked *Pride and Prejudice*, which they'd already seen many times. One of them picked it at least three times a year.

Halfway through the movie, Kora got up to get another Coke from the fridge. "Where are your dad and Sam?" she asked on her way back to the couch. Sage sighed. She had been expecting this question, but it wasn't one she particularly wanted to answer.

"Dad is already asleep," she said. Sometimes, he didn't get out of bed much except to move to the couch, but Kora didn't need to know that. "Sam's on one of his ghost hunts."

Kora's expression turned to surprise. "He's still doing those? I thought he would snap out of it by now."

Sage shrugged. "Me too," she said. "He's full of surprises."

"Doesn't he have class?" Kora asked, cracking open her drink.

"He dropped out," said Sage. The Coke was almost to Kora's lips, but she held it there in surprise.

"Sam dropped out," she repeated, incredulous. "Of college? To look for ghosts?"

Sage nodded. Talking about it made her think about it, and she didn't really like thinking about it too hard. She didn't want to be angry at her brother; she didn't want to care what he did at all.

"I'm gonna kick his ass," said Kora. Her face looked so determined Sage had to laugh. She couldn't picture Kora kicking anyone's ass.

"Good luck," she said. "He's a lot bigger now than he was when we were kids."

Kora rolled her eyes. "Yeah, but I think I could take him," she said.

Sage was relieved that it seemed to be the end of the conversation. The details of their family's life post-mom were not very pretty, and she wanted to hide the worst of it from Kora. She couldn't bear Kora's big, round, pitiful eyes whenever she was worried about Sage.

They fell back into the movie. Sage laughed at Kora for still tearing up at the scene where Mr. Darcy walks across the moor, even though they'd seen it so many times before. Then she found herself sniffling at the end.

When it was over, they decided to bring all the pillows and blankets down to the living room so they could sleep on the floor in front of the TV like when they were little. They turned all the lights out in the house and put on a cartoon with the volume way down so they could fall asleep to it.

Kora scooched closer to Sage, putting the tops of their heads together.

"The house feels so empty," she said. "Without Sam and your dad and—" She stopped herself, but Sage knew what she meant.

"Yeah, it does."

"Do you think Sam doesn't like being here?" Sage glanced at Kora's face, which was blue in the light of the TV. She hadn't really thought about it much. She had been too wrapped up in worrying about their dad and getting mad at Sam for ditching them.

"Maybe," she said. "Probably. I don't either sometimes."

Kora was quiet for a while, watching the cartoon characters run across the screen. Without the sound, the scene was surreal. The old house creaked as it settled.

"I still like it here," Kora said softly after a while. Sage rolled over to face her. "Better than home. I'm sorry I haven't been around much."

"It's okay," said Sage. "We have all summer." She found that as she said it, the house didn't seem quite so empty.

CHAPTER 3

The Riveras' house was old. In the 1800s, a local family built it as a small farmhouse. Since then, most of the surrounding farmland had been sold off to build new subdivisions. The house was registered with the city as a historical property.

Kora never slept well there. She was already prone to insomnia, but something about the old house made her restless.

She supposed if ghosts were real, there were probably some wandering around the Rivera house. Somewhere in the attic, there was a portrait of the family that had lived here when the house was first built, which Kora had always found unsettling.

But she had never felt unsafe in that house, even in the dark. When she heard inexplicable noises late at night, she never thought it was malevolent spirits. Instead, she liked to imagine that the house itself was taking deep breaths, the old wood expanding and settling into bed to sleep with the rest of them. The house wasn't haunted, it was just a bad sleeper, like her.

When she had nightmares—which was often—she couldn't really find it in her to blame the house. She wasn't sure what caused her sleep problems, but it wasn't an old farmhouse.

She woke up from a fitful sleep in Sage's bed, but Sage was already gone. She worked summers as a swim coach and had already left for the pool without waking Kora, for which she was grateful. Kora pulled clothes out of her overnight bag and got dressed, then put everything back in the bag. She didn't always remember to keep her things tidy in Sage's room, but she did her best. She tracked down the toothbrush she kept in the bathroom cabinet for such occasions.

It wasn't until she was walking out the front door that Kora realized she didn't have any plans for the day. With graduation over, the consistent rhythm of her school routine was disrupted. Soon, she would have to start looking for a summer job, but in the meantime, the empty day stretched before her.

She got in her car and turned on her stereo, nodding along to the mixtape CD she had burned and left in the player. She wasn't sure where she would go, but it was a beautiful day, and with the music playing and the windows down, it didn't matter. It was truly summer in Pinebrook now with fast winds whipping through the mountain lanes and brilliant, balmy sunshine making the asphalt sparkle.

She drove through Sage's neighborhood and watched as the houses got bigger and the lawns got greener. The Riveras lived on one of those winding Southern roads where the houses grew more grandiose the further in she drove. Their sprawling old farmhouse sat apart from the rest of the neighborhood, a historical monument that couldn't be placed in the financial hierarchy. Then came the one-story Colonials and Tudors with white wood or plastic siding. Then the two-story Victorians and brick Manors with longer drives and more expensive-looking cars. And finally, toward the end, the monumental five- and six-bedroom mansions, glorious and ostentatious.

This was the part of the neighborhood where Connor lived. His sprawling, red-brick mansion was legendary. It had an enormous yard full of expensive sports equipment and dotted with impressive crepe myrtle trees. As she passed by, Kora remembered all the days she had spent lounging on the wide front porch and swinging in the hammocks out back.

Whenever she drove through this neighborhood, she was struck by how many kids she knew who lived there. Were it not for Oakcrest, she didn't think she would have had reason to meet many kids from this side of town. Oakcrest was free to attend, but students had to undergo a rigorous application process and maintain a high GPA. It was not a coincidence, in Kora's opinion, that so many of them happened to be rich.

Just past Connor's house was the neighborhood's handsome and charming park. It was lined with poplars, and wide, stretching oaks scattered around the green. In the center was a mulched playground. Last summer, she and Sage had spent their nights trespassing in the park, which closed at dusk. They would hop the fence and use the flashlights on their phones to light their way, playing games and lying on their backs on the roundabout.

Before she really thought about where she was going, she had already pulled into the park's tiny dirt parking lot. She grabbed her sketchbook from the front seat and tossed it into her bag, thinking she might lounge under the trees and draw.

Sitting under one of the oaks, she started with the trees. She smiled as she covered her page in sharp, short strokes. The leaves were lush, and she could smell the grass beneath her legs. When she had filled several pages with different trees, she moved on to the playground, drawing the swings with the back of a child's head.

It was then that she saw him. Connor's fine, curly, white-gold hair blew around in the wind, hanging low over his eyes. He was laughing, a deep, full-body thing that consumed him. His fingers were lean and strong, grasped around a bar of the jungle gym as Caleb, his little brother, climbed it.

She realized after a moment she was holding her breath. Of course, she should have expected to see Connor here, he lived down the street. It wasn't a shock. But, as she took in his grin and his dimples and the soft lines of his eyes squinting into the sun, she remembered sitting on a swing last summer while he stood behind her, pressing his lips to the top of her head while she swayed gently, her feet dragging little bits of mulch around.

Her body was moving without her permission, standing up and walking over. She put her hands in the pockets of her dress, bag slung over her shoulder, as she approached him. He closed his eyes, laughing again as Caleb tumbled through the bars and caught himself, and when he opened them again, he saw her. His eyes widened, and his laugh cut off abruptly.

"Hey, Kora," he said, smiling nervously. He glanced at Caleb and back at her, unsure of what to do. She wished she hadn't made it obvious she was coming to talk to him. Maybe she should have given him the opportunity to ignore her.

Caleb had no such reservations. He shouted her name, quickly untangling himself from the bars of the jungle gym. When he got to the ground, he sprinted for Kora and crashed into her torso, his head coming just to the bottom of her chest. She hugged him back.

"I saw you at graduation," he said. "We all clapped for you."

She smiled and patted his soft golden hair, even curlier than Connor's.

"You're all too sweet," she said.

He laughed, though she hadn't said anything funny. He got this from his brother: neither of them ever needed an excuse to laugh.

"You keep getting taller," she said. It had only been a few weeks since she had been over to their house, but it seemed true.

He puffed out his chest proudly and put his hands on his hips. "Mom says I'm going to be taller than Connor," he said. She smiled. He was tall for an eleven-year-old, but he still had a ways to go for that.

"Well, that's not that hard," said Kora, and she nudged Connor playfully with her elbow. He glared back at her, but those looks never worked on his friendly face.

"Want to go for a walk?" Caleb asked. "We were just gonna go on the trail."

She looked up at Connor. His face softened, and he nodded in invitation.

"Sure," Kora said. "Will you show me the way?"

He took off ahead of them, leaving Kora and Connor to follow behind together. They walked from the playground back through the field of oaks and on to the winding trails just outside the park.

"Did you have fun at the party?" Connor asked, not meeting her eyes. She remembered his face when he saw her talking to Hunter and felt a resurgence of guilt.

"Not as much as Sage did," she deflected. "I was afraid she was going to puke in my car."

He laughed, and the sound was different from when she had heard him from across the park; warmer and more familiar.

"Wouldn't be the first time," he said. "Remember homecoming?"

Kora laughed, too, remembering the sloppy dancing and bad decorations, followed by Sage's vodka vomit covering the outside of Kora's car. Connor had helped her clean it off the next morning. That was the worst of Sage's drunken antics.

"Her pride is bigger than her liver," said Kora.

Ahead of them, Caleb had reached a small bridge and was leaning over the railing, watching a duck dip its head underwater.

"Have you decided where you're going to college?" she asked. Last she had heard, he was torn between going to the local community college while working with his dad or going away to UCLA to study business before coming back to take over. The decision had prompted several late-night phone calls in which Kora talked him down while he ate his way through his hidden stash of processed sugar.

"Yeah," he said, looking away. "I'm going to UCLA."

It was strange to hear this way, by happenstance, that he was moving across the country. A month ago, she wouldn't have had to ask; she would have been there with him when he pressed the submit button on his acceptance, would have read aloud the number from his credit card with the ridiculously high limit while he typed it in to submit his deposit. Now, she could only offer a friendly congratulations.

They stopped at a bench in the middle of the trail, a bright spot in the dappled shade of the forest. Caleb had stopped to pet a dog someone was walking.

"He's a good kid," she said.

Connor didn't reply, his eyes far away, watching the dog lick Caleb's face. His hair was speckled golden in the rays of sunshine streaming through the pine trees.

She remembered afternoons spent swimming in his family's pool, playing Marco Polo and diving for toys. Then another memory: lying in Connor's bed on a hot day—so hot that the sweaty sheets stuck to their skin. It was one of the rare times they had the house to themselves; his parents had taken Caleb out for ice cream and left them alone for an hour. In this memory, her fingers were tangled in his hair, and she couldn't move them. They touched only with their arms, their toes, their foreheads, their noses; lying lethargic in the sun under the window like bugs on a windshield.

She wondered if he remembered it and looked away from his bright face, into the green shade of the pines.

"Yeah, he is," he said after a while, too late to be a natural response. His voice was thick with feeling, and she wanted to smooth his Adam's apple with her palm, take away the pain that stuck in his throat.

He put his arm on the back of the bench, around her shoulders but careful not to touch. She rested her hand on the bench between them, fingers only a few inches from his knee.

They sat like this for a few more minutes, not talking, not touching, too close but not close enough.

◆

When Kora got home, she realized she hadn't seen her mother in several days. Ronnie was busy trying to sell Kora's childhood home before the end of the summer, when she and Kora's stepdad would be moving out west to Santa Fe. Kora wasn't happy about the idea and was putting up passive resistance by refusing to clean her room for the open house. Closing the door to her room while her mother talked on the phone to the realtor in the kitchen, she dropped her overnight bag on the floor and didn't bother unpacking it. Soon, she would have to pack up the rest of her things.

This room was full of keepsakes and souvenirs, the walls crowded with artwork that celebrated her improvement over time. In some places, there were paper mache dolls and crayon drawings from grade school. In others, there were the pieces she was most proud of, that she had submitted in her portfolio for her college applications. Gifts from family members, small stuffed animals, a picture of Kora with her grandparents on their farm in West Virginia. Now that she was going off to college and her mom was moving away, there would be no family left here in Pinebrook; no reason to come back here for holidays.

No, that wasn't true. As long as Sage was here, she had a home here. She had at least one more year before she had to worry about Sage being off to college, too.

Kora's mom knocked on the door and then opened it without waiting for a response. She had the phone pressed to her shoulder, still on a call.

"The open house is on Saturday," she said, trying to be quiet so it wouldn't be picked up by the receiver. "Clean this up please." Her tone indicated that the *please* was a formality. The door was closed again before Kora could respond.

Kora looked down at her duffel bag, still mostly full of clean clothes. She always kept a bag packed, something she could easily throw into the backseat of her car that kept her from having to go home if she didn't want to. She cleaned the dirty clothes off her floor, made her bed, but kept the bag packed. When everything else in her room was clean, she brought it back out to the car. Sage wouldn't mind another sleepover, she was sure of that. Her mom would be mad that she was spending so much time away from home, but every time she came home she was reminded that it wouldn't be hers for much longer.

Before leaving again, Kora stepped outside to walk through her mother's garden. Since she had heard about the move, the worst part was knowing that someone else would inherit all her hard work. They could tear it all down if they wanted to, replace their complex maze of local fauna with a plain, grassy backyard with a grill. Kora remembered when she was little and the garden was just a few flower beds. During the summer, she would sit in the dirt listening to blues music on the radio while her mother dug into the fresh soil with her hands. She couldn't remember those hands without dirty nails. Now, they were freshly painted, waiting to sign the closing papers.

Kora walked toward the back gate, along the winding path of mismatched stones pressed into the ground. Different breeds of wildflowers tickled her ankles. Leafy vines covered the ground. And then, rising over the gate, roses wound through the chipped white paint of a massive arbor. Not the pampered, curated bushes that the neighbors two doors down kept in their lawn; these roses grew in all different directions, branches bowing over from growth. Kora pulled her sleeve over her hand to move the stray stalks away, careful to avoid the thorns.

She left through the back gate and walked around the house to her car, careful to avoid her mother and the meticulously staged house.

For the second time that day, Kora found herself driving aimlessly. Sage worked eight hour shifts at the pool and wouldn't be home for a while. She could wait at Sage's house, but her dad would be there, and these days she didn't like being around him without one of the kids as a buffer. He took up a lot of the air in the room.

She passed through the main street in Pinebrook's small downtown. It was lined with two-story brick buildings with lots of eclectic boutiques and antique stores. Several restaurants had patios that spilled out onto the sidewalk. To the north, just past the last of the shops, the road made a steep turn up the mountain. You could just see the peak of Pine Mountain from where Kora was stopped at a light.

It was almost sunset, and shops were starting to close. Restaurants were switching to their dinner menus, turning the lights on in their signs. The glowing neon open sign of Cabin Fever just next to the old post office caught her eye. She remembered getting her first tattoo there not so long ago. The cafe next door had changed owners since then, but the shop looked just the same.

Hunter had told her to stop by, but Kora wasn't sure if she meant it. It was possible she said that to all the girls or she was just trying to be nice. But she parked her car anyway.

A bell chimed as she opened the door. Hunter leaned over the front counter, sketching with charcoal. The side of her hand had turned silvery-black from the process. She was so engrossed in her drawing that she didn't hear the door. Kora snuck a peak at the notebook. It was a beautiful geometric bear's head. Further down the page, there were some older sketches of a skeleton hand and a rabbit's foot. Kora smiled.

"Is that for you or a client?" she asked. Hunter jumped at the sound of her voice, and for a second, Kora regretted showing up unannounced. But when her eyes focused on Kora's face, that crooked smile from the bonfire returned.

"That depends," she said, turning the notebook around so Kora could get a better view. "You interested? I did offer to do your next one."

"I'd rather you designed one just for me," she said, leaning over the counter to trace the edge of the paper with her finger.

"Well, I'll have to get to know you first," Hunter grinned. "So I can get it just right."

Kora was certain that was not true of all clients. She smiled back. Maybe this flirting thing wasn't so hard.

"Sorry, am I distracting you from your work?" Kora asked, not at all sorry.

"Actually, I was about to close up," said Hunter. "We don't have any more appointments today, and we don't get a lot of walk-ins. Most of Jeb's clients make appointments by texting him." She started moving things off the counter and putting them away. When she was done, she turned back around to Kora. "Want to grab a coffee next door?"

Kora nodded, and Hunter grabbed a large key ring and a leather jacket from the back. Once they were out the door, Hunter turned the key and pulled on it to make sure it was locked.

They walked next door to Common Grounds. It was a nice place with planters full of pansies in the windows and wrought iron chairs outside.

Hunter got a black coffee and spooned in some local honey. Kora got a caramel mocha with extra whipped cream. Hunter gave her a look and she shrugged.

"I like sugar," she said.

"Clearly," said Hunter, but her tone didn't show any signs of judgment.

They chose a little table outside. It was just getting to the time of year that didn't require a jacket in the evenings, and Kora couldn't stand to be inside for too long. The patio was full of eclectic furniture and twinkly lights, which were already on despite the fading pink skies.

"So, how long have you been doing the apprenticeship with Jeb?" Kora asked.

"Not long," said Hunter. "I moved here from the Cherokee area a few months ago. Jeb is a friend of the family, and I came out here to work with him." She took a sip of her coffee, and Kora liked the way the tendons in her hand flexed around the mug.

"That explains why I don't know you," said Kora.

"Oh yeah?" Hunter asked, a confused smile pulling up her lips.

"Pretty girl, small town. Not to mention the motorcycle. I'm sure I would have heard about you by now." Kora held her coffee mug in front of her face. She wasn't good at flirting, and she shouldn't even be trying. The memory of sitting on the bench with Connor this morning replayed in her mind, and she felt a stab of guilt.

"You make me sound like I'm in a biker gang," Hunter said with a grin. "I bought the motorcycle because it was cheaper than a car. I used to ride dirt bikes with my cousins when I was a kid, so it wasn't too much of a learning curve."

"Okay, but it would be pretty cool if you were in a biker gang," said Kora.

"Good to know you're into that," Hunter laughed. "So, I take it you're from around here?"

"Born and raised. Just graduated from Oakcrest—you were at my graduation party."

Kora looked up, suddenly nervous. She wasn't sure how old Hunter was, considering she was already working, and she didn't know if just having graduated high school put her outside the acceptable dating age range. But Hunter didn't seem surprised or worried, so she relaxed.

"What's next for you?" Hunter asked, looking genuinely interested.

"Art school," Kora said. For some reason she couldn't conjure up her typical amount of enthusiasm.

"You don't seem too excited about it," Hunter said, raising an eyebrow.

"It's pretty far away," said Kora. She felt an urge to change the subject. "What about you? How did you get into tattooing?"

"I've always been an artist," said Hunter, absentmindedly rubbing her hand over a rose tattoo on her forearm. "I graduated high school early so I could take some drawing classes at a local community college. When I heard Jeb was looking for an apprentice, I decided it was time to turn it into a career."

Relief flowed through Kora. So they weren't that far apart in age after all.

"How do you like it so far?" she asked.

Hunter smiled, looking away. It was softer than her usual charm.

"I love it," she said. "It means so much to me that people let me practice on their bodies. I don't take that for granted."

Kora could tell she meant it.

"So what about you," Hunter asked. "What kind of art do you do?"

"Painting, mostly," said Kora. "Some drawing. I like flowers. My mom has a garden."

Words were tumbling out of her mouth in a nervous rush. She shook her head subtly enough that she hoped Hunter couldn't see it, trying to get her thoughts straight.

"So how do you like Pinebrook?" Kora asked.

"It's great," said Hunter. "Cool shops, good hiking. Nice people." She grinned.

Kora smiled back. "So you like hiking?"

"I've pretty much spent as much time as I could outdoors since I could pitch a tent," she said.

"You must be pretty good," Kora said, taking another sip of her coffee. She looked past the patio at the mountain peak that rested just beyond Main Street. The sky had faded to a smoky purple.

"I know my way around an REI," said Hunter. Kora laughed.

"You'll have to teach me," she said. "I'm hopeless on camping trips."

"You can't be that bad."

"I go every year with my best friend and her family," said Kora. "Without fail, every year I come home with some kind of dramatic injury." She reached out her hand to show Hunter a light pink scar on her finger. "This is from my one and only attempt at gutting a fish."

Hunter took Kora's hand so she could get a closer look at the scar. Kora tried to control her heart rate when their fingers touched. For someone who was obviously strong and outdoorsy, Hunter had remarkably soft hands.

"That's nothing," she said, dropping Kora's hand. She couldn't help but be a little disappointed. But then, Hunter pulled up her shirt almost to her chest. There was a patch of raised red skin over her ribs. "Falling out of a tree in a bathing suit."

Kora's breath caught a little at how much of her skin was showing. Her hand twitched unconsciously. Hunter noticed, and gestured at the scar. "Go ahead," she said. Kora leaned over the table and ran her fingers over the rough mark. The skin on Hunter's torso was soft. Kora's eyes drifted down to her belly button. She pulled her hand away and took another sip of coffee.

"Impressive," she said into her mug. Hunter was smirking. Kora felt flushed and reached to press a hand to the back of her neck, which suddenly felt hot. She quickly changed the subject. "So, do you live nearby?"

Hunter laughed. "Very nearby, actually. Jeb lets me rent the apartment above the shop." She pointed back toward Cabin Fever and the little windows on the second floor.

"I'd love to see it sometime," said Kora, and then looked down at the table, embarrassed at how that sounded.

Hunter feigned ignorance. "Definitely."

The rest of the sun seeped from the sky as they talked, and the sparkling lights of the patio started to stand out more. They reflected in Hunter's shiny, dark hair. The baristas started to put chairs on top of tables, and Kora knew that was their cue to leave.

Hunter walked her to her car. Kora shivered as the wind picked up, and Hunter took the leather jacket that was wrapped around her waist and draped it over Kora's shoulders. She shrugged into it. It smelled like campfire and some kind of spice.

When they got to the car, Kora became very aware that it was officially dark outside. Away from the lights of the coffee shop, she could hardly see Hunter's face. She turned around and leaned against the door.

Hunter took a step closer—close enough that Kora wouldn't be able to open the car door without them both moving. But she didn't want to move. This close, the smell of the jacket was stronger and mixed with something sharp, like gasoline. Hunter's grin faded to a soft smile. Kora's heart raced, and she felt sweaty.

Hunter noticed the change in her expression. "You okay?" her voice was soft, almost a whisper, like they were swapping secrets in the dark.

Kora decided to go with honesty. "You make me nervous," she said.

"In a good way or a bad way?"

Kora thought back to Connor's face at the party, how deflated he'd looked when he saw Hunter. And she thought of all the complications in her life, dividing her attention—her mother packing up the house, Sage's family drama, preparing to leave for art school. There were a lot of reasons to steer clear of this.

"I can't really commit to someone right now," she said. "I'm leaving at the end of the summer, so I need to keep things casual."

Hunter nodded, looking thoughtful but not upset.

"Casual," she said. "I can do that." She leaned in a little closer. "Does that mean you don't want me to kiss you?"

"No," Kora breathed, "it does not."

In the dark, leaning against the car, the kiss seemed to last a long time and not long enough. Kora liked the soft curve of Hunter's face and the way it felt to hold it with her palm. Her hair was thick and pin-straight as Kora ran her fingers through it. She felt a chill up her spine as Hunter wrapped her hand around Kora's neck, pulling her closer.

It occurred to Kora that it had been a long time since she had kissed a girl. Since she kissed anyone other than Connor, really. Kissing Hunter was sharp, electric. It felt immediately right, like they had done it before.

Hunter pulled away and gently kissed Kora's cheek before leaning back and running a hand through her hair. Kora started to take off the jacket so she could return it.

"Hold onto it," said Hunter, grinning. "You can give it back next time."

Kora smiled back. "Sure."

And just like that, Hunter was rounding the corner, back toward the tattoo shop. Kora's heart was still racing when she got into the car. She waited to calm down before starting it. Hunter's last words ran through her head over and over: *Next time.*

CHAPTER 4

I t was still dark outside when Sage woke up for swim practice. She turned off her alarm, blinked heavily for a few minutes, and then shoved a handful of pills in her mouth.

She had been on the same cocktail of medications for a while, and it was hard to remember what each of them was for, but she knew they struck a difficult balance to offset her brain's various troubles. Things had gotten worse after her mom died, the tension pulling her toward the darker end of the spectrum. But she had more or less evened out since then.

Her body moved slowly as she got out of bed and started getting ready, but once her meds kicked in, it was a little easier. It had been a long time since she had woken up unaided by pharmaceuticals. Even longer since she had slept past sunrise. Before, when Sam was still at home, he would begrudgingly give her rides to swim practice and Kora would bring her home after school. Now, her dad hardly ever left the house, so his car was free for her to use.

Driving to practice was her favorite part of this morning routine. The roads at 5 a.m. were empty except for long-haul truckers and baristas driving to their opening shifts. She could drive fast without the glare of the morning sun in her eyes. When the moon was bright, she could see fog over the mountains as she passed over bridges and through sparse patches of trees.

She had been swimming with her teammates for so long they didn't blink at each other's naked bodies as they changed in the morning. Sage didn't bother finding an empty stall in the locker room anymore. She was fast and efficient at switching from her shorts and t-shirt to her suit. Everyone else liked to talk while they got dressed and warmed up. Sage could remember when she did the same thing, but now, nothing seemed worth talking about so early in the morning.

The summer season had started, which meant using the outdoor pool, but it was still too early in the year for the water to be warm. Somehow it never got easier diving into the cold first thing in the morning, even after months and years of the same routine. But eventually, she got used to the water, and then it was just as jarring getting back out. At least the air was clear outside. In the small confines of the indoor pool, the air was thick with chlorine.

Practice always passed by quickly to Sage. The rest of the team would probably hate her for thinking that, but moving her body meant she had something to focus her mind on. Anxiety was starting to creep up on her. She had the horrible feeling that there was something she was forgetting, but she couldn't remember what it was. It was pretty much a hallmark of her ADHD, and she hated it. Whenever she felt this way, distractions were the only thing that really kept panic from building up in her chest and squeezing her lungs.

Swimming meant that she couldn't think about her family or her final grades or what she was going to do when Kora left for school. She had to focus on moving her arms in exactly the right way to push her forward.

Today, she had a coaching shift after practice. She wasn't usually good with kids, but she liked teaching them about swimming. This sport was hard on the body and the mind. It took discipline and focus. She had had many coaches that pushed her past where she was willing to go, and she could still feel the results in her body. When she stretched too far or lifted too much, her muscles protested, and her joints struggled to keep up. With these kids, she had the chance to teach them differently. Under her leadership, they could learn to listen to their bodies and respond to its cues rather than working it into the ground. Not that she could ever follow that guidance herself.

As she dried off from the pool and got ready to coach, her teammate sat next to her on the locker room bench.

"We missed you at practice last week," the girl said. Her name was Shania. Sage liked her, but she couldn't help but wonder why she had stuck it out this long. Her times weren't good enough to make it to Regionals. If she had no chance at a swimming scholarship, what was she doing here?

"Yeah, I wasn't feeling well," Sage said, wringing her hair out with a towel.

"Did you go to the senior bonfire?" Shania asked, a knowing smirk on her lips. Sage glanced over and decided her expression wasn't judgmental.

"I've been told I attended," she said. "Don't remember it too well myself."

Shania laughed. "At least you had some fun before the summer session," she said. "Sometimes I wish we could have a normal summer off."

Sage nodded. She had felt that way every summer since she could remember.

Shania stood up and walked toward her locker. She turned back to look at Sage.

"Your times were looking good today," she said with a gentle smile. "We're lucky to have you on the team."

Before Sage could respond, Shania was around the corner. She wasn't sure what she would say anyway. As fast as she was and as hard as she worked, her presence on the team didn't feel lucky. She was as good as she needed to be to excel. It had always been a means to an end.

She stretched her shoulder and felt the twinge of pain that came with certain movements. The summer had just started, and she couldn't wait for it to end.

◆◆◆

Buried under a pile of blankets on the couch, Sage refused to move when Kora arrived, even after she held up a bag of microwave popcorn and a DVD of *Jurassic Park*.

"It's my turn," Kora said triumphantly.

While Sage stayed put in her blanket cocoon, Kora popped the disk into the DVD player and cooked the popcorn. She was already munching on a handful when she sat down on the couch. After one attempt at stealing the corner of Sage's blankets, she realized it wasn't going to happen and went in search of another one. Sage grabbed some popcorn and watched the menu screen for the movie.

"Okay," said Kora when she came back, blanket in hand. "Ready for some dinosaur action?"

"Hold up," said Sage. She sat up and unwrapped part of her blanket. "First, you have to spill about your date with Hunter." Kora had texted her the other night that she had spontaneously met up with her new crush, and Sage had to know the details.

Kora looked up to the ceiling like she did when she was experiencing complicated feelings. Sage didn't really understand why, but knew to be on the lookout for it, because it usually meant they were going to have to talk about them. She almost regretted asking–she loved Kora deeply and wanted her to be happy, but her friend occasionally veered too far into the sappy, woeful, or otherwise intense emotions Sage was not particularly equipped for.

"It was really nice," she said, running her fingers through her hair. "She's actually really nice. I didn't expect that, because she's also really cool. And I think she likes me."

"Well, good," said Sage. "She should. Everybody likes you."

Kora sighed, and Sage fought the urge to roll her eyes. *Here we go*, Sage thought. Kora's dramatics were never a good sign.

"I just," she began, then huffed another sigh. "I just don't know what I want right now. I mean I'm supposed to be going to New York at the end of the summer." She leaned forward and rested her chin in her hand, propped up on her knee. She glanced at Sage with a guilty expression. "And then there's Connor."

"Forget about Connor," Sage groaned. "You guys didn't work out for a reason. And you don't have to know what you want yet. Just give yourself a chance to figure it out. Like by going on more dates."

Kora smiled and sat back up. "You're right," she said. "You're always right."

"Now you're getting it," said Sage. She re-cocooned herself and picked up the TV remote. "Now let's watch some dinosaurs eat some people."

They had each watched this movie too many times to count, mainly because Kora always insisted on it. It was the only movie she still had on DVD. Sage shoved Kora when she kept saying the lines at the same time as the characters.

Onscreen, Alan Grant and the little kid Tim raced to climb out of a tree while a car fell through the branches above them.

"Okay, see, this has never made sense to me," said Sage. "Why do they climb directly down? Couldn't they just climb sideways out of the way of the car?"

Kora shushed her.

"Yeah, but how great is this score?" said Kora, waving an imaginary conductor's baton. "John Williams at his best. This movie is perfect."

Sage rolled her eyes.

"You just like it because you think Laura Dern is hot," she said.

Kora glared at her. "Laura Dern *is* hot," she insisted. "How can you not see that?"

"She's wearing khaki shorts!"

"It was the 90s!"

They'd had this argument so many times, Sage could predict what she was going to say: the CGI was groundbreaking, the writing was clever, the message of corrupt capitalism was still relevant as ever. There was no convincing her otherwise, obviously, but Sage knew they both enjoyed playing out the argument over and over.

It was better than watching a movie with Sam, who always sat in enraptured silence, no matter what was on.

Just as that thought crossed her mind, something occurred to her. Horror coiled in her stomach as she went around in a circle of wanting to be wrong and realizing more and more she was right. She unwrapped her blankets, paused the movie, and jumped up from the couch.

"Where are you going?" Kora asked. "We're almost to the frog DNA scene. I bet I can recite it from memory."

Sage couldn't respond for a moment. She was going over and over it in her mind, making sure she had something to be worried about before she spoke. But, there was no way around it.

"It's Sunday," she said.

Kora tilted her head, clearly worried by Sage's tone. Her answer took a second longer than Sage had the patience for.

"Uh, yeah," she said. "What about it?"

Sage began pacing back and forth through the den. Onscreen, the T-Rex was frozen mid-roar, chasing after the Jeep. It mimicked the fear pumping through her veins, making her hands shake. By the time she turned back to Kora, she looked like she was about to leap out of her seat.

"What? What's wrong?" asked Kora. "Tell me what's going on."

"Sam said he would be back by Friday," said Sage. "He's supposed to be back by now. He always calls if he's going to be longer than he said."

Kora shook her head, her brow furrowed. "Maybe he doesn't have cell service," she said. "I mean, he is in the middle of the mountains somewhere, right?"

Sage stopped her pacing and stood still. She could feel the blood pumping in her chest and hear it racing past her eardrums. Her fingers were twitching in a way she couldn't entirely say she was controlling.

"Of course, he doesn't," said Sage. She realized too late how harsh her tone was. Kora rarely saw her freak out like this. Actually, no one really saw her freak out like this. But her brother was missing. She was sure of it. "He has a sat phone. And even if he didn't, he would drive home to tell me before staying out past when he said he'd be home."

She sat down on the coffee table, facing Kora on the couch. They were at eye level now, and Sage focused on Kora. She rarely maintained this kind of eye contact, but she wanted Kora to understand the importance of what she was about to say.

"He wouldn't do this to me," she said. Her voice sounded strange and foreign to her, more level than she felt inside. "He promised not to worry me like this."

The memory surfaced without her permission: a long night of waiting, waiting, waiting, and then the blue lights of the cop car in the window. A short conversation with a sympathetic cop who Sage would nevertheless always detest. Sam and her dad's matching vacant expressions, like haunted twins.

Then Kora and her mom had showed up as soon as they could, ready to cook food and hug everyone and cry together. Instead, they arrived to find a family already shuttered away in their individual rooms, grieving in private. Kora had waited for days while Sage refused to speak to anyone.

Sage didn't like to think about it, but whenever Sam was gone too long, the memories got under her skin. She could see in Kora's eyes that she understood why Sam's absence would fill her with anxiety.

Kora stood up. Sage thought she would start pacing, too, but she just walked to the kitchen.

"Now is not the time for more popcorn," said Sage.

Kora pulled a jar of jam out of the fridge and set it on the counter. Sage looked at the clock. It was well past midnight, much too late to head out on a search mission.

"Listen," Kora said as she got bread from the pantry. "I believe you. Let's figure out what we're going to do about it."

"That idiot," said Sage, pacing again. "Hiking all the time, not telling anyone where he is. Camping out in the woods, where bears live. Bears! What is this, *The Revenant?*"

When she got back to the kitchen, Kora was taking a bite out of a sandwich. Sage sighed and poured herself some juice, stopping to take a bite of Kora's food.

"Why didn't you put peanut butter on this?" she asked with mild disgust.

"I've decided I don't like peanut butter," said Kora, mouth sticky with jam. She put her plate in the sink and put her ingredients away. Then, she turned her attention back to Sage.

"So you don't have any idea where he is?" Kora asked, still chewing. "Not even like a general direction?"

Sage shook her head. "He doesn't say much to me about it. All he said was he still had some leads to follow."

"Maybe there's something in his room that could tell us where he is."

They agreed to check. Sage felt strange going into Sam's room when he wasn't there. It reminded her of when Sam was a teenager and kept his door closed all the time. Sometimes she would stand outside with her ear pressed to the white wood, trying to hear what he was doing. During her particularly ill-advised rebellious phase, she would pick his door lock with a pair of child-size scissors and barge in uninvited.

Sage didn't move, so Kora opened the door. At first glance, his room was much the same as she remembered it. The dark wood paneling and small lamp meant that it was full of shadows. The bed was made but had only one pillow and a simple red comforter. His dresser was covered in memorabilia from high school, including his Eagle Scout certificate.

Behind the door, his desk stood out as very different from the last time she had been in there. It was covered in half-open books, sticky notes, and scraps of paper. The bulletin board leaning against the wall was cluttered with articles he had printed off and highlighted, along with maps he had cut out and pinned with locations. His own scratchy handwriting was everywhere. It had always been cluttered, but this was a different beast. It was obsessive, erratic. Sage's eyes jumped from one page to another, not taking in any of the words. She could see there were a lot of blurry black and white images of mysterious figures. The contents of the desk spilled out onto the floor, with a pile of books that came up to Sage's knees. A library card sat on top of the stack.

"I didn't even know he knew where the library was," she said, showing it to Kora.

"There are a lot of books here," said Kora. "I can't believe they let him check out this many at once."

Sage found a folded-up paper on the corner of the desk and opened it. It was a notice of an unpaid late fee from the local library branch, dated last month. "I don't think they'll be letting him check out anything for long."

She wanted to start sifting through the papers, but it was hard to tell where to start. She could see no indication of which books he had read most recently or which notes he was working on now.

There were two metal filing cabinets built into his desk. The bottom one locked with a key. She pulled on it with no luck.

When she opened the top drawer, she found a large, overstuffed journal, with more sticky notes than seemed probable coming out of the sides. The cover was a burnished leather that had been worn down over time. Sage pressed down on the front so she could see what was embossed into the leather: SAM RIVERA. It seemed like the kind of gift their dad would have given him.

Sage pulled it out and set it on the desk. It was so stuffed that it couldn't stay closed on its own. As she flipped through it, she saw pages and pages of Sam's handwriting, diagrams and photos that he had been printed out and glued onto the pages, and loose-leaf papers folded inattentively between pages.

The journal was the central account of Sam's research, that much was clear. But it was like it was written in some code that only Sam could understand. It was impossible to navigate, seemingly because it was organized according to the inside of his brain. Sage felt scared to touch it any more than she already had, like it belonged in a museum.

She frowned at the mysterious notebook. It was their best clue to finding Sam, and it was indecipherable. She let out a frustrated sigh and ran her fingers over a library copy of *Mountain Madness: A Firsthand Account of the Phantom Hiker* by Thomas J. Elliot.

"We should go to the library," said Sage. "Maybe they can tell us which books he checked out last so we have a place to start," said Sage.

"It's worth a try," said Kora. "Let's get out of here. The lighting in this room gives me a headache."

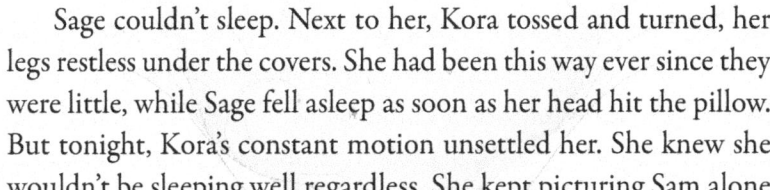

Sage couldn't sleep. Next to her, Kora tossed and turned, her legs restless under the covers. She had been this way ever since they were little, while Sage fell asleep as soon as her head hit the pillow. But tonight, Kora's constant motion unsettled her. She knew she wouldn't be sleeping well regardless. She kept picturing Sam alone in the woods, stubbornly trying to find his way. In the dark, she glanced over at Kora, who always seemed to be glaring in her sleep.

Another memory kept coming back to her. After her mother's funeral, they had a reception at their house. Most of it was spent nodding politely at family members she hadn't seen in years, but then Sam had walked downstairs. He was holding one of their mom's scarves, one that had been hanging in her closet. It was small and made of silk, and he clutched it in his hand like a handkerchief. Sage saw him from across the room. His eyes were red-rimmed and hollow, though she hadn't yet seen him cry. For a moment, she forgot all the family and the food and just looked at her brother and remembered that she wasn't the only one suffering. Their mother had fallen, and the rest of them were tumbling like dominoes in her wake. He crossed the room and handed her the scarf. She took it and grabbed his hand. They stood side by side, not saying anything.

It was that look from across the room, and the feel of his hand in hers, that she couldn't stop thinking about now. Her brother was older than her, but he needed her just as much as she needed him. This grief was shared between them, and they each had to pull each other back from it sometimes. Wherever he was, she was responsible for him.

Sage woke up at 5 a.m. automatically, still attuned to her swim practice sleep schedule. Kora had finally settled into a relaxed sleep, snoring softly into the pillow. Sage gently climbed out of bed, careful not to wake her.

She figured since she had time to kill before Kora woke up, she would go through her normal morning routine as if she were going to practice. Shower, clothes, coffee, breakfast. She also called her swim coach and successfully pretended to be too sick for practice. That excuse wouldn't hold up for very long, especially if Coach tried to talk to her dad about it, but she would deal with that later.

After she finished getting ready, she still had some time to kill, so she went for a run.

The early morning mist was soothing to her nerves. She loved moving her body. That was the one part of swimming that she actually liked.

When she had first started, she had also liked the rigidity, the strict schedule, the clear wins and losses. It had provided a protective cage around her ADHD to keep her from getting distracted. Between school and swimming, her free time was all accounted for. But now, that cage was feeling a little too tight. She had the rest of her life mostly under control–missing brother notwithstanding—so she wasn't sure she needed a team sport to keep her on track.

When she got back to the house, Kora was up, munching on the toast Sage had left for her. As usual, Kora's hair stuck out in three different directions, and she looked like she was asleep standing up. Sage silently made her a coffee, and Kora took it gratefully, then poured several spoonfuls of sugar into it.

"What time does the library open?" Kora asked, shoving half a piece of toast in her mouth and washing it down with coffee.

"Nine," said Sage, She glanced at the oven clock. They still had half an hour before they would need to leave. "Can we go now, though?" she asked. Kora's expression was unkind, so she added, "We can get better coffee, with all the sugary stuff you like."

Kora reluctantly agreed.

While Kora was getting dressed, Sage took Sam's notebook from his room. She wanted to bring it with her, but it was big and unruly, and she wanted to keep it hidden from the general public. She found an old messenger bag of her dad's that was the right size to keep it in.

Kora came downstairs and laughed at the sight of Sage holding the bag over her shoulder.

"Professor Rivera," she greeted with a little bow.

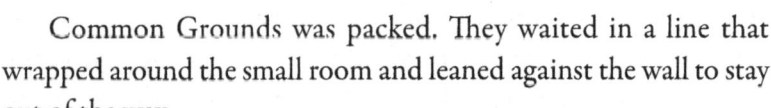

Common Grounds was packed. They waited in a line that wrapped around the small room and leaned against the wall to stay out of the way.

Sage looked at her watch: 8:42. The library wasn't open yet.

She tried to calm her anxiety but she couldn't stop her rubber-soled heel from tapping against the baseboard. Kora lay her head on Sage's shoulder, which was one of the primary forms of physical contact Sage was comfortable with.

When they got to the front of the line, Kora's head suddenly spiked up, nearly clipping Sage's ear.

"You look tired," the barista said in a very suggestive voice and a sly smile. Sage took a step back and looked between the two of them. Did they know each other? It wasn't exactly uncommon for people to flirt with Kora, but they seemed familiar with each other.

"Remember my order?" Kora asked. She looked suspiciously less tired than she had a moment before. The barista nodded.

Sage ordered an Americano and put it together. It was Hunter, Kora's new crush. Short black hair, tattoos, a confident, relaxed way of moving. She had to admit, Hunter seemed cool. But Sage would reserve judgment until she had tried Hunter's espresso.

They found a table in the crowded room. When the coffee was ready, Hunter brought it to them personally, passing the line of customers off to another barista. Kora's face brightened as she wrapped her hands around the warm cup.

"You're my hero," she sighed into the steam.

Hunter smiled. "Not a morning person," she laughed. "Got it."

"Definitely a night owl," Kora said, smiling back. "I didn't know you worked here."

"Yeah, tattooing isn't exactly a full time gig yet," said Hunter.

Sage cleared her throat pointedly.

"Right," Kora said, "Sorry. Sage, this is Hunter."

Sage took a sip of her drink and then said, "Okay. I like you."

Hunter gave her a confused look, but with a smile.

"Thanks, I guess?"

Sage just nodded.

Kora and Hunter continued to flirt while the other barista shot Hunter nasty looks for abandoning him. Sage looked at her watch.

"Kor," she said. "It's 8:53."

She watched with vague interest as they said goodbye and promised to text each other or whatever, before physically pulling Kora from the building.

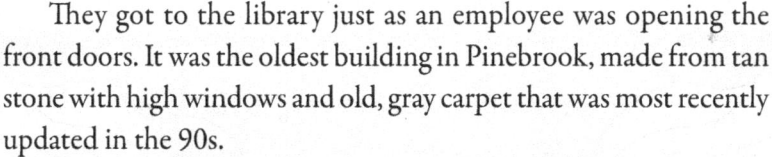

They got to the library just as an employee was opening the front doors. It was the oldest building in Pinebrook, made from tan stone with high windows and old, gray carpet that was most recently updated in the 90s.

Inside, the library was totally empty. Sage had never seen it without its usual population of elderly perusers and stressed out college kids. It was a little creepy.

Sage hadn't been much since she was a kid, when her mom would bring all three of them for the library's weekly story time events. Since Oakcrest had its own library on campus, she hadn't needed to use the public one.

At the checkout desk, a young man scanned returned books and placed them on a cart. He looked a little older than them. He was tall and thin with dark skin and short, curly hair. He pushed a pair of glasses further up the bridge of his nose as he took a closer look at the spine of a book. A laminated staff identification card hung around his neck on a lanyard.

"Hi," said Kora, walking up to the desk. The boy looked up, seeming surprised to hear her voice. He set the last book onto the cart.

"What can I help you with?" he asked. His smile was bright and earnest. Perfect for a librarian, Sage thought.

She stepped around Kora and pulled out Sam's library card from her pocket.

"Could you tell us the last few books that were checked out with this card?" she asked.

The boy took the card and looked it over. He raised his eyebrows and looked back at Sage, eyes wide.

"How did you get Sam Rivera's card?" he asked.

Sage's eyes narrowed. "You know my brother?"

"Oh, you must be Sage," he said brightly, pointing a finger gun at her. "Sam has talked about you before. I'm Noah. Your brother comes in a lot."

Sage remembered the stack of books in Sam's room and the unpaid late fee. "Are you the one that keeps letting him check out more books?" she asked.

Noah laughed and looked down at his hands. "Yeah, my boss isn't really a stickler for the rules."

"So can you look up his records?" Sage asked impatiently.

"Is there a reason you need to see them?" Noah asked, raising an eyebrow. "It's not really library policy to pull someone's borrow history without them present."

"It's important," said Sage. She tapped her finger tips against her leg, her anxiety quickly turning into irritation.

Kora stepped in again. She was much better at being polite than Sage was.

"He hasn't been home in a few days," she whispered, leaning over the counter, even though no one else was there. "I'm sure he's fine, but we'd like to see if we can trace his steps."

Sage worried that Noah would question why they weren't handing this over to the cops, but he just looked around conspiratorially, matching Kora's vibe.

"Was he looking for something?" he asked, looking back and forth between the two of them intensely.

Sage crossed her arms. "Did he tell you what he was looking for?" she asked.

Library patrons started to come inside. Mostly old people there to use the computers.

Noah looked around the desk until he found a small placard that read "Be back in 15 minutes!" with a little clock holding a thumbs up. He placed it in front of the computer and gestured for them to follow him.

He led them to a back room full of office supplies and old books that needed to be rebound. Sage didn't waste any time.

"What did he tell you?" she whispered, her tone a little more hostile than she intended.

"I've been helping him research ghost stories," said Noah. "I'm a history major at the community college, and I'm really interested in local history. I know a lot about historical ghost sightings, so when he came in looking for books on local legends, I talked to him about it."

He leaned back against a small table that held an ancient desktop. Next to him, a large, gray copy machine hummed inharmoniously.

"So, how long have you known Sam?" Kora asked. She used her friendliest voice to balance out Sage's interrogation.

"I guess it's been over a year now," said Noah, looking up while counting the months. "Wow, time flies."

"Did he say why he wanted to know about that stuff?" Sage asked.

Noah nodded, his face somber. "He told me he was trying to find out if any of them were real."

"And you didn't think he was crazy?" asked Sage.

Noah shrugged. "I don't think anybody's crazy," he said. "People have reported the same sightings over decades and centuries around here. Reading the history, it's hard not to believe it's possible."

"You sound like Sam," said Kora. Sage had to agree, although Sam rarely talked to them about it.

"He has a habit of rubbing off on people, it seems," said Noah with a soft smile.

Noah seemed totally harmless and trustworthy, but Sage still had her arms crossed. It was a painful reminder that this stranger knew more about her brother than she did lately.

"So," said Kora, bringing attention back to the issue at hand. "Do you know where he was headed most recently?"

Noah shook his head, disappointed. "But," he said, "I can look up his records like you asked. Maybe the books he's been reading will point you in the right direction."

At that, Sage finally relaxed a little. They followed Noah back to the front desk. He took down the placard and logged into the system. Then he scanned Sam's library card and handed it back to Sage. A loud, angry printer slowly began to spit out a sheet of paper.

"This is a list of all the books he currently has checked out, along with when he got them," said Noah.

Sage pulled the page from the printer as soon as it finished inking the last line. She pored over the words, but Kora could see that the titles didn't reveal much.

"Oh, and he talked sometimes about a contact in Cherokee," said Noah. "There's a guy who owns a bookstore called Shortleaf Books. Sam mentioned running things by him a few times. That might be a good place to start."

Kora nodded and wrote the name on the printout.

"These books are probably all in Sam's room," said Kora. "Let's go home and read through the recent ones."

Sage nodded and turned to leave.

"Can I ask—" said Noah, stretching his hand out as Sage walked away. "What are you planning on doing once you figure out where he was going?"

"Find him," said Sage, and she kept walking toward the door.

"She means thank you," Kora said.

"No problem," said Noah. "Sam's a good guy. If he really is missing, I hope you two find him."

"Me too," said Kora.

CHAPTER 5

Kora and Sage spent all afternoon scouring Sam's books, cross-referencing it with the journal and trying to find any clues as to where he might have gone. They still didn't have much to go on.

The journal continued to confound them. It was like it was written in code—the pages were filled with seemingly random coordinates and scribbled half-thoughts. Sam's handwriting was difficult to decipher and many pages showed signs of spilled coffee and smeared ink.

When it started to get dark, they headed for the diner—Pinebrook's only 24-hour restaurant and primary destination for intoxicated college kids and high schoolers with no curfews, which happened to include Sage and Kora. It was their favorite place to go at 3 a.m. to share a huge plate of shoestring fries and a milkshake. They rarely came during the dinner rush, so it was strange to see the parking lot so full.

They got their usual booth in the back, and Sage's knee was bouncing, knocking against the bottom of the table. Kora wanted to lay her hand on top of it but figured it was a good outlet for Sage's nervous energy.

"I'm sure he's fine," Kora said. "Sam's an expert hiker. There must be some other explanation for why he hasn't come home."

"He's been doing this for a long time," Sage agreed. "But for two years, he's always come home when he said he would. Or he's called."

"Do you really think he's in trouble?" she asked, though she already knew the answer from the look on Sage's face.

"Yeah," she said. "I do."

"Should we call the park ranger?" Kora asked.

Sage shook her head. "We don't even have it narrowed down to one forest," she said.

"Plus he's not exactly the respect-for-authorities type," Kora said. "I doubt he checked in with them before going out there."

Suddenly, a third person appeared at their table. "Talking about me?" said the unmistakable voice of Connor Riley. Sage glared at him. Kora almost laughed at her glowering expression; Sage was not often in the mood for Connor's particular brand of humor, but even less so when she was already distressed.

"Connor, you are literally the physical embodiment of respect for authorities," said Sage.

Connor looked her up and down. Her leg was still bouncing, and her hand was clenched into a fist on the table. She seemed to notice his attention, because she pressed her hand down on her knee to stop it from bouncing.

"What's wrong?" Concern had dripped into Connor's voice once again. Whenever Connor was feeling earnest, his parents' Southern Appalachian accent came out stronger.

"Nothing," said Sage.

"Sam might be missing," Kora said.

Sage glared at her, and Kora gave her a challenging look back. She knew that Sage was protective over him and didn't want anyone knowing his business who didn't have to. Kora wasn't sure exactly why she was so intense about it—Sage had rarely even talked about it before he went missing.

But the situation was too important to worry about secrecy.

Connor's eyes widened. He dropped into the booth next to Kora. She briefly remembered how many late nights the three of them spent in this same configuration in this same booth.

"What do you mean by missing?" he asked.

"He went looking for something," said Sage. Kora raised an eyebrow at the vague wording. "He was supposed to be back by now, but we haven't heard from him."

"What was he looking for?" Connor asked.

Kora and Sage had another of their silent conversations, in which Sage's expression said, *He doesn't need to know the details,* and Kora's said, *What harm could telling him do?*

Sage sighed. "Ghosts."

Connor didn't seem phased, which surprised Kora. They hadn't talked much about the supernatural, but he wasn't usually quick to accept the unexplainable.

"Any ghost in particular?" he asked. It was common knowledge that the mountains had a lot of rumored hauntings.

"We don't know," said Kora.

"Have you told your dad?" Connor asked Sage.

As she considered it, Kora realized it hadn't occurred to her to involve him until now. He had faded into the background recently, becoming a shadow in his own house. She wished there was a capable adult that they could appeal to who could make everything better. But Sage's mother's death had thrown their entire makeshift family out of orbit and into a new dimension of care and responsibility. All of them had grown up too fast.

"I'm not bringing this to him until I have to," said Sage, echoing Kora's thoughts. "He's had enough to worry about."

"Are you going to call the cops?" Connor asked. This also had not occurred to Kora. She turned to Sage, who was rolling her eyes.

"If it were you, sure, I'd call the cops," said Sage, disdain clear in her voice. "But they don't give a shit about Sam. And I doubt they'd be able to find him anyway. Like Kora said, he doesn't exactly broadcast his intentions to the park rangers."

Kora had to agree. Pinebrook was a small town, and the Riveras were well-known and well-liked, with plenty of money and influence. But, unlike Sage, Sam had inherited their father's darker complexion. With their last name, Sage could often pass for Italian, but Sam didn't get the same kind of treatment.

Kora glanced over at Sage's profile. Her jaw was set. Sage had her own reasons for disliking cops. The night her mother died, the cops had been the ones to come to her door to tell her the news. She hadn't been particularly courteous to them in response.

Connor didn't ask any further questions. Sage's expression must have been enough to convince him.

Sage put her hand down on her knee to stop it from shaking again.

"I need to go look for him," she said.

They were silent for a minute. Connor and Kora glanced at each other. The waitress brought them their signature giant plate of fries, but no one took one.

"We don't know for sure he's missing," said Kora. "Like I said, there has to be another explanation."

"Either way, something's wrong here, and I need to find out what it is," said Sage.

"Even if he is missing," said Kora, "you could get lost, too." She could picture Sage traipsing through the woods with a compass, dirt smeared on her cheeks, growing scrawny from lack of food.

"I won't," said Sage.

Kora could feel Connor's eyes on her, but she met Sage's gaze, trying to gauge how serious she was. Sage didn't blink.

"I think you're right," said Connor. Both of the girls turned to look at him in surprise. "You need to find him."

Sage smiled tightly. With him on her side, Kora didn't really have room to argue. "It's settled then," she said. "I'm going."

Kora sighed. "Okay," she said. Sage's knee finally stopped bouncing without being forced to. "Obviously, I'm coming with you." She wasn't sure about anything except that she wouldn't let Sage go alone. She leaned back in her seat and ate some fries.

Sage frowned. "It's probably nothing," she argued, seemingly more to herself than anyone else.

"Either it's so worrisome that we both need to check it out, or it's nothing, in which case there's no need for you to go," said Kora. "Can't be both."

Sage's frown deepened, but she didn't have a response to that.

"If it turns out to be for nothing, then we'll get some good hiking in," Kora said. She smiled triumphantly.

"Fine," said Sage. "But we're leaving tomorrow morning."

"I'm coming, too," said Connor.

Once again, they turned to him at the same time with identical incredulous looks.

"I don't remember inviting you," said Sage. "Kora is family, but you barely know Sam. Why would you want to help us look for him?"

Connor was kind and had always liked Sam, but Kora had a feeling there was more to it than that. She was pretty sure she saw his eyes flicker toward her. This could be his way of getting more time with her. She didn't feel great about that idea.

"I'm not going to let you two go alone," he said, picking up a fry and tossing it into his mouth. "I don't trust you not to take stupid risks."

"What do you think we're going to do, jump off a cliff?" said Sage.

"Maybe," he said, dismissing her sarcasm. "You two have done a lot of stupid things."

Kora rolled her eyes. Connor's tolerance for risk-taking was pretty low. He didn't think she and Sage should be sneaking into the park at night to hang out on the playground, and that was pretty harmless, in Kora's opinion.

"Plus, you need my car," said Connor with a triumphant look of finality. "Kora's car shouldn't be driven more than five miles from the nearest auto shop."

That stung a little, but he was right. Kora's car was an ancient station wagon with bad suspension and a cracked windshield. It broke down frequently, and Kora had already eaten up all her AAA towing miles for the year. The trunk was also currently full of blank canvases she had bought when the craft store had a sale.

"Fine," said Sage. "But I pick the music. None of your folksy acoustic strumming music."

Connor was visibly offended, but he threw back, "Kora also likes 'folksy acoustic strumming music,' if I remember correctly."

Kora looked away. That was exactly the kind of situation she was trying to avoid with him. Reminiscing about all the concerts they had gone to together was not going to help with the whole "being broken up" thing.

"Sage doesn't let me pick the music either," she said, grabbing a handful of fries.

They both looked satisfied enough. But thinking about his car reminded her of another problem.

Sam was an Eagle Scout. He regularly went for overnight backpacking trips and climbed mountains. His capabilities far exceeded theirs. And if they were going to find him, they were going to have to follow in his forest-trekking footsteps.

"You guys are forgetting something," said Kora. "We're not particularly good hikers. We don't have any backpacking experience. Plus, we don't even have the right equipment. Our family camping trips did not prepare us to follow Sam into the woods. If we don't bring someone who knows this area and is prepared to hike it, we're going to trip over a rock and fall off a cliff way before we find Sam."

Kora hadn't mentioned anything about Hunter, but she knew immediately that Sage could read her mind. Sage narrowed her eyes at Kora skeptically and she felt her face flush.

"Let me guess," said Sage. "Hunter just so happens to be like a young, hot, lesbian Bear Grylls?"

Kora knew it seemed like she just wanted her crush to come along. But truthfully, she would not invite Hunter on a road trip with her best friend and her ex after two encounters and one kiss. In fact, she felt like it was probably a terrible idea romantically. But they had gone to school with a bunch of pale skinny nerds. They didn't have many friends who were good with the outdoors.

"Do you have any better ideas?" she asked. Connor was included in that question, but Kora didn't make eye contact with him.

Both of them were silent, but she could tell neither of them were happy about it.

"I'll ask her," said Kora, putting an end to the conversation.

Despite her hesitance to invite Hunter, once the plans were made, Sage's knee stopped bouncing. She relaxed into the plump vinyl booth.

Kora texted Hunter: *Are you up for a camping trip tomorrow? I know this is weird and last minute, but it's important.*

Her response: *I'm in.*

Kora gulped down the last of her tea and swirled around the ice with her straw. When she looked up, Sage's shoulders dropped below her ears for the first time that night. And that was the most important thing.

The Riveras were as close to her blood as friends could be. She loved them fiercely and unflinchingly. They would find Sam, whatever it took.

CHAPTER 6

Sage sat on the front porch with a coffee. It was nearly dawn, and the sky was starting to lighten. She couldn't remember the last time she watched the sunrise from anywhere other than the pool. Her stomach was full of bile as she thought about telling the coach she had mono. Searching for her maybe-missing brother would have raised some red flags, and she was sure it would not be considered an acceptable excuse to miss practice.

The swim team was no joke; if they found out she was lying, she would never be able to swim competitively again and would likely be expelled from Oakcrest. She had called from Sam's room, looking at the pile of dusty books on his desk to remind herself why it was vital for her to go.

Kora wasn't awake yet, and since they still had to wait for Connor and Hunter to show up, there was no point in waking her. But without her and without swimming, there was no distraction from worrying about Sam. The coffee made her jittery, and she needed something to do with her hands.

After the sun came over the horizon, she heard the porch door open and close. It was far too early to be Kora. Her dad's familiar scent settled over her as he sat on the wicker loveseat.

"Don't you have practice?" he asked, voice still gravelly with sleep. He was wearing a robe over a white t-shirt and sweatpants.

"I'm going camping with Kora," she said.

In all her planning, she hadn't really given much thought to what she would say to her dad. She had forgotten he might be opposed to her skipping swim practice to go on an impromptu camping trip.

"That sounds fun," he said. He leaned back and closed his eyes.

Sage found herself disappointed. She didn't want her father to pose an obstacle to the trip she knew she needed to make, but he didn't ask where they were going or why she hadn't told him before now. With Sam, it was different; he was an adult and was hardly home enough to qualify as living under their dad's roof. But Sage was still in high school. A few years ago, she couldn't wait to live on her own and make her own rules. Now, it felt like she'd been tossed out of a plane without a parachute.

Her dad didn't open his eyes again, and after a while, Sage realized he had fallen back asleep.

———— ◆ ————

Connor knocked on the door in the garage. He, like Sage, was fully dressed and held a half-empty coffee in his hand. They started loading camping equipment into the back of his Jeep while Kora trudged around, half-heartedly loading her duffel bag and then trying not to fall asleep on the stairs. She was still wearing her pajamas, and her sleep mask was around her neck. It was pink and embroidered with the word "Princess" in cursive, probably something she'd had for a long time.

Sage caught Connor smiling at her as he shoved a tent on top of a plastic storage bin.

"Guess you're still not a morning person," he said, giving her a sip of his coffee.

"What would give you that idea?" Kora monotoned.

"No offense, but I'm glad we're not carpooling anymore."

"It's your fault we had to get to school early for your debate meetings. Maybe if I had slept in the extra hour I would have been more pleasant."

"Unlikely," he said, grinning. She shrugged in reluctant agreement.

Just as Sage tossed her own bag onto the pile in the back of the Jeep, Hunter pulled into the driveway on her motorcycle. Kora scowled at the noise and put her hands over her ears. When Hunter turned off the engine, Kora sighed in relief and walked up to her.

"Some of us are still waking up, you know," she said.

"You're lucky I'm here, princess," said Hunter. She pulled at the sleep mask around Kora's neck and smirked. "You're welcome for not letting you get lost in the woods."

Sage had no idea what Kora had said when she asked Hunter to come on this trip with them, only that she had agreed. She was very wary of getting involved in any romantic drama while they were trying to find her brother. It was not the time for fraternizing.

Sage showed Hunter where she could store the motorcycle in the garage while they were gone. There was space next to her mom's car, which had gathered a thick layer of dust. Her dad never came out here, so he probably wouldn't notice it. Hunter poked at the car inquisitively.

"What happened here?" she asked.

"It was my mom's," said Sage.

She waited for Hunter to ask follow-up questions, but she just held a curious expression. When Sage didn't elaborate, she drew a little line in the dust and kept moving.

The car was supposed to be handed down to Sam for his graduation, at which point Sage would get his car, but neither of them wanted to drive it after she died. Sam kept his car, and Sage borrowed their dad's. Most of the time, he didn't miss it, but she couldn't take it on a multi-day trip.

She was annoyed to realize that if her mother had lived, she wouldn't be relying on Connor right now. She pressed her toe into the rear tire, which was going a little flat. Her mom's death had screwed up a lot of plans.

Sage heard a knock on the front door. She looked around; Connor was leaning against the Jeep, and Kora and Hunter were talking in the driveway. Only strangers ever used the front door.

She crossed through the house to answer it, expecting to see a mailman delivering a large package or a missionary attempting to proselytize.

Instead, she saw Noah, the guy from the library. Sam's friend.

"What are you doing here?" she asked, trying to disguise the animosity in her voice. It wasn't Noah's fault that Sam hadn't told her much about his trips, she had to remind herself.

"I couldn't stop thinking last night," said Noah, looking at the ground. "About Sam."

Sage raised an eyebrow. "What about him?"

"If he really is missing, I want to help find him," he said. The worry in his face was genuine, but Sage was still wary of inviting a stranger.

"Trust me, we've got it covered," she said. "Our search party is already over-bloated."

"I guarantee you no one knows these stories like I do," he said. "That's why he talked to me about it."

From the doorstep, Sage could see that the sun was already over the treetops. Losing daylight.

"We're probably going overnight. Camping. We might even be gone for a few days."

"I packed a bag."

Sage glared at him. Something about his preparation made her suspicious.

Noah looked in her eyes for the first time. "I know you don't know me," he said, "but I know Sam. He trusted me with his research, and you can trust me, too. I can help you with his notebook."

Sage couldn't help her surprised face. She hadn't mentioned it to Noah and had kept it tucked away in her tote bag while they were in the library.

"I'm the only one who can understand it," said Noah.

Sage didn't have time to argue. And it occurred to her that it couldn't hurt to have another buffer between the love triangle drama.

"Fine," she said.

She led him back to the garage where Kora seemed to be awkwardly fielding a conversation about football. She shot Sage a glare for leaving them all alone, but turned it into a smile when she saw Noah. She introduced him to Hunter and Connor.

"He's going to be joining us," said Sage. It didn't look like anyone was going to object, but just in case, she raised a hand. "I didn't invite any of you, so this is my call."

It took a while to finish packing up the car. With the five of them and their camping gear, the Jeep was stuffed.

Sage headed for the driver's seat, but Connor held up his keys. "Where do you think you're going?" he asked.

"I'm driving," she said.

"No way," he said. "If you wreck my car, my parents will kill me."

"They can afford it."

Kora came up from behind Sage and reached for the keys.

"How about a compromise," she said. "I'll drive. Sage, you can ride shotgun and navigate. You know where we're going, and you'll need to look at the map anyway."

Sage nodded, but Connor didn't look appeased. "What makes you think I want you driving my car either?" he asked.

"Connor, I've driven your car a thousand times," she said. "One more won't hurt."

His face looked pained, and Kora looked guilty. Connor dropped the keys into her hand without a word. Sage climbed into the passenger seat while the other three squeezed into the back.

"What a clown car," Sage muttered under her breath.

—◆—

Their first destination was Chimney Rock, an hour-long drive from Pinebrook. Sage didn't like sitting in the passenger seat, but she focused her energy on navigation. She tried to keep herself from tapping her fingers on the dashboard because she knew it annoyed Kora, but whenever she stopped paying attention, her fingers twitched on their own.

It didn't help that there was no highway to take them to Chimney Rock. Getting through the mountains, they had to rely on winding, two-lane roads that passed acres of farmland and cut through thick forests. Kora was a good driver, but the sharp curves always made Sage queasy.

"I think there's a gas station coming up," said Kora, as if reading Sage's mind. "It might be our last opportunity to stop for a while."

"Sounds good," said Sage.

The gas station in question was small and ancient, blending into the surrounding bushes. Vines grew over the white brick siding, and the sign had long since faded past recognition. The pumps were old, not the digital ones you could find at a BP or Exxon. While Kora struggled to figure out how to swipe her debit card, Sage went inside to find a restroom.

The general store was filled with most things you could find at a gas station: cigarettes, beef jerky, 6-packs of beer. It also housed a collection of eclectic local trinkets. She passed a shelf of t-shirts with camping and hunting-related wordplay. She also noticed a section devoted to buying ammunition. She tried not to think about hunters out in the woods where Sam was hiking.

The restroom was as expected, and she spent as little time in there as she had to. When she came out, Connor waved her over to the candy aisle. As she rounded the corner, he shot her a conspiratorial look.

"Let's buy out all the peach rings so Kora can't get any," he said with a sly grin. "Make her think they're out."

Peach rings were Kora's favorite road trip snack—the kind you can only really find at gas stations—and they were very important to her.

"She'll kill you," said Sage, remembering more than one instance of Kora pouting when she was forced to travel without them.

"Not when she finds out she has five packs of them," Connor smirked.

Sage had to admit it was a good prank—the nice kind where nobody really got hurt, which was very much Connor's style.

"Do it," she said.

He pulled each of the packs of peach rings off the hook and brought them to check-out. The cashier looked confused as Connor piled them onto the counter but didn't say anything. Connor paid for them all and started hiding them in his clothes. He put two in each of his back pockets and asked Sage to hide the fifth one in hers.

They heard a chime as Kora came through the door. She looked frustrated, having given up on paying at the pump. She walked absentmindedly to the candy aisle and frowned at the empty shelf. Dejected, she paid for the gas and walked back to the car. Sage and Connor followed, grinning at each other.

Kora slid into the driver's seat, and her shoulders slumped miserably as she turned on the car. Hunter and Noah, still in the backseat, looked confused as Sage got into the passenger seat and Connor took his place in the back.

"What's wrong?" Hunter asked.

"They were out of peach rings," Kora said quietly.

"What are peach rings?" Noah asked.

"They're just this candy I like," said Kora with a pitiful sigh.

"Actually," said Connor, sending a look to Sage, "they look something like this." He pulled the four packs from his pockets and tossed them over the center console so each of them tumbled into Kora's lap. She looked behind her and laughed as Sage passed her the last one.

"You guys are the worst," she said, still smiling. She popped open one of the packs and shoved several peach rings into her mouth. She passed the pack to Noah. "Try one. They're great."

Kora passed another of the packs to Hunter for her to try one, too. Sage couldn't miss the way her grin seemed to shift to the corner of her mouth when she looked back at Hunter. Their hands almost touched when she passed over the pack. Connor didn't look too pleased at this side effect of his prank.

Kora pulled out of the parking lot, satisfied with her road trip snacks.

The rest of the hour passed quickly. Hunter connected her phone to the car's stereo, and she and Noah took turns adding songs to the list. Sage zoned out as she watched the trees pass through her window and paid little attention to the music.

"I'm sorry, but *To Pimp A Butterfly* is a classic," she heard Noah say. "It redefined the genre."

"Yeah, but *Damn* gained so much mainstream success for a reason," said Hunter.

Sage tried to tune out their banter. The dashboard told her it was already after nine. The sun was speeding across the sky, and with it, her chances of finding Sam today. She hoped they would find him safe at the ranger's station, broken sat phone in hand and a panic blanket wrapped around his shoulders. Or better yet, so absorbed in his quest that he hadn't bothered to check what day it was. She would try her best to stay mad, but she would really be relieved.

Memories were pulling at her focus again. Her mom had left that morning for a work trip, and the house felt creepy and even older than usual without either parent. Her dad wasn't picking up the phone, and it was already dark outside. Sam was pretending there was nothing to worry about, but Sage could see the wrinkles in his forehead. When the blue lights had darted through the window, she knew immediately what they meant.

Sage examined Kora's profile as she focused on the road. Kora had been there her whole life—every birthday, every Thanksgiving, every vacation. She held an honorary place on their mantle, another type of sibling. She should be just as worried about Sam. But Kora shoved peach rings into her mouth with one hand while driving with the other, occasionally adding something to Noah and Hunter's conversation.

Sage sighed. She should have guessed. No one was ever as worried as she was.

CHAPTER 7

Kora drove through the main road of Cherokee as Sage navigated from her phone. The address from Sam's contact brought them to a shopping center full of tourist traps. They parked and walked into a narrow, wooden walkway in front of a stretch of short buildings, all connected and covered in different colored metal roofs. Sage walked ahead of them, counting under her breath until she found 1400-G. Signs plastered the front displays: "Ice cream" and "Mocassins" and "Souvenirs." Finally, Sage stopped and looked up.

It was an old bookstore, the front window cluttered with used copies of the classics and local travel books. A red-orange neon sign read "BOOKS" instead of "OPEN." They couldn't see inside because the glass door was covered in posters for local poetry readings and open mic nights. A faded sign above the door identified it as Shortleaf Books.

"Have you ever been here before?" Kora asked Hunter.

Hunter shook her head, looking around with a frown.

"This part of town is really just for tourists," she said. "I didn't come over here much. It sucks that this is what a lot of people think of when they think of us. Just a bunch of tacky souvenirs."

Kora squeezed Hunter's shoulder.

"Maybe, when this is over and Sam is home, we could come back here," said Kora. "You can show me where you grew up. The parts you like the best."

She realized that the outing she was describing was a trip to Hunter's hometown where she would presumably meet Hunter's parents, which was a pretty presumptuous suggestion at this stage of a not-relationship. She stuttered and tried to backtrack, but Hunter just grinned at her and pulled her into the bookstore.

Sage was already inside, standing at the front counter while the boys spread out, wandering through the store. There was no one behind the counter, so Sage rang the service bell. Kora caught up with her and waited. She picked up a small wooden bear carving from a rack on the counter, turned it toward Sage, and made exaggerated growling faces. Sage was not amused.

Footsteps echoed through the dusty room as someone came out to greet them. A boy about their age emerged from the back. His shoulder-length black hair was tucked behind his ear on one side. A dusty, brown hand straightened his rumpled Metallica t-shirt, and he leaned over the counter.

"What can I help you with?" he asked cheerfully.

Sage spread a crumpled piece of paper on the counter. "I found this address in my brother's notes," she said. "His name is Sam Rivera, and I think someone here was a friend of his."

The boy's face brightened.

"Oh man," he said, "are you Sage? Sam's talked about you before."

Kora and Sage glanced at each other. Sage's face said *Why do people keep saying that to me?*

"That's me," she said, tentatively.

"I'm Austin," he said with a smile.

"It's nice to meet you," said Kora. She introduced herself and shook his hand.

"Okay, how do you know Sam?" Sage asked. She was not tolerating small talk.

Austin seemed taken aback by her aggression. He stepped back and busied himself as he organized some books.

"Oh, uh, he's a customer," said Austin.

"Do you know all your customers by name?" Sage asked. She leaned over the counter and very obviously looked to see what kind of books he was looking at. "Why do you know who I am?"

Kora rolled her eyes. She understood Sage's frustration better than anyone, but she also knew that Sage had never been particularly patient or friendly to strangers. She felt the need to intervene.

"What she means is," she said, nudging Sage out of the way, "we know Sam was working on a... research project. Do you know anything about it?"

Austin relaxed a little and nodded.

"He comes in sometimes asking about Cherokee stories," Austin said. Absent-mindedly, he swept away some of the dust from the counter. "We have tons of books on the stuff."

"That's great," said Kora with a polite smile. "Do you remember the last time you heard from Sam?"

"Sam doesn't really like me telling people about what he's working on," said Austin. "He's pretty secretive. I'm not sure why. Is there a reason you're asking?"

Sage nudged Kora back, though her nudge was a bit more forceful than Kora's had been.

"Sam was supposed to be home a couple days ago," Sage said.

"We're hoping he just forgot to call," Kora added. It wasn't necessarily untrue, and she didn't want this kid to call the cops. She sent a glance at Sage, silently telling her not to argue.

Austin looked back and forth between them.

"One sec," he said, disappearing behind the curtain to the back room. When he came back, he had a notebook stuffed full of looseleaf papers. He flipped it open to the very end.

"I kept a record of the stuff we talked about, in case he called and asked for the information again," he said. He ran his finger down the page, looking through his writings. "Here we go. He called a couple weeks ago wanting to know about the Siren of the French Broad. He already had plenty of intel on the story, but the original version mentions the Cherokee, so he wanted to know if there was anything similar in tribal stories." Austin looked up. "I haven't seen him since then, but maybe he's been around there."

"Thank you," said Sage scribbling frantically into a small notepad she pulled from her pocket. "This is really helpful."

"What can you tell us about the siren?" Kora asked.

Austin thought for a second and then turned around, rifling through a very precarious-looking stack of books behind him. He pulled one out, careful not to topple the rest, and handed it over.

"This book has some more information about it, I think. I gave him the title when he asked."

Sage took it. "How much?" she asked.

"Take it," Austin said. "If you find him, tell him to give me a call. I want to know he's okay."

Kora thanked him profusely while Sage rifled through the pages, but something behind her caught Austin's eye.

"Hunter?" he said, grinning. "Hunter Lane?"

Kora turned to see Hunter peeking out from one of the aisles, surprised to hear her name. Her surprise turned to recognition.

"Hey, man," she said. "It's been a while. I didn't know you worked here."

"Yeah," said Austin with a wide smile, "my dad owns the place."

"No shit?" she said, smiling and looking around at the tall bookshelves. "That's great."

"It's great to see you," he said, coming around from behind the counter to give her a hug. The boys noticed and came to see what was going on. "Are you guys friends with Hunter? She and I used to go to elementary school together."

Kora was excited to meet someone from Hunter's past. She didn't know much about her history yet, and for some reason, it delighted her to picture little Hunter in elementary school.

"I heard you moved to Pinebrook," he said. "How's it treating you?"

Hunter shrugged. "I like my job. And the people I've met have been nice." She glanced over at Kora and then slid her eyes to Sage, as if not wanting to single anyone out. Kora grinned. It was generous to imply that Sage was "nice." Hunter had not met them at a particularly good time for Sage to be anything but standoffish at best.

Austin put his hand on Hunter's shoulder, turning to the rest of the group. "You know," he said, "Hunter and I got married once."

Hunter covered her face with her hands.

"I'm sorry," said Sage. "Say that again?"

"Yeah, when we were five," Austin said. "It was a small ceremony on the playground, officiated by our friend Ben. I gave her a ring made out of yarn. Do you still have it?"

Hunter was looking very pointedly at the hardwood floor. "I, uh, I'd have to check," she said.

Kora laughed. "That's a yes," she said.

Hunter rolled her eyes. "It's at my parents' house," she said, her cheeks turning a little pink. "My mom doesn't throw anything out." Austin grinned.

"All right, well, if we have everything we need, we should go find your brother now," Hunter said quickly, turning toward Sage and corralling them all toward the door. "Nice to see you, Austin."

"Bye, wifey," he said back. Everyone laughed.

Before going back to the car, Connor suggested they go into a couple other stores to look for snacks. Most of the stores were souvenir shops, so all they found was novelty candy and gourmet trail mix.

While Sage and the boys walked further down the strip, Hunter looked at campfire coffee mugs that read "Visit Cherokee." Kora found her way over and stood next to her, pretending to examine the merchandise.

"Why didn't you tell me you were already hitched?" Kora mocked. "Could have saved me an awful lot of trouble flirting with a married woman."

"I'm pretty sure it wouldn't hold up in court," Hunter said. Kora laughed. Hunter slipped her hand into Kora's. She glanced around to see where the boys were but smiled surreptitiously. She liked seeing Hunter around someone she had known for a long time.

Connor and Noah checked out at the front desk with their souvenirs, and Sage steered them back to the car. The bright summer heat had warmed the Jeep's interior in the short hour they were gone, and getting back in the car was brutal. Kora leaned forward on her knees, trying not to touch her back to the seat. Buckling her seatbelt and avoiding the metal tip was an act of acrobatics.

"God, I hate the South," said Connor, his face covered in sweat.

Hunter laughed. "What, you can't handle the heat?"

Kora looked pointedly out the window and pretended to ignore the bickering happening in the backseat. It was going to be a long day.

———— ✦ ————

It took a while for Sage to arrange a campsite for them along the French Broad River, just north of Asheville, and it was another hour to drive there.

Sam's notebook mentioned several different ghosts rumored to appear along the river. The French Broad ran through the heart of the mountains, cutting into downtown Asheville. It had seen a lot of death. The main legend she could decipher was the one Austin had given them a book about—the Siren of the French Broad, a mysterious figure who pulled men into the river to drown. Of course, people had reported spotting the siren at lots of different points along the river, which didn't make their job easy.

They arrived just as dusk was falling, so they hurried to set up the tent before dark.

Connor had brought his enormous family tent and was the only one who could understand it, so he put it up. He agreed to let Noah share and directed him on how to help.

Hunter set up the girls' tent—one she had brought from home—with no help. Kora and Sage stood around the fire pit frowning at it until she was done.

"Want me to start the fire?" Hunter asked, dusting her hands off on her shorts.

"That would be good," said Kora. "We can get the food ready."

"Sam is an Eagle Scout, so he never let us help with the fire when our families went camping," said Sage, looking sheepish about her lack of camping skills.

"No worries," said Hunter, already collecting logs and kindling from the nearby woods.

Sage and Kora pushed hot dogs onto spears, so by the time the fire was ready, they could cook them by turning them over the flames.

Dinner was quiet except for the sound of hot dog juices dripping into the fire, and Kora couldn't stand the silence.

"Anybody want to play a game?" she asked.

"Sure," said Hunter. "I'm always up for a game."

Noah shrugged his acceptance. Connor looked uncomfortable but nodded.

"Never have I ever?" Sage suggested. Kora glared at her. That wasn't exactly what she had had in mind, but Hunter's eyes lit up conspiratorially. Plus, anything to get Sage's mind off Sam.

"We don't have any booze," said Kora.

"We can do it the middle school way," said Sage. She turned to the whole group. "Okay so you start with five fingers." She held her hand up in front of her, fingers outstretched. "If you've done the thing someone says, you put your finger down. The last one to lose all their fingers wins."

Kora and Connor both nodded. They'd played with Sage plenty of times at parties.

"I'll go first," said Hunter. "Never have I ever had a brother."

Sage rolled her eyes as she put her finger down, along with Connor. She was sitting to Hunter's left, so it was her turn. "Never have I ever gotten a tattoo."

Hunter haughtily curled her bicep, showing off her most prominent tattoos, and put a finger down. Kora put one down, too.

"I feel targeted," said Hunter. "Noah, your turn."

Noah considered. He still had all his fingers. They didn't know much about him, so Kora was curious what he would say.

"Never have I ever seen a ghost," he said.

Everyone looked around at each other, but no one put a finger down. Kora felt a chill and wrapped her jacket closer to her chest.

Connor's turn. "Never have I ever ridden a motorcycle," he said. Hunter was the only one to put a finger down. Kora sent him a pointed glance, knowing he was targeting Hunter, but he seemed to be watching to see if Kora put one of her fingers down. She could feel her face heat up, so she looked away and focused on taking her turn.

"Never have I ever gotten in trouble for pulling a kid's pants down on the playground," she said, deciding that targeting Sage with specific memories was the easiest way to play. With her non-playing hand, Sage gave her the finger.

"Never have I ever kissed a boy," said Hunter.

Kora was surprised. She put a finger down, and she noticed that Noah did, too. Kora didn't want to call attention to it just in case he was shy, but she did send him a small smile of non-hetero solidarity.

"Wait a second," she said, realizing. "Didn't you kiss Austin when you married him on the playground?"

Hunter rolled her eyes. "Fine," she said. "Never have I ever kissed a boy *with tongue*." Sage and Connor were still the only holdouts.

"Never have I ever lost my virginity in a Mazda," said Sage. Kora knew this was just Sage getting back at her, but now was so not the time for this. She tossed a pinecone at Sage's head, subtly putting her finger down. She intentionally didn't look at Connor to see how obvious he was being as he put his down, too.

"Noah?" she nudged, eager to move on to the next question.

"Never have I ever gotten an A in science," he said.

Sage snorted and lowered her finger. Connor and Hunter did, too. *Great*, Kora thought. *My type is nerds.*

She scoffed. "I'm an artist," she said. "I don't need to balance chemical equations."

"Word," said Noah. "Humanities, bitches." Kora nodded in his direction.

Sage wiggled her pinky in the air. "I only have one left," she said.

It went to Connor. Kora wondered if he would try to get Sage out or target someone else. She had a bad feeling when he glanced at Hunter.

"Never have I ever smoked a cigarette," he said.

To everyone's surprise, Hunter's finger stayed up, but Sage was out. Kora made a fake-shocked look at Sage, though she knew. Someone with that much going on mentally was bound to have a bad habit or two. Kora knew that from experience—she relied way too much on coffee and sugar to get through her day.

Sage had lost, so the game was over. Connor started getting ready for bed. Sage pulled out a lantern and started pouring over Sam's notebook, occasionally skimming the book Austin had given her. Noah sat down next to her to help.

Kora and Hunter stayed by the fire, putting marshmallows on the hot dog spits.

"How do you like yours?" Kora asked.

"Burned to a crisp. You?"

"Same." Kora smiled and let her marshmallow catch fire. She turned it over, letting the fire catch on all sides, and then blew it out. She held it out for Hunter. "You can have the first one."

She expected Hunter to take the marshmallow with her fingers, but instead, she steadied the spit with her hand and pulled it off with her teeth. She watched Hunter's tongue slide across her lips and knew it wasn't just the fire that was heating up her chest.

"Perfect," said Hunter.

Kora heard Noah head for the tent. Sage tried for a little while longer to decipher the notebook, but eventually let out a frustrated huff, turned off the lamp, and trudged toward the tent.

"Make sure you put out the fire before you come to bed," she said absent-mindedly, still turning over the gears in her head. Kora nodded.

She became suddenly aware that she and Hunter were alone for the first time since they'd left Pinebrook. But she was also aware that Connor was lying on an air mattress mere feet from them, not to mention Sage and Noah.

"Why did you want to come with us?" she asked, her voice nothing but a whisper. The forest was alive with sound, and the fire crackled loudly, but she leaned in close enough that Hunter could hear her.

Hunter kept looking into the fire, pushing her marshmallow close to the embers but not letting it catch yet. The flames cast a lovely orange glow on her skin and shadows danced across her cheekbones just like the night they met. Kora thought of how she would draw that sharp jawline, smudge the shadows into her cheekbones.

"We need you. I'm not saying we don't," Kora whispered. "We need all the help we can get. But you just met me. Why would you give up your whole weekend to come on some mysterious mission with people you don't know?"

"I've always been up for an adventure," said Hunter, her mouth splitting into a wry smile. Kora's heart skipped a beat.

She looked back at the fire. Maybe she shouldn't flatter herself. Maybe it was just an adventure, and the kiss was nothing new to Hunter. Maybe she made a habit of going from town to town, kissing girls and going on road trips with abandon.

"And it seemed like a good way to impress you," Hunter said so softly Kora almost didn't hear her.

Kora grinned, keeping her face toward the fire.

"But we can hold off on... whatever this is, if you want," said Hunter, suddenly pensive. Kora looked up but couldn't decipher her expression. "Until we know Sam is okay. I know it must be weird, having me and Connor both here. We can just be friends for now, no messiness."

For a moment, Kora was hurt, and then she remembered that she was the one who wanted things to be uncomplicated. It was out of necessity. So much was changing this summer; her mom was moving away, she was going to college, and something less certain was shifting in Sage's family. It was bad enough that she had brought Hunter into this mess. To carry on with whatever they started with that kiss would be ill-advised. She nodded, trying to keep the disappointment off her face.

"That makes sense," she said. "Just friends helping friends find a missing brother."

Hunter grinned. "Exactly. Just gals being pals."

Kora laughed. "Well, this trip has already been good for our friendship. I'm learning more about you."

"Well, that's not hard. I'm an open book," said Hunter without a hint of irony. Kora scoffed. "What?"

"You don't seem like an open book," said Kora, an involuntary smile spreading across her face. "You seem all broody and mysterious."

Hunter rolled her eyes. "All right then," she said. "Ask me anything, oh buddy of mine."

Kora raised one eyebrow. She thought about all the things she wanted to know about Hunter. There were too many to narrow down. She thought back to the day they'd had, to their short trip to Cherokee, Hunter's hometown. But other than running into Austin, she hadn't mentioned her childhood once.

"Do you get along with your family?" she asked, voice still soft to avoid waking the others. It felt like she was asking for a secret.

Hunter's confident smile faded almost imperceptibly. She started at the fire for a minute.

"It's complicated," she said.

Kora couldn't keep the smirk from her face. "Open book, huh?" Hunter grinned, but she felt compelled to add, "You don't have to tell me if you don't want to."

Hunter sighed, relenting. "I get along with my mom. She's the best." There was something sad in her eyes while she spoke, and Kora was content to listen. "She's worked for the tribe my whole life, and she's on the council now. She takes it really seriously and was always signing me up for extracurriculars and Cherokee language lessons."

While Hunter spoke, Kora watched the way the flames flickered over her face and listened to the sounds of crickets chirping in the woods. Hunter paused, but Kora just waited.

"I never really got along with my dad. I don't know what he expected having a daughter would be like, but I guess *I* wasn't it. He named me Hunter and took me on all these camping trips when I was little, but then at some point, he suddenly wanted me to wear dresses and go with him to church on Sunday. It was like he saw me turning into too much of a tomboy and needed to correct it. And he didn't ever seem to care about my mom's work with the tribe. He's not Cherokee, so I guess he just didn't get it, but it sucked that he was so dismissive."

Kora started rotating another marshmallow while she listened just to have something to do with her hands. She was sitting close enough to feel the rise and fall of Hunter's shoulders as she took a deep breath.

"He's not... a bad guy. He just doesn't get me," she said. "Or my mom, really. And I never understood why they were together. My mom is so caring. She's always there for people, you know? And it's like he just doesn't see her. And then with me," she drifted off, her face falling a little. "When I came out, my mom was totally fine with it, immediately supportive. And it's not like he ever said anything homophobic or anything, but it was like he had just given up on me ever living up to his expectations. He started acting like I didn't exist. He didn't even say anything when I decided to start tattooing."

Without thinking, Kora reached out and took Hunter's hand. It was warm from where she had been leaning toward the fire. She offered up the toasted marshmallow, and Hunter pulled it off the stick with her fingers this time, sucking on the tip of her thumb to get rid of the stickiness. When she finished, she glanced back at Kora, who nodded for her to continue.

"Now, I just don't really see either of them much anymore," she said. "Because seeing my mom means seeing my dad. And it's not like I'm estranged from them, but most of the time, I just... don't want to."

Kora nodded while she listened, rubbing her thumb over Hunter's knuckles. She wasn't sure she could ever understand the intricacies of another person's family; sometimes she was still on the outside of the Riveras, and she was practically one of them. But she was glad that Hunter was talking to her. It felt good to know her better, to listen to the gentle cadence of her voice, the one Kora had found so intimidating at first.

"Thank you," she whispered.

Hunter smiled back. "Told you," she said. "Open book."

"You can ask me something if you want."

Hunter tilted her head back as she considered, and Kora's eyes wandered over the expansive column of her throat.

"I'll ask you the same thing," she said.

Kora laughed quietly. "Cheater."

Hunter grinned.

As she considered her answer, she grabbed another marshmallow and squashed it between two of her fingers.

"It's always just been me and my mom," she said. "We've had our issues. I've spent my whole life trying to figure out our relationship, and then when she married Paul a few years ago, I stopped trying. I never really even got to know him. But she and Paul are moving away soon, and I'm..." she paused, not wanting to remind herself or Hunter of her plans to go to New York in the fall. "I'm not going with them."

As she paused, she listened to the chirping crickets, loudly singing in the trees.

"What about your dad?" Hunter asked softly, squeezing Kora's hand.

"I don't know much about him," said Kora with a small shrug. "He was a farmhand on my grandparents' farm when my mom was a teenager. He got her pregnant and then moved on. I guess I just didn't think it was worth putting in a lot of effort to care about someone who obviously didn't care about me."

Her throat felt tight. That wasn't quite true. Sometimes she did wonder, but her stubbornness to shove him to the back of her mind always won out. It wasn't that her mom made up the difference—though for the most part she did everything a parent needed to do. Kora just didn't think he was worth thinking about.

"That's why I'm so close with Sage's family," she said. "Mom was close with Liz—Sage's mom—before she died, and they basically raised us together. I've known them since we were babies. When I think of family, I think of them."

When she finally looked up, she found Hunter's eyes on her face, unwavering. It made her cheeks flush. Hunter was roasting another marshmallow, but all her attention was on Kora.

"I'm glad I can help you find Sam," said Hunter, barely a whisper. "Now that I know how important he is to you."

"I'm glad you're here," said Kora, smiling gently.

Kora heard someone turn over in the tent behind them. She remembered that they weren't alone. And she remembered that she had a lot of reasons to keep this platonic. She didn't want to hurt Connor. She was leaving at the end of the summer, and there was still so much she didn't know about Hunter. Even though the weight of everything they had shared felt heavy between them.

But then Hunter looked up at her, her eyelashes casting long shadows across her cheeks, embers warming the color of her lips. Kora wanted to reach out and run a finger down Hunter's face, pull her forward, and see if those lips were as warm as they looked. She tucked her hands underneath her thighs to keep herself from doing something she shouldn't.

"We should probably put the fire out," she said, her voice barely an exhale.

Hunter nodded, catching her marshmallow on fire and blowing it out seconds later. "You want this one?" she asked. Kora imagined eating it the way Hunter had, but she decided it wasn't a good idea.

"Go for it," she said. Hunter ate it in one bite.

Kora got up and looked for a water bucket. She threw it quickly over the fire and noticed her hands were shaking.

She couldn't remember the last time she had wanted to kiss someone so bad. Maybe when she and Connor had first got together, but maybe not even then. The memory of her kiss with Hunter ran through her head as she listened to the fire hiss and watched the steam and smoke pour into the sky.

When they climbed into the tent, there was room for each of them on either side of Sage. Kora was relieved. She wasn't sure how she could lie next to Hunter in the dark right now. As they settled in for the night, all she could really think about was the way Hunter's lips looked in the light of the fire.

Then she heard Sage's deep, measured breathing and remembered what they were there for. She felt guilty for thinking about anything but Sam. This trip was pulling her in all different directions, and her heart ached. Outside, an owl hooted. She hoped it would be over soon—with Sam back where he should be and her heart settled back into place.

When she slept, she dreamt of fire.

CHAPTER 8

The sun was beating down when they started on the path. The small dirt trail was dappled by the shade of the trees, but the heat couldn't be stopped. Summer turned everything technicolor, and Sage could feel the waves of heat bouncing off the ground and soaking into her skin.

Swelter was a word invented in the South. Even having lived here her whole life, she never seemed to get used to it.

The sweat on her neck made her feel like bugs were crawling on her. Heat only made her anxiety more palpable.

The French Broad was 218 miles long and surrounded by a combination of highways, neighborhoods, and dense hiking trails. Much of it could not be accessed directly. Sage and Noah had put together a list of points referenced in Sam's notebook, assembled from messy lists and places he had circled on looseleaf maps, but Sage already felt lost in a vast, unknowable space. She doubted her ability to find her own way through, much less get to Sam. If he was even here. The doubt got worse every day they didn't find him. She wondered if she should have called the police or told her dad.

But something about these woods told her nobody else had a chance of finding him. She didn't believe in the world of ghosts and spirits that Sam did, she could feel him out there. Science has disproved twin telepathy and other types of psychological connections between siblings, but Sage had known the night her mom died that something was wrong. She knew she would feel it if Sam were gone. Her brother was out in the Appalachian wilds somewhere, waiting for her to find him.

They completed a trail loop that took them by the river. Sage was looking for any evidence along the waterline that Sam had been there. Maybe he had gotten lost. Maybe he had waded into the water and gotten caught in a sudden flood. Those happened all the time in the mountains. She focused on the map in front of her, his hastily scrawled notes about potential sightings.

After a couple hours, they stopped on the riverbank to eat and cool off. Kora laid out a blanket and sat down with her feet in the water while Connor and Hunter brought out bags of food from their backpacks. They picked apart sandwiches and munched on chips. Sage shared her liter-sized water bottle. A ladybug crawled over Kora's sandwich bag. Slowly and carefully, she pulled her sketchbook out of her bag and started to draw it.

Sage grimaced against her will. Kora noticed the face and raised an eyebrow inquisitively.

"I just don't like ladybugs," said Sage.

"Who doesn't like ladybugs?" Kora asked incredulously.

"Me."

"What don't you like about them?" Kora gently caught the ladybug as it tried to leave her knee, coaxed it onto her finger, then placed it gingerly back in the center. She returned to sketching it.

"One bit me once."

"Ladybugs don't bite."

"Yes, they do!" Sage insisted. "Not that often, but it hurts."

She turned to Connor for backup. He shrugged.

"That's true," said Hunter, still chewing on her sandwich. "They can bite."

"Thank you!"

"But they're also super important for the ecosystem."

"Whatever," said Sage. "They can nourish the ecosystem away from me."

"I think they're pretty," said Kora, slowly pulling her knee up to her face to more closely admire the bug.

Sage noticed that both Connor and Hunter were tracking Kora's movement with their eyes. Kora's curls were pulled into a messy bun on top of her head, revealing a neck that was slick with sweat from their hike. Her eyes were lit up in the sun, turning them from light brown to gold. Sage had seen it a million times, but the two yahoos were staring like they'd never seen a pretty girl in their lives. Sage resisted the urge to fake barf. She turned to Noah, hoping to find some camaraderie that wasn't vomit-inducing, but he was placidly reading a book on a nearby rock. She sighed and scooched another foot away from Kora and her ladybug.

They continued on their path after lunch even slower than before. Once they finished the loop, they got back in the car and drove to the next river entrance point on the map. This one was just on the side of the road. After looking around for a while, they kept driving and headed for a campground for the night. By the time they got there, the shadows were long and the orange sunset bled through the trees.

Sage sat against a tree, dropping her backpack to the side. Connor and Hunter each set up a tent while Noah built a small fire. Kora snacked on pre-packaged waffles and Cocoa Puffs.

It was still unbearably hot, and Sage knew from experience that it would never really cool off. After dark, the temperature would sink to a tepid 75 degrees, cool enough to sleep but still humid and stifling. Every summer since they were kids the high temperatures were creeping up, becoming more dangerous and unsettling. Summer was not her favorite season. She preferred cool breezes and sweaters and a set class schedule.

For dinner, Connor used a pan to make a huge pile of nachos that they all shared. Sage watched the fire flicker as the light dimmed around them and listened to the rest of the group's chattering.

"You're only saying that because you had a crush on her sophomore year," Kora was saying, her voice amused. Sage didn't bother to try and remember back that far. Connor's crushes were usually predictably lame, present company excluded.

"I did not," he protested a little too loudly to be believable. "She and I worked together on a few group projects. I liked her dog! I did not have a crush on her."

Sage could hear Kora's eye roll without looking up.

"What kind of dog?" Noah asked, as if that mattered to his decision of whether or not to believe Connor.

"Corgi," said Connor confidently.

"Royal breed," said Hunter, laughing. "You are so predictable."

Connor was startled into silence. "I have no idea what you could possibly mean."

"That proves it," said Kora. "Whenever he gets defensive, he starts speaking like landed gentry from the 19th century."

"You're all hooligans and scoundrels," said Connor, leaning into the accusation with a reluctant grin. "I would best any of you in a duel."

"Oh, I'd like to see that," said Kora. "Hunter, will you be my champion? I'll give you my last bag of peach rings."

"That's not fair," Connor whined. "Face me yourself like a real man, Mason."

"Nah, I think I'll have a woman do all the hard work for me and take the credit for myself like a real man, Riley."

"Damn, dude, she really got you there," said Noah. "I gotta side with her on this one."

Connor and Hunter leapt up and began mock-jousting with last night's hot dog skewers.

Noah turned to Sage. "I'm learning all about the social dynamics at your weird hipster school," he said, taking a bite from the nachos and reaching for the bag of marshmallows. "Sam told me a little bit about it, but it's totally different hearing it from you guys. Is it true you had to maintain a 3.0 to stay enrolled?"

"Yup," said Kora, popping her lips on the P. "But there's a lot of flexibility with class, so you can choose to take ones that suit your learning style. If, for example, you hate taking tests like me, you can mostly focus on your specialty subject, like art."

"What's your specialty subject?" Noah asked Sage.

"I'm in the STEM program," said Sage, skewering a marshmallow to roast. "Science, technology, engineering, and math."

"Oh, like your dad," he said with his mouth full of s'more.

Sage looked up at him. Logically, she knew that he and Sam had spent a lot of time together, but their family was pretty private. Neither she nor Sam made a lot of friends. Having someone she barely knew already know so much about her and her family was unsettling. She just nodded.

"Do you want to be a professor like your parents?" he asked, undeterred by her hesitation.

"I just want to survive high school," she said with a shrug.

"Did you have any scandalous crushes or forbidden loves like Kora and Connor?"

Sage really hoped Noah wasn't asking because he wanted to ask her out. That was just going to make everything more awkward and uncomfortable than it already was, thanks to Kora and her bisexual melodrama.

"Yeah," said Kora before Sage could say anything. "With the chem lab. It was explosive."

Sage rolled her eyes. She had never really been interested in anyone like that. While everyone else was having crushes and getting all giddy over asking each other out, she was finding obsession after obsession to fuel the ADHD goblin that lived in her brain and demanded entertainment. She was lucky that there were at least some school subjects that were interesting enough to hold her attention, otherwise she never would have kept her grades up enough for Oakcrest. But when she wasn't swimming or doing extra reading from the chem and physics textbooks, she was playing Skyrim and learning to skateboard and teaching herself complicated sailing knots she would never need to know.

It hadn't really occurred to her that it was weird she didn't like anyone until further into high school when some of her peers were in their second year of relationships and were talking about staying together after graduation. That seemed silly and frivolous to her, though she had respectfully cheered on Kora and Connor until their inevitable end.

And then her mom died, and Sage lost her chance to ever ask her about it. She also stopped caring about what she was supposed to be doing. It was easy to reject society's expectations for her when it was hard enough just to keep breathing.

She realized Noah was still waiting for her answer.

"No need," she said dryly. "Kora had enough crushes for the both of us."

Thankfully, Kora took the cue and launched into the story of her first kiss, which had resulted in their principal installing security cameras in the orchestra room storage closet. No one asked Sage any more questions.

Once the fire started to die down, the group divided up between the tents. Sage considered asking Connor if she could crash with the boys so she wouldn't have to third-wheel, but she thought pointing out Kora and Hunter's sexual tension would probably upset him.

She stayed by the fire while everyone else got ready for bed. Their campsite was only a few yards from the river. She could see the reflection of moonlight on the surface and closed her eyes. The beauty only made her angry.

She wasn't there to camp or hike or admire the natural splendor of the great outdoors. She wasn't there to eat dinner with her awkward and haphazardly assembled friend group. She wasn't there to sleep in a tent with two people who just started dating.

She didn't blame any of them for enjoying themselves when they could. It was hard for anyone to understand how Sage knew that Sam was in trouble. He was known for his disappearances.

Still, their lack of progress ate at her. It felt like every hour the forest expanded around them, the mountains growing taller and the valleys deeper. Even with Sam's notes, it seemed like the trees moved around while no one was looking. Sage wanted to punch something.

This feeling happened to her a lot. Sometimes at swim practice when the coach yelled at her, sometimes at home when she got frustrated with her dad. It used to happen whenever Sam came into her room to bother her. Now she wished she had paid more attention.

Her hands shook. Punching a tree would be satisfying but would probably require a trip to urgent care. Instead, she pulled out a pack of cigarettes and a lighter from her backpack and walked down to the river.

Sage knew smoking was bad for her. She was an athlete and a scientist. She had seen the commercials that showed you what a smoker's lungs looked like—black shriveled-up meat sacks. But there were only so many ways she could keep herself from breaking her hand on a 150-year-old birch.

They all needed an outlet—Sam had loud music, driving too fast, and ghosts. Kora had art, getting into arguments with her mom, and crawling out onto the roof at the Rivera house. Sage had swimming, running, and cigarettes and, when those failed, punching things. And it was too dark to go for a run. She sat on a rock and lit one.

A branch cracked behind her. She turned to see Kora navigating her way down to the rock, using her hands to guide her through the trees.

"World-class camper, and the girl forgets to bring a flashlight," Sage could hear Kora muttering to herself, swatting away a gnat from around her face. She sat next to Sage and wrapped a blanket around both of their shoulders.

"Busted," said Sage, taking a drag from the cigarette.

Kora rolled her eyes. "You really thought I didn't know?" she said. "You're not that sneaky."

"I could be if I was really trying," said Sage. "I was just never trying to hide it from you."

"Sure," Kora said, drawing it out with a smirk on her face. She held her hand out. Sage passed the cigarette over, and Kora took a drag.

"Since when do you smoke?" she said.

"I don't," said Kora, coughing on the exhale and frowning down at the burning tip. "Well, only when someone else is."

"Smokey the Bear would be disappointed in us," said Sage.

"I think he'd be lenient, given the circumstances," Kora sighed. "You should put the butt somewhere we can take with us when we go, though."

For a minute it was silent, the two of them passing the cigarette back and forth and watching the slight ripple on the river's surface.

"I don't think we're going to find him here," Sage whispered in the direction of the water.

"Why not?" asked Kora.

"I don't know," said Sage. "I just don't."

Kora contemplated that for a while, and then said, "Lie down."

Sage raised her eyebrows, but she stubbed out the cigarette on the rock and did as she was told. Kora lay down next to her. She took Sage's hand and pressed it into the dirt between them.

"Can you feel it?" she asked.

"Feel what?" Sage said, skeptical.

Kora was looking up at the stars. Sage looked up, too. They blinked at her. She could hear the river running over stones. Far away, she thought she could hear a coyote howl something melancholy.

"This place is magical," Kora whispered. "We're on the right track."

Sage wanted to protest, but lying on the ground made her feel better, closer to Sam. She closed her eyes.

"Okay," she breathed.

After a moment, Sage whispered to the darkness. "If you can hear me," she said, "if you're in trouble, we're coming for you. If you're not in trouble, you will be."

Kora nodded, her head rustling the leaves on the ground. "Yeah, what she said."

It was quiet for a while. Then Kora asked, "What's the story here?"

"What do you mean?" said Sage.

"The ghost," said Kora. "Did you look at the book Austin gave you?"

"Oh, supposedly there's a siren here that calls to men and lures them into the river," said Sage. "Dark eyes and hair like moss. When they enter the river, they find that her arms are slimy and her face is a skull."

Kora made a grossed out face and laughed. "Spooky," she said.

Sage rolled her eyes. "Don't be tempted by any beautiful women in rivers," she said pointedly. Kora laughed again.

"I'll do my best," she said.

CHAPTER 9

Kora slumped in the front seat of the Jeep with a small metal mug filled with instant coffee they had made by boiling water over the fire. It was mediocre at best.

She wasn't a good sleeper. Sage, her mother, several psychiatrists and a sleep therapist had called it persistent, severe insomnia with a tendency toward nightmares, but she liked to think of it more as a personality quirk. Sleeping in was less of a luxury and more of a harm reduction mechanism.

But sleeping in a tent meant being woken by the sun as soon as it cleared the horizon. After two mornings like that, the sleep deprivation was weighing on her. She had dreamt that she was trying to put her shoes on but she only had one of each pair.

When everyone piled in the car behind her, she asked Sage where they were going.

"The Grove Park Inn," said Sage. "Apparently it's burned down multiple times, but it's still open."

"A hotel," said Kora, dreamily imagining crisp white sheets and thick, dark curtains. Right now, the thought of a real mattress made her light-headed. "We should stay there tonight after we search it. Take a night off from camping."

Sage scoffed. "It's, like, four stars. Upwards of $300 a night. Definitely not in our budget, which is—oh yeah—approximately zero dollars."

Kora rested her head on the steering wheel and groaned. She heard a familiar noise from the backseat. When she looked up, Connor was making tentative eye contact with her through the rear-view mirror.

"No," she said, leaving little room for argument.

"I wasn't going to!" he said, sounding guilty.

This was a fight they had had before, and it was like they entered into the middle of it, already angry.

"You totally were," she said, letting irritation bleed into her voice. "And the answer is no."

Sage hummed. "I mean, it couldn't hurt." Kora cut daggers at her. "Okay, okay, I'm just saying. You wanted a hotel for the night."

"Does somebody want to clue me in?" asked Hunter, glancing back and forth between them.

"Connor wants to slap his steel-plated mega-rewards credit card down at the Grove Park Inn and expense it to Daddy's non-existence credit limit," Kora said icily. "Even though it's about 50 hours of minimum wage labor for one night in a hotel. And that's assuming we all pile into one room."

Connor's head was lowered in the backseat. Kora immediately felt guilty. She knew it was harsh—Connor was being nice, offering to help. But it was far too early in the morning, and this was already a contentious issue between them, and Kora hated, *hated* having to argue against something she really, really wanted. She resented having to be the one to say no. But she couldn't have a $300 bill adding to the already desperately uneven tab between them.

The tension was reaching uncomfortable levels for everyone in the car, she could tell.

"I have a coupon for a stay at a Ramada," said Noah, piping up unexpectedly. "I think it's like $20 off a single-night stay. I got it while I was at a conference for library staff in Charlotte."

Kora's shoulders slumped, relieved. "How much is a night after the discount?" she asked.

"I don't know, probably like 40 bucks?" he said.

"That's eight dollars each if we split it," said Sage. "I'm willing to pitch in. You guys?"

Hunter and Connor both nodded. Visions of a full night's sleep swam back into Kora's mind, and she sighed.

"Thank you, Noah," she said. "That's very generous of you." She shot Connor an apologetic glance, and he nodded graciously. She pulled out of the campsite parking lot and onto the interstate.

◆

As they pulled into the Grove Park Inn's expansive campus, Kora felt more and more embarrassed for having suggested they spend the night there and more and more glad she hadn't let Connor pay for it. It wasn't even in the same species as a Ramada. It was a castle, something transported from the south of France or the English countryside, where King Arthur could have hosted the Knights of the Round Table 500 years ago. She had grown up going to Biltmore, which was majestic and huge, but it was also a museum with guided tours and a security check at the entrance. It was absurd to her that you could pay to sleep in this place. The $300 a night suddenly seemed cheap.

The facade was built from old, weathered stone, and the broad roundabout where guests dropped off their luggage was entirely made of brick. She avoided the hotel staff directing cars toward the valet and drove around to find a place where they could self-park.

Luckily, the hotel had several cafes, restaurants, and stores that were open to the public, so it wasn't suspicious for non-guests to wander around. The place was huge. It was less of a hotel and more of a resort full of historical exhibits, manicured gardens, gift shops, expensive restaurants, and luxury amenities. Kora felt conspicuous walking through the halls to read the historical documents on display.

That may have been why Connor offering to pay bothered her so much. She knew he felt perfectly fine making his way through the hotel. Guest or not, he looked the part. He had his hands tucked into the pockets of khaki shorts and wore a mint green polo shirt. His posture was relaxed, unbothered.

She, on the other hand, had been raised by a single mother who did odd jobs on top of her landscaping gigs to make a living. The house they lived in was beautiful but small, and they wouldn't have been able to afford it if her Great Uncle Pat hadn't left them his pension when he died in a mining accident. Here, she felt like her poverty was an aura she couldn't hide. Somehow she knew that these guests could smell her grandparents' farm on her skin even though she hadn't been there in years.

The Grove Park Inn was very committed to its historical relevance. Locked display cases housed artifacts from the inn's early days in operation, like dinner menus and letters from famous guests. There were not many articles that described the fires that had forced the hotel to be rebuilt over the years, but there was a small exhibit on the Pink Lady, the hotel's resident ghost. A mannequin wore a silk pink dress inspired by the story in a large upright glass case, along with long white gloves and a gold necklace.

The exhibit didn't seem to imply that they had actually belonged to the dead woman, though. Kora knew Sam would roll his eyes at the display. It did nothing to help his search.

"How do we know if Sam was here?" asked Kora. "I doubt the staff would tell us if he booked a room."

"He couldn't have afforded to stay the night anyway," said Sage.

"Noah, didn't you say the ghost was supposed to haunt a specific room?" asked Connor, carefully looking over a display of old brochures.

"Yeah," said Noah. "Room 545. People book it on purpose because of the story."

"Maybe he tried talking to the people who are renting that room," said Sage, already making her way toward the elevators.

Sage and Kora went to knock on the door alone while the rest of them waited around the corner. Kora figured a large crowd might weird the guests out.

The door was large and made of vertical slats of light brown wood. It was old-fashioned and rustic, like everything in the hotel. Kora knocked lightly.

An older woman answered the door, her hair in curlers despite it being the middle of the day. She looked bewildered to see two teenage girls instead of housekeeping or room service.

"Hi there, ma'am," Kora said, channeling her Southern charm. "Would you mind telling us how long you've been staying in this room? We think our brother might have been by here sometime in the last week."

The woman seemed to recover from the surprise and gathered herself, pulling a cardigan around her shoulders.

"Well, that would have been us," she said with a heavy Appalachian accent. "We've been here a week already. Checking out tomorrow."

Sage pulled up a picture of Sam on her phone. It was from his high school graduation, smiling in his cap and gown.

"Have you seen this boy?" she asked. "He might have come by to ask you some questions about the room you're staying in?"

"No, I don't reckon anyone's come by to ask us anything," said the woman, squinting at Sage's phone screen. "He doesn't look familiar. Why would he want to talk about our room?"

Kora glanced at Sage. She knew people sought out the room for its supernatural connections, but in general, the hotel tried to keep it quiet, not wanting to invite controversy. But, she decided, that wasn't really her problem.

"This room is supposed to be haunted," she said. "You haven't seen any ghosts around here, have you?"

The woman laughed. "I think I'd remember that," she said. "No, the only ghost around here is my son when he stays up too late playing video games."

Kora laughed with her politely. "Well, thank you for your time, ma'am," she said. The woman nodded and closed her door.

They rounded the corner and reported back what they had learned to the group.

"Is there any way he could have come here and not talked to them?" asked Hunter.

"No, there's no way," said Sage. "He wouldn't have bothered with any of the other stuff around here. If this was next on his list, he'd be pestering that poor couple night and day."

They took a collective deep breath.

"Onwards to the Ramada then?" asked Noah.

The lobby of the Ramada smelled like tobacco, and it took ten minutes of ringing the service bell for someone to come help them. Kora smiled to herself. This was much more comfortable to her, more familiar than the hotel's ridiculous golf courses.

Noah used his coupon to get them a room with two queen beds. There was a Denny's within walking distance, and they converged on it for dinner. Kora ate a stack of blueberry pancakes smothered with maple syrup. It improved her mood tremendously.

When they got back to their room, it was dark but too early to go to sleep. Sage grabbed the remote and started flipping through channels before landing on the seven o'clock news. Kora groaned.

"Can't you put on something fun?" she complained. "I guarantee you nothing important is going on."

Sage squinted angrily but didn't take her eyes off the screen. "I'm just keeping an eye out in case they've found, oh, I don't know, a nineteen-year-old male body?" She finally turned the glare on Kora, who felt appropriately chastised.

"I'm positive your dad would call you far before it ended up on the news," she said, her voice softer. "But we can keep it on. I have my headphones anyway, I can just listen to a podcast or something." Sage returned her gaze to the T.V. and nodded.

As Kora settled back with her earbuds in, Hunter and Noah decided to look for a vending machine. Connor watched the news with Sage for a little while, then made his way to sit on the bed beside Kora. He held out his hand in a silent request for one of her earbuds, and she gave it to him. She had been in the middle of a true crime podcast, but she switched it to one of her many playlists. She chose something neutral, avoiding all the emotional breakup music she'd been listening to lately.

"I'm sorry about what I said earlier," she said after a few songs had played. She kept her voice down so Sage didn't hear, but she didn't think Sage was paying attention to them. "I know you meant well, and it was really nice of you."

He shrugged. "I get it," he said quietly. "I know it bothers you how much money my parents have."

"It's not that I think they shouldn't have it," she said. "I just can't wrap my head around how easily you can spend it. Like, do they even check your statements?"

Connor turned away. "Not really."

"So you could be hitting the limit on diamonds and superyachts, and they wouldn't even notice?"

He laughed. "That's not really my style."

She smiled and had to give him that.

"I try not to spend it recklessly," he said, face serious again. "I know what it means that we have it. I never want to take it for granted." He turned to face her, his eyes full of something deep.

"I wasn't offering because I wanted to stay in a nice hotel," he said. "Everyone here has something they're bringing to the table. Hunter is good at hiking and camping. Noah knows about the ghosts. My thing is money—that and my car, which I have because of money." He looked at her earnestly. "Whatever it takes."

Kora took that in, playing with the cord of her headphones. They were all giving up a lot to be here. Kora was spending precious nights that could be spent saying goodbye to her childhood home, though she was a little grateful to be avoiding her mom. Hunter, Sage, and Noah had all bailed on responsibilities. Connor had nowhere to be and nothing but time. But it wasn't nothing, what he was offering.

His car, his time, his money—and spending time with her. Being here, watching her with Hunter. Remembering the feeling of riding around in his car with her driving. It had to be hurting him.

When she turned back to look at him, he was pretending to watch the news.

Before she could say anything else, Noah came back inside by himself.

"Where's Hunter?" Kora asked.

"She said she wanted to go for a walk," said Noah.

Kora handed the second earbud to Connor and slipped outside. It was properly dark now, the night air still humid and sticky. Even this close to downtown, the cicadas were louder than the traffic.

Hunter wasn't by the vending machine or the icebox. Kora wandered around the side of the building toward the designated smoking area. She'd never seen Hunter smoke, but Sage wasn't the only one who could have secret vices. Hunter wasn't there either, but from where she was, she could see a silhouette sitting by the pool.

The sign clearly said the pool closed at nine, and Kora found the gate was locked. She glanced over to confirm that it was Hunter and then vaulted over the fence.

A familiar pair of combat boots was tossed aside along with two inside-out socks. Hunter had her feet in the water as she leaned back on her hands. The light from the pool made her skin look blue. Her sharp eyes were even more intimidating. Kora couldn't tell what she was thinking about or what kind of mood she was in.

She shucked off her sandals and slumped down next to Hunter, slipping her feet into the water. It was surprisingly cold despite being outside in the sun all day. She shivered, and Hunter finally looked at her.

"Are you hiding out here?" Kora asked. Her voice echoed across the pool. She quieted herself, remembering they weren't supposed to be there.

Hunter shrugged, looking back out over the water. Something was tense about the way she held herself up, her shoulders too high and tight. Kora frowned, not sure what to say.

"What did Connor want?" Hunter asked, better about keeping her voice down.

"What?" Kora asked, confused.

"I saw you through the window," she said quietly. "Sitting on the bed together."

Kora considered this. She hadn't thought it was a big deal. It wasn't a big deal. They had shared some music and chatted.

"He probably just wanted to make sure I wasn't mad at him anymore," she answered honestly. "After this morning. I was kind of mean when he tried to pay for the hotel room."

Hunter nodded, still not looking at her. Her eyes were dark with a blue glow in the center, her lips unreadable.

"We always got in fights about money," Kora said, "before." She swallowed. Hunter had said she thought they should be friends. It should be okay to talk about this. Right?

"So, why'd you come out here?" Hunter asked.

"You left," said Kora. Hunter finally looked back at her, searching Kora's face for something. "Are you okay?"

"Yeah," Hunter said. "Fine. You should go back inside. He's probably messing with your playlists."

Kora huffed a laugh. He wouldn't dare. Connor was kind but spineless, and Kora was notoriously territorial about her music collection.

"Do you want me to go?" she asked, voice quiet. The water was cool on her toes, and she liked the feeling. Hunter smelled like leather and jasmine. She instinctively leaned in to smell it better. Hunter turned back to look at her again, this time turning her shoulders so they were almost face to face. Kora realized how close she had gotten; they were only a breath away from each other.

"What I want," Hunter breathed, "is not of consequence right now."

Kora felt those words in her chest. It wasn't true. What Hunter wanted was all she could think about right now, her scent mixing with chlorine. It made Kora dizzy.

Instinctively, her hands reached out to Hunter, but she didn't know what to do with them once they got there. She glanced down and saw Hunter's phone in her pocket. Kora gently slid it out, careful not to touch her fingers to Hunter's thigh. She set it down a few feet behind them next to Hunter's shoes. Then she slid into the water.

It was colder than she expected, her toes having gotten used to the temperature. She gasped and froze in place, unable to move until the rest of her body recovered from the shock. Once she could move around, she glided through the water until she was in front of Hunter's legs and grinned up at her.

Her implacable expression was persistent, but Kora could see a shine to her eyes and a quirk to her lips. Kora held out her hands, palms up, just over Hunter's knees. Hunter placed her own on top of them and allowed herself to be pulled into the water.

Hunter was much better about keeping her composure, despite the chill. She made slow movements through the water. Even with languid strokes, Kora could tell that Hunter knew how to swim properly. She could mostly only doggy paddle and was grateful the pool was only five feet deep. She could stand on her tiptoes with her face above the water.

The loose t-shirt Hunter wore billowed around her, while her shorts stuck close to her body. Kora reached out under the water and grabbed a handful of the wet shirt, pulling Hunter toward her slowly. The water made everything smooth, easy. The chill made her want to huddle close. The smell made her want to press her nose against the side of Hunter's neck, breathe in her scent to drown out the chlorine.

Connor and the others were just around the corner, back in the room. She had no idea how they would explain their soaking wet clothes. They could be caught by the motel staff and have to explain themselves. But she could hear nothing but the water moving around them, cicadas in the distance, and Hunter's deep breathing. The quiet was hypnotic.

The fist that held Hunter's shirt was pressed all the way against Kora's chest. Their eyes met, hovering just over the water. Kora moved forward, keeping hold of the shirt, until she had Hunter pushed up against the side of the pool.

She let go of the fabric and instead wrapped her hand around Hunter's side, splaying her fingers across ribs. Their eyes never moved from each other.

It was a bad idea.

She kissed Hunter anyway. Their lips tasted like chlorine from where they had drifted under the water, and Kora wondered for a moment if chlorine was toxic, but then she stopped thinking. Her fingers wrapped around Hunter's neck and burrowed into hair, feeling where it went from wet to dry. She could barely keep their mouths above water.

As the hand on Hunter's side moved around to the small of her back, Kora saw a light flicker out of the corner of her eye. She turned her head and saw that it was a fluorescent light on the outside of the building that detected motion. Through the bushes that lined the pool area, she could see that a maid was walking around the outside of the building.

Kora's face was still just an inch away from Hunter's, and she pressed her finger between their lips and shushed them both. They breathed for a few seconds, trying not to make ripples in the water until the maid was gone.

"We should head back," Kora whispered and looked Hunter in the eyes. For a moment, they just watched each other.

"Yeah," Hunter breathed. Kora pushed off the wall and floated toward the stairs.

Luckily, they didn't have to climb over the fence to get out. The gate could be opened from the inside. Less luckily, they were dripping wet with no towels. Hunter texted Sage and asked her to bring them some. The thought of Connor questioning why she was bringing towels outside was embarrassing, but the thought of knocking on the door soaking wet was worse. Sage raised an eyebrow when she came around the corner but said nothing. They dried quickly and went inside.

She didn't have to worry about it. Connor had fallen asleep listening to the music on her phone. That was supposed to be the girls' bed, but Noah had already climbed in next to Connor's sleeping body.

Once they had taken turns drying off and changing into pajamas, Kora and Hunter climbed into bed on opposite sides of Sage. This was becoming a routine. Kora thought they had the same reasons. The idea of laying next to Hunter in the dark with Sage right next to them made her heart race, and she was already flushed from the pool. Better to keep things separate.

Kora knew it would be better for everyone if she kept her hands to herself.

CHAPTER 10

In the early morning light before everyone else woke up, Sage climbed into the shower and turned the faucet as hot as it could go. Scalding water poured over her shoulders as she stepped in, trying to soothe her muscles after a night of fitful sleep.

When she was done, she set to work on the motel coffee maker. It was a relief not to have to make coffee over an open flame.

By the time she was done, the others started to stir. She stepped outside to let them get ready. The motel was sparsely occupied, and she saw only a few other people in the parking lot. A family of five was piling into their minivan, probably getting back to their road trip. A young couple leaned against the supports of the building smoking cigarettes.

Sage took the last sip of her coffee and walked over to join them. "Can I get one of those?"

The girl looked her up and down with a frown. "How old are you, kid?"

"Forty-two," said Sage with a blank face. The girl huffed a laugh and passed her a cigarette. The man lit it for her.

"What brings you around here?" he asked.

Sage considered telling them the truth, just for fun. They didn't seem like the type of people who would question a story about wayward brothers. Still, she wasn't sure she wanted to open up to strangers.

"Enjoying the view," she said, gesturing out to the half-empty parking lot.

The couple looked at each other questioningly but said nothing. She didn't ask about them, just finished the cigarette and stomped it out on the asphalt.

When she got back to the room, everyone was getting ready. They were all sleepy-quiet, moving around each other in silence and drinking coffee before they hit the road.

It was a short drive to downtown Asheville, but all the parking lots they passed were full, so Kora dropped them off on the street and drove around to look for a parking garage.

Sage had been there plenty of times for school field trips and with her family but not enough to navigate it without a map. It looked a lot different than Pinebrook's sleepy main street. The roads were wider and more populated, and the buildings were taller and more modern. Still, like most mountain towns, it was filled with strange, eclectic shops that seemed to exist outside of time.

By the time Kora had parked and made her way to meet them, Sage stood under an awning of a storefront, frowning at the map on her phone. Noah had uncovered several locations Sam had mentioned in the notebook that were around here, and it would take hours to find them all. Sweat was already gathering on the back of her neck from the stifling summer heat.

"Do you know where we're going?" Hunter asked, shading her eyes with her hand.

"Maybe," said Sage.

They walked along the streets, weaving through roads packed with moving cars until they stumbled on a small shop. The window was filled with antique animal statues, hanging terrariums, and ancient-looking books. Posters papered the outside, advertising music festivals and poetry readings. Fairy lights hung from the ceiling, made visible in the unrelenting sunlight by the dim lighting inside. If it weren't for the "Come in, we're open!" sign on the door, Sage would have thought it was closed.

The sign on the door proclaimed "Psychic Readings $25."

"Maybe someone here can tell us about the ghosts," said Kora.

Sage wasn't a fan of the idea, but she figured Sam might have had the same thought. She pushed open the door and heard a loud chime, punctuated by the strong scent of patchouli. The shop was filled with rows and rows of tiny beads in large plastic bins, satchels of herbs, crystals, and trinkets. In the middle of the room, a middle-aged woman with long gray hair waved a bundle of burning herbs over a large claw-foot bathtub set atop a huge pedestal.

Sage glanced at Kora and noted the crease in her eyebrows that said she was just as confused. She glanced behind them to check that yes, in fact, they had entered a place of business and not a private residence. She saw a cat in the windowsill, lazing over a pile of books.

"Is that a bathtub?" asked Sage.

"Come see for yourself, darlin'," said the woman, without looking up.

They stepped up to the edge of the bathtub, which was level with their torsos. Peering inside, Sage could see two large koi fish circling the bathtub lackadaisically. The bottom was coated with colorful rocks and assorted playthings. The fish blinked at her. She blinked back.

Seemingly satisfied with this explanation for the bathtub, though it was no less confusing than before, Kora asked, "What are the herbs for?"

"I'm cleansing the fish," the lady said. "They've seemed all out of sorts lately."

"Ma'am, we were hoping you could answer a few questions for us," said Connor. He dipped into the accent he always reserved for when he wanted something. He smiled sweetly, and the woman melted. "My name is Connor Riley, and these are my friends."

"Nice to meet you, Connor," said the lady, tamping out her herb bundle on a small ceramic plate. "My name's Evangeline. I'm the owner of this old place."

"It's lovely," he said, looking around like it was a fine piece of architecture he was admiring, covering his eyes even in dim lighting.

"Well, thank you, dear," she cooed. She walked around the bathtub and placed the bundle on an overstuffed counter where Sage could barely make out an old cash register.

"We're looking for my brother," said Sage, decidedly less charming than Connor. "We think he might be nearby. Has anyone come by asking about ghosts?"

"People come through here most days asking about spirits of some kind," said Evangeline. She pulled a handful of immensely long hair from her back over her shoulder and began to braid it. It reminded Sage of Kora's habit of unbraiding and re-braiding her hair when she didn't have anything to do with her hands. She frowned and hoped she wasn't getting a glimpse at Kora's future.

Sage pulled up a photo of Sam on her phone and handed it to Evangeline.

"Nope, I don't recognize him. I'm sorry darlin'," she said. To her credit, it sounded like she meant it. Sage frowned. "Let me do a reading for you, free of charge, help you find him."

Sage and Kora looked at each other. Kora's face said *Why not? It can't hurt.* Sage's face was surely the picture of skepticism, but she resigned.

"Thank you," said Sage. "That would be great."

Evangeline led them to a deep maroon curtain that separated a small, dark room from the rest of the store. Sage and Kora went in, while the rest of them waited outside by the fish bathtub.

The room consisted of a short, round table with several pillows strewn about around it. Evangeline sat on one, and Sage and Kora took two across from her.

Evangeline lit a candle in the center of the table and brought out a basket full of tarot cards, herbs, and some other, less recognizable objects.

"All right, tell me what happened," she said.

"Aren't you supposed to tell me that?" said Sage.

"I can tell you where you're goin' from here, but I don't know where you've been already," said Evangeline, as if it should be obvious.

Sage told her about her brother's obsession with spirits, leaving out the part about her mother's death. She explained how he went on these little research excursions, but he hadn't come back from the last one. As she gave a rundown of their trip so far, Evangeline nodded empathetically.

"Well, bless your hearts," she said. She slapped her hand against her chest. "I can't imagine." She looked at Kora then. "And who are you, little missy?"

"Kora," she said.

"My goodness, what a wonderful name," said Evangeline. "Like the goddess of the underworld."

"Yes, ma'am," said Kora. Sage noticed her sitting a little bit higher on her cushion.

"And how are you connected to all this?" Evangeline asked.

Kora glanced at Sage. "I'm her sister," she said after a moment's hesitation. "Sam is my brother, too." They often said this to strangers. It simplified things.

"Well, we'll get everything sorted out now," said Evangeline. Without any further ado, she held her hand so close to the candle that it seemed like it should have hurt her. Her eyes were closed, and she hummed as she worked. Sage expected it to be some kind of somber dirge or old folk song, but it was more upbeat than that. She thought she recognized the melody of an eighties pop song. The small room filled with an earthy smoke. By the light of the candle, Sage could barely make out Kora's face next to her.

"I see a mother," she said. Sage's shoulders tensed up, and she could feel Kora's eyes on her. She didn't look back. "A mother spirit."

Sage just glared at the woman. It was a lucky guess. She didn't like the idea of this woman using the memory of her mom to score psychic points.

Evangeline opened her eyes. "I'm so sorry, sweetheart," she said. Her face was kind and empathetic, and it made Sage want to punch something.

"Do you see my brother?" she asked, trying to hide her grimace. She knew that fake psychics interpreted people's body language to decide if they were on the right track, but she didn't feel all that able to hide her reactions.

Evangeline looked down at the candle and swayed from side to side for a moment. "No ma'am, I'm afraid he's well and truly lost, even to me," she said.

"I thought you said you could find him," Sage said icily.

Evangeline clicked her tongue. "There are some magics more powerful than mine," she said with a sigh. "The mountains are a strange and mysterious beast. If they're hiding someone, they won't be found. I can tell you, if he's alive, he's in danger for sure."

Sage stood up. "You don't know what the hell you're talking about," she yelled. She had entertained this nonsense long enough. If she had believed in psychics before, she definitely didn't now.

Evangeline held a look of pity that infuriated Sage. She grabbed Sage's hand. Evangeline's smooth palm was warm from the flames. In the dark room, their joined hands were all Sage could see.

"You don't understand this place," she said. "But you were born here. The mountain blood runs through your veins, just as it does your brother's. The magic is strong, but blood is stronger. Trust in yourself, and listen to the mountains, honey. They've seen a lot more than we have."

Sage's eyes filled with angry tears against her will. "You can't help me," she whispered.

Evangeline put her hand back over the flame in a rush and burned herself. She hissed and shook her hand but put it back up close to the fire. Humming for just a second, she closed her eyes and opened them again so fast it was like a blink.

"I see a bridge," she whispered. Somehow the room was full of her voice, soft as it was. "A bridge between here and there," she whispered. The room was cool despite the candle, and Sage felt Kora shiver next to her. "You may be able to find him there."

Sage shook her head. Part of her wanted to believe this woman, if only to have some bit of hope, but she couldn't put her trust in something so flimsy. "This is bullshit," she said, standing up and pulling back the red curtain. She stalked toward the exit, and her friends followed.

Evangeline blew out the candle and emerged from behind the curtain. "I'm sorry I couldn't be of more help to you," she said, looking earnest and sad. "Look for a bridge. The spirits may see fit to guide you."

Sage walked out the front door of the shop, anger bubbling under the surface of her skin. Realizing the boys and Hunter weren't so used to seeing her rage, she quickly cooled off.

"Let's go," she said, walking down the street in a random direction, not waiting to see if the others were following.

After twenty minutes of trying to find the first location on her list, Sage was ready to set something on fire. Or she would be if it wasn't already so damn hot. Her t-shirt was soaked in sweat, and the little hairs that usually hung around her face were plastered to her forehead.

She stepped inside a museum to get out of the sun and found that it was blissfully air-conditioned. She ignored the glares of the guides and slumped into one of the plush leather chairs in the lobby, not caring that her sweaty back was probably sticking to the material. The others followed her lead and found places to sit, gulping water and wiping their necks.

When she finally felt cool enough to move, she looked around at the museum—something about Asheville's not-so-interesting history. But she caught a glimpse of the sign over the check-in desk. They did tours around the city. One of them was a ghost tour.

"Okay," she said and waited until she had everyone's attention. "How about this: we wait until the cursed sun goes down so we can stop sweating our asses off, and then we do one of these ghost tours. That way, we don't have to waste more time wandering around looking for these stupid places."

She received a chorus of nods in return and closed her eyes again, satisfied.

At 8:30, they bought tickets for the next tour and stood in line with a small group of tourists. Their guide was a bubbly brunette with a curly ponytail who informed them that when she wasn't doing tours, she taught first grade at a nearby elementary school. Sage instantly disliked her for no good reason.

As soon as they stepped outside, it started to rain. Sage was relieved—at least it would cool off. She had an umbrella in her bag, but for now, she just let the rain wet her shoulders with something cooler than sweat.

The tour began at the Thomas Wolfe house, which was supposedly marked by tragedy and the sight of many ghostly occurrences. Sage cross-checked the house on her list of ghosts from Sam's notebook, didn't find it, and moved back to let the other tour goers get close enough to see. Noah, however, stood close to the guide the whole time, peppering her with questions when she wasn't speaking to the group.

He continued to follow close behind her, asking about local historical figures and what kind of records they had of each location. Sage simply followed behind the group, listened for the details of the hauntings, and then checked them against her list. Her feet ached, and the misty rain continued to stick to her eyelashes.

"Some theorize that Asheville is so haunted because of the sheer number of violent deaths that have occurred here," she heard the tour guide say. "Oftentimes, the dead have unfinished business to attend to."

Sage rolled her eyes. She hoped they got something useful out of this.

The tour walked them through the streets, weaving back and forth, stopping outside old churches, firehouses, public buildings.

The stories told of bootleggers and police chiefs, adulterers and nuns. Cemeteries were moved, and the dead were forgotten. Some of the names mentioned were from families that were still around.

As the tour guide discussed how many of the buildings had connections to the Freemasons, she mentioned Helen's Bridge. While it wasn't downtown, and therefore not on their tour route, it *was* on Sage's list. She listened closely as the tour guide continued.

"The bridge is said to be haunted by a woman named Helen who lost her daughter in a fire and then hung herself from the bridge," said the tour guide, her brown curls bouncing in her ponytail. Sage felt a familiar clench of grief in her chest. "Some say it's a site for Satanic worshippers now. If you look closely, you can see Masonic carvings in the stonework."

"Where is the bridge?" Sage asked.

"It's a ways out of town," the girl said. "It doesn't have an exact address, but there's directions in one of the brochures we have back at the museum."

Sage was impatient through the rest of the tour, eager to get back to the museum and find Helen's Bridge.

She felt relieved to have a new destination. She was running out of ideas, and the longer Sam was gone, the more anxious she got. But Helen's Bridge was on her list. Sam had extensive notes on it, she remembered. And it wasn't far.

The rain had subsided, but she still felt damp and claustrophobic as she waited for the tour to end.

The tour guide talked about a haunted apartment building and different methods for contacting spirits, which Sage barely paid attention to, and then finally they rounded the corner back onto the block where they started. While Noah stayed and chatted with the tour guide, Sage ducked inside the museum and went digging for the brochure.

By the time she found it, the rest of their tour group had dispersed, and Noah was explaining some of the tour's more interesting findings to Connor, who had trailed along the back with Sage.

"All right, gang," she said. "I know where we're going next."

⟡

Sage's heart was beating fast in her chest as they drove too fast down narrow mountain roads. This bridge was proving impossible to find. It was old and no longer a part of the intricate system of roads that criss-crossed up the mountain, so it didn't have a direct address. Once the directions from the tour brochure failed, the best they could do was some ancient website filled with popups. Sage was reading out loud to Kora and looking at the map on her phone, searching the path illuminated by headlines in front of them. There was no noise from the backseat, everyone presumably noting that Sage needed absolute silence other than her own curt directions. Anxiety was nearly spilling out of her, and she could feel her fingers tapping on her knee.

She knew it was unlikely they would find anything, psychic be damned, since it was nearing midnight and they were in the middle of nowhere, but the pitch-black roads made everything seem more dire and urgent. The idea of getting lost out there made her more afraid than was reasonable, considering there was decent cell service.

They doubled back on the same road they had gone down three times, pulling into someone's driveway to turn around. The headlights flashed into the house's front windows. Sage felt strangely exposed, like the headlights were a beacon that announced their strange intentions.

Kora made a left where she had made a right before and wound around a sharp turn. Sage heard someone in the backseat inhale a quiet gasp. Connor's Jeep was made for this kind of difficult road, but this was old country, and the streets weren't exactly up to code. They were hastily paved versions of shoddy mountain paths, and she could feel it in the way the car rocked back and forth over uneven asphalt. In the dark, it felt treacherous.

Sage didn't see the bridge until they were almost right under it. Everything in her stilled. She could barely see its outline in the dark, but it was unmistakable, an archaic piece of stonework overgrown with leaves and ivy. As they passed under it, Sage caught glimpses of graffiti that covered the sharp, jagged lines of the stone arches. She directed Kora to pull over at the nearest gravel turnoff.

Everyone climbed out of the Jeep, and Connor pulled out some flashlights. Sage headed back in the direction of the bridge.

When she turned around, she saw lights flickering on top of the bridge. It had only taken them a couple of minutes to park the car and get out, but she was sure there had been no one up there when they had driven under it. From that angle, she couldn't see any people, but the light darted around like a flashlight.

The street ran under the old bridge, but Sage could see a beaten footpath around the side to the top. She dug her Converses deep into the wet dirt to get a good grip as she climbed up.

When she got to the top, the bridge was dark, lit only from above by the moon and stars. Whoever or whatever had been making the light was gone.

The top of the bridge was just as overgrown as the sides had been. She knew from looking below that it was made entirely of stone and would have once been a flat cut across the valley, but it had been taken over by a dirt path, indistinguishable from the surrounding woods except for stone railings on either side. There were empty cans of energy drinks and spray paint that littered the ground. She turned her phone's flashlight to full brightness. She could see graffiti tags in bright neon pink and orange. It should have made the place seem less otherworldly, more solidified in time and space, but for some reason, the idea that teenagers trampled through there on weekend nights made her wary. The combination of timeworn stone and evidence of modernity was jarring. Who had she seen up there?

She heard the others come up the footpath behind her, and several other sets of flashlights illuminated the bridge. More bodies only added to her uncanny feeling.

"What are we looking for?" Kora asked, and Sage was grateful for the task. She shook her head and turned to find Kora's face in the dark.

"Let's see if we can find anything of Sam's, any evidence he was here," she said.

The five of them spread out on either side of the stone pathway, going a short ways into the woods. There was plenty to find—old liquor bottles and candy wrappers and fast-food bags. Sage thought she saw an opened condom wrapper and decided not to investigate too thoroughly. Occasionally, she came across something interesting, but it turned out to be an old baseball cap or a tarnished, broken necklace. Nothing familiar, nothing of Sam's.

She smacked at mosquitos that landed on her legs and wiped the sweat from her forehead. Searching felt pointless, but the idea of returning to the car—and back to Pinebrook—with nothing felt worse. They were no closer to finding him than they were when they set off on this ridiculous quest, and Sage felt silly, both for worrying everyone into a panic and for not doing something more dramatic, like telling her father or calling the police. Sam was fine until proven otherwise but missing until found. She had no idea what to do.

"Hey, Sage, do you recognize this?" came Noah's voice from the other side of the bridge. She scrambled over and found everyone converging over Noah's outstretched hand.

In it was an old watch with a basic gold face and leather band, hands still and edges scuffed with wear. Sage recognized it at the same time as she heard Kora's quiet gasp.

Kora took it from Noah and flipped it over, turning it for Sage to see the engraving, dirty but unmistakable on the back.

Her mind swirled with memories. It had been her father's first, a gift from the Physics department when he secured tenure. When he tried it on, it didn't feel right, he said, too tight. He gave it to Sam, who had slender wrists and liked the feel of leather. Most of the time it had sat on Sam's nightstand, where he forgot to put it on in the mornings. But he had worn it on special occasions: his graduation, their mother's funeral.

The watch was in her hand without her noticing Kora passing it to her. She traced the scratched surface, the time stuck at 2:47. When had she last seen him wear it? Why would it end up here when he was so reluctant to wear it out? Even without answers, hope and horror were blooming both unbidden in her chest. He had been here. It was something. Was he the one whose light she had seen?

The answer struck her—a conversation from weeks ago, another time that Sam had come into her room to bother her while she was studying. She had taken some extra Adderall to pull an all-nighter before finals, not her proudest moment. Sam had dug through the storage bins on her bookcase, making too much noise. She had turned around, irritated, ready to kick him out.

"Have you seen my watch?" he'd asked, agitated.

"It's not in your room?" she said, trying and failing to sound sympathetic.

"No, I can't find it." His voice had sounded more worried than she felt it should, but she ignored him and turned back around to her textbook.

"It'll turn up," she had said, not bothering to check if he was leaving her room.

Now it was in her hand, plastered with mud on top of a bridge.

Several thoughts occurred to her at the same time. One: he had been there. Sam had come on his secret crusade, hoping to catch a glimpse of Helen herself. Two: for some reason he had brought his precious watch with him and managed to leave it behind. Three: he had been home since then, she had seen him afterward, which meant they were really no closer to finding him.

Hope and horror in equal measures. They were no closer, but it was something.

"He was here," Sage whispered.

She looked up to find four faces looking at her in varying expressions of shock. She knew then that none of them had really expected him to be missing, though she had suspected as much. She also knew that they believed her now and were ready to keep looking.

Somewhere too close for comfort, an owl hooted, followed by a rustling of feathers. A bead of sweat traced down the side of her neck. She tucked the watch safely into her jacket pocket.

"Let's get the fuck out of here," she said.

CHAPTER 11

When she walked up the steps of her beloved childhood home, Kora wanted to feel relieved to be back. But the loose ends of their trip tugged at her.

She worried about Sam.

In the beginning, she had gone along to make Sage feel better, but she hadn't truly believed that he was in danger. Lost, maybe, or obsessed with some story. Maybe he met a girl and was holed up in a cabin. Maybe he was on a bender, forsaking ghost hunting for a more depressive coping mechanism. But Sam couldn't be hurt. He was Sage's smart, sarcastic, obsessive big brother. He would be fine.

But they had been out there for days and still had no idea where he was. And it was becoming more and more worrisome that they hadn't heard from him. The anxiety was starting to work its way through her.

Above all else, she was exhausted. Not just from trekking through the mountain, but from managing everyone's conflicting emotions. She felt wrung out to dry.

It did not help that as she walked up the steps she noticed that they had been recently painted, presumably to up the house's market value.

Inside was even worse. All of the knick-knacks on their bookshelf had been removed, leaving only neat rows of spines. The coffee table, which was usually full of empty coffee mugs, house keys, and dying plants, had just a large book about sailboats that Kora had never seen before. She defiantly dropped her duffel bag in the front hall, not bothering to move it to her room.

She found her mom in the back garden, lounging in a deck chair and drinking a glass of pinot grigio. This was her favorite version of her mom: loose white linen shirt, bright-colored wraparound skirt, brown leather sandals. Her skin was tan and wrinkly from years outside without sunscreen, and it didn't make her any less beautiful.

Kora's frustration deflated a little. She understood why her mom was moving. And now that Kora had graduated and would be moving on herself—a thought that still hurt, no matter how long she had to get used to it—her mom didn't have any more obligations there. But Kora didn't like thinking about Pinebrook as an obligation. She loved it. And she thought her mom did, too.

"I'm gonna miss this garden," she said, sinking into the chair opposite her mom. She pulled out her sketchbook and started drawing some of the flowers.

"I've got lots of ideas for the house in Santa Fe," her mom said. "We'll be able to have more cacti and succulents."

"Yeah, but I like the flowers here."

"Me too."

It was quiet then. Kora thought about pouring herself a glass of wine too, but she was still thinking about the boxes inside full of her childhood treasures. She wasn't sure if all of it would survive the move. Would she have any physical reminders of her youth anymore?

The sun quickly heated the top of Kora's head, making the skin where her hair parted start to burn. She adjusted in her seat so that she wasn't in direct sunlight. She supposed there were things she wouldn't miss about Southern summers: the sunburn and mosquito bites and stifling humidity. But she couldn't bring herself to hate the sun, not this time. It danced over the flower petals in her drawings.

"Any bites on the house?" she asked, holding a hand over her eyes so she could see her mother through the sharp rays.

"We've had some interest," her mom said. "No official offers yet, but Sandra thinks it won't be long."

Kora frowned. She didn't care for Sandra, their real estate agent. She was an older blonde woman who attributed all of her financial success to God, rather than the ruthless way she approached her business.

"I'm going back out camping with Sage in a couple days," Kora said. Part of her didn't want to say anything about their trip to avoid suspicion, but she didn't want to disappear on her mom, either. She just hoped she wouldn't ask too many questions.

"Hmm," her mom hummed as she took another sip of wine. "I talked to Leo the other day, and he seemed a little worried. Sage has missed a lot of swim practices this summer."

Kora hadn't thought about that. She was never a sports person, but she did remember Sage bailing on a lot of plans because she had practice. It hadn't occurred to her that this would be a big deal to the coach. But she knew that finding Sam was much more important for Sage.

"I don't know," she said. "Maybe she's not really into swimming anymore." It seemed as good an excuse as any.

Her mom drained the last of her wine and stood up. "Well," she said, "I better call Sandra. She wants to do another showing tomorrow." She kissed her hand and tapped it to Kora's shoulder before heading inside.

Kora sat outside for a while longer. The heat was heavy and cicadas buzzed loudly in the nearby trees. The flowers scented the air, and her thighs were warm against the metal frame of the chair. She closed her eyes and let the golden afternoon sun light up her eyelids.

———— ◆ ————

When she walked back inside, Kora picked up her duffel bag and brought it to her room. But when she walked through the door, she dropped it again.

The walls were bare. The light blue paint was marred by ugly splotches of spackle where nails had been removed. Her picture frames, posters, and tapestries were gone. Kora could have lived with that. She knew her things were being packed up and put in storage. Memorabilia from her childhood, little things she couldn't remember, had been disappearing for weeks.

But now, her paintings were gone. Every single one of them had been stripped from the walls. Since she could hold a marker, her room had been covered in her art. It was a little gallery just for her. As she got older and started taking lessons, her art improved, and she could see the changes in her work mapped out on the walls. In the upper corner were her kindergarten scribbles, drawings of childhood dreams that only she could make out. Then her early experiments with depth and texture, attempts at faces. And toward the middle, her most recent works, the ones that got her into art school. She was so proud of her portfolio, she had made copies before she submitted the pieces so she could keep them forever.

She looked down at the storage bin where her mother had collected all her works. Some were torn from where they had stuck to the wall too well, some were crumpled and folded under heavy frames, developing permanent creases. They would be shoved down, a lid forced over them, and then moved into a storage unit where they would yellow and wither until Kora could rescue them.

Kora dumped the dirty clothes from her duffel bag into the hamper and grabbed random shirts and shorts from her dresser. She shoved in enough pairs of underwear for a week and some mismatched socks. Her toothbrush and shampoo were still in the bottom. For the first time since she had left for the trip, she grabbed her laptop, charger cords, and sketchbook. She didn't want to come back until she had to.

She could accept that her mother was moving, if she tried hard enough. She could even get past the idea of leaving her childhood home behind forever. But her art was her world. It had decorated the landscape of her inner thoughts, an outer representation of her passion, her skill, her growth. It was how she saw the world and how she wanted the world to see her. And she thought her mother understood that. She had always encouraged Kora to go after what she wanted, to paint and draw until her fingers were calloused and raw. She delighted at every piece of paper, even after Kora had colored thousands. But now, they were buried in a careless stack, ready to be discarded. And that was something Kora could not accept.

She left without telling her mother where she was going. She didn't know yet, either. The last few weeks had her driving around aimlessly more than usual. But she supposed that was her future, now—with her mother gone and the house sold, she wouldn't have a home anymore. As she drove through town, she memorized every tree, every yellowed grassy median, every graffitied stop sign. If she couldn't have a home to come back to, she would have to make all of Pinebrook her home.

She had a sort of home at Sage's house, but she didn't think she could stand it right now. She had always tried so, so hard not to be jealous of Sage, and most of the time, it worked. But there was something about the comfortable warmth of the Rivera house—the way they fit together easily as a family—that had always pulled on Kora's insides. When the Riveras chafed against each other, it was the kind of thing that came from knowing each other deeply. Even after their mother had died, the house still smelled the same, like old wood and tobacco smoke and cloves. There was a timelessness and surety about it that Kora wanted so badly for herself, to belong somewhere so thoroughly you didn't notice it at all. Her own childhood home was like a toy she clung to even though its fur had always been a little too coarse. She cherished it, but it wasn't quite what she wanted. She felt similarly about her mother.

She made the turn downtown without thinking about it. Usually, her meandering led her up the mountain, but this time, she found herself looking for parking along Main Street. When she turned her car off, she laid back, exhausted. Her lack of sleep was catching up with her, aches spread up her spine and dirty curls fell into her face.

Suddenly, she remembered somewhere with a bed nearby. Kora got out of the car before she could stop herself and walked the short block to the tattoo shop. She had never been to the apartment above it, but she knew the entrance was through the side alley. She found the stairs that clung to the side of the building and took them two at a time. When she knocked on the door, she was out of breath.

For a few moments, there was just the sound of Kora's panting. Her heart raced, and she felt her face flush. Maybe Hunter wasn't home. Of course, she thought. Part of her was relieved, the same part that was becoming embarrassed, exposed on the small landing. She imagined Hunter coming home and finding her lurking outside her door. A girl she had only been on a couple of dates with, if they were getting specific.

But then the door opened.

Hunter stood there in boxers and a large t-shirt with holes along the collar and faded lettering on the front. Her hair was sticking up like she'd been asleep. Kora remembered that she had just been thinking about how exhausted she was and realized maybe Hunter had been catching up on sleep after their late night. She felt guilty and even more embarrassed.

But Hunter smiled. She didn't seem angry to see her, or even surprised. She just looked pleased.

"Hi," said Kora, not sure what to do now. "My mom sucks. And I don't want to be home. And I know I've never been here before, but you said maybe I could see it sometime, and I thought maybe sometime could be now."

Hunter didn't say anything, she just stepped aside.

The apartment was small but cozy. Kora could tell that Hunter had recently moved in because there were still a couple of small boxes stacked near the kitchen that hadn't been unpacked. But she could also tell that Hunter lived there. The desk was littered with papers, some showing sketches of tattoos and some random bits of writing. The shelves were full of books, alternating between horizontal stacks and vertical rows. The walls were filled with eclectic original art of all kinds, paintings and hanging sculptures and collages. It smelled like coffee and something else, a spice that Kora couldn't name.

"I like it," she breathed, relieved. The panic at seeing her own bare walls was receding now that she was once again surrounded by artful disorder.

She looked over and realized that Hunter was studying her reaction with a nervous face. She had closed the door and was leaning against it with her arms crossed. While Kora was looking around, Hunter had clearly run some fingers through her hair, as it wasn't sticking out quite as bad anymore.

Kora looked over Hunter's crossed arms and once again admired the intricate tapestry of her tattoos, an elaborate, intentional work of art created over years of thought and creation.

Hunter was still watching her. She looked up and caught her eyes for the first time.

"Is it okay that I'm here?" Kora asked, breathless. "I can go to Sage's."

"No, it's cool," said Hunter with an air of nonchalance. Then, quieter, "I want you here."

After several days of trying to convince herself there was nothing special about Hunter, nothing worth causing more drama and giving herself another painful goodbye at the end of the summer, Kora stopped thinking. She just kissed her.

Hunter seemed surprised but not upset. Kora pushed her against the door, one hand running through the still-tangled hair and one feeling the soft cotton t-shirt as she grabbed Hunter's waist.

It was nothing like she had felt before. Not with Connor, not with the girls she had made out with at Oakcrest parties, not with any of her school crushes. Even sleep-deprived and dirty from a long trip, smelling like campfire and sweat, it felt inevitable. Like all the time she had spent wondering and waiting was wasted effort because there was an irresistible force bringing her back. It scared her and thrilled her, and she ignored it completely.

And the little thought that she had tried to suppress at the campfire, that had wondered if Hunter felt the same way, it was quiet now. She knew there was something between them, something stronger than she knew what to do with. She felt it in the way Hunter pushed back, fingers wrapping around the back of Kora's neck and hand pulling her closer. It was in the way Hunter kissed, like she was falling from a cliff, scrambling for a ledge; desperate and instinctive.

Hunter pulled her to a bedroom, and Kora vaguely registered deep blue walls before she was lying on the bed, eyes closed, feeling electric. She felt a soft bedspread beneath her and breathed in Hunter's scent on the pillow. As Hunter's fingers ran down her sides, Kora couldn't help thinking that this had turned out to be the perfect escape.

⸻ ◆ ⸻

Later, after the sun went down and Kora had taken a much-needed shower, a decision had to be made.

"Are you staying for dinner?" Hunter asked. They were laying in her bed listening to some old vinyl records. Kora's wet hair was splayed out on Hunter's pillow, but she didn't seem to mind.

"Am I invited?" Kora asked. She caught herself chewing on her bottom lip and forced herself to stop.

"You can stay as long as you want," said Hunter, her face open and genuine. Warmth filled Kora's chest.

"In that case," she said, "would it be okay if I spent the night?" She quickly felt guilty for inviting herself and rushed to add, "if it's too soon that's totally okay."

Hunter grinned at her. She grinned back.

"Stay," she said. "You like pasta?"

Kora did like pasta. Hunter made it from a box and served it in two large mugs. They watched reality T.V. and made fun of the contestants. It was perfect.

After a while, Hunter turned the T.V. off and sat back on the couch. "Do you want to talk about it?" she asked.

Kora frowned. She knew she probably owed Hunter an explanation for why she showed up unannounced and asked to stay the night. But, more than that, she did want to talk about it. She wanted to tell someone who wasn't Sage, someone who hadn't grown up with Kora's mom as a third parent. Someone who was completely on Kora's side and maybe didn't know she was being selfish and childish. She just wanted to complain, for once.

So she told Hunter. Not just about Sante Fe and the boxes and Paul, but about growing up in Pinebrook. She explained how it felt to ride around town with her windows down and know every building and what it used to be. She talked about the feeling she got at night when she listened to the cicadas, like she would never truly be alone. How it was her home, and now she would have no anchor, like belonging had been ripped away from her after 18 years. While she talked, she laid back on the couch and stretched her legs over Hunter's lap. Hunter listened intently and nodded and ran her fingers over Kora's shin. It felt nice.

When she was done, she looked at Hunter and played with her hair, embarrassed for having talked so much. But Hunter didn't look bored or annoyed. She had a soft expression on her beautiful face.

"If you love it here so much," she said, slowly, "then why are you going to school so far away?"

Kora stared at her. Nobody had asked her that before. Everyone assumed that she was overjoyed to be accepted at a prestigious art school in New York. It was the dream—everyone she went to high school with talked about wanting to get out of Pinebrook, go somewhere with better opportunities.

"I want to be an artist," she said. "I guess I just thought it would be easier to make a living there. Not a lot of job prospects for an artist here."

Hunter shrugged. "I managed," she said, like it was just that simple.

Kora nodded. Maybe it was that simple. But everyone expected her to go somewhere expensive and far away, move to a big city and never look back. Even her mom was counting on it. She had waited until Kora was leaving to pack up and move away. How could she go back on all of that without even a plan or a job? Art school would give her a path. And right now, she didn't have one.

She continued to think, chewing on her thumbnail. When she looked back at Hunter, she saw that Hunter was watching her, curious.

"I don't know," said Kora. Hunter nodded, satisfied with a non-answer.

When it was time for bed, Hunter gave Kora a soft gray henley to wear as pajamas. She offered some sleep shorts, and Kora hesitated, rubbing the back of her neck with her hand. "I don't usually wear pants to bed. Is that okay?"

Hunter grinned. "Sure."

When the lights were off, they faced each other in the dark. Kora could just make out Hunter's long eyelashes framing bright, inquisitive eyes. She felt like she was an animal being observed by a nature documentarian, but she kind of liked it.

"Are you sure you're okay going back out with us?" Kora whispered. "I know you have work."

"Work can wait," Hunter whispered back. "I'm coming."

Kora smiled, unwilling to argue. "Okay," she said. "Good."

Hunter exhaled slowly, and Kora breathed in the scent of her toothpaste.

"Are you worried about Sam?" Hunter asked.

Kora thought about the creeping anxiety she had been feeling, Sage's nervous leg-tapping, Sam's convoluted notes amounting to very little trace of him out in the world. She remembered when they were little, how she would find Sam's little hiding spots all over the Rivera house, secret nooks where he would leave small treasures, like empty birds nests and lost keys. He was always full of little mysteries.

"Yeah," she breathed, exhausted again. She felt like she had been trying to figure him out for a lot longer than the summer and didn't feel any closer to understanding. And she had a hunch that they would have to really know him to find him.

Hunter reached out in the dark and brushed a piece of her hair back over her ear.

"Whatever we find," Kora said, "I'm glad you'll be there."

Kora dreamed about a house full of empty rooms. She walked down a long hallway, then turned a corner onto an identical hallway. Each one was lined with doors, and each door opened to nothing. She kept searching but couldn't remember what she was looking for. In one of the rooms, she saw a bird with a broken wing, trying and failing to make it to the window.

She woke up with a start. It was dark, and it took her a second to remember where she was, but Hunter's scent reminded her. She turned over and saw Hunter's eyes blink open.

"Sorry," she whispered. Hunter shook her head a little.

"Can't sleep?" she asked, voice hoarse.

"Weird dream." Kora stretched a little and felt strangely wired. "And now I'm awake."

Hunter slung an arm over Kora's waist and inhaled deeply. She sounded tired.

"Go back to sleep," said Kora. She traced the lines of Hunter's cheekbones in the dim light of the moon through the curtains.

"Are you going to sleep?" Hunter asked, eyes still open.

Kora knew from experience with nightmares she probably wouldn't be able to fall back asleep. At home, she would put on a podcast or sit up and sketch with a small book light. At Sage's, she would walk downstairs and watch infomercials on the living room T.V. Her family was used to her wandering around at night and usually slept through it. But she didn't want to keep Hunter awake.

"I might go hang out on the couch," she said. "Maybe make some tea, if that's okay."

Hunter narrowed her eyes. For a second Kora thought she might have upset her and felt a shot of panic in her chest. But then Hunter gave her a troublemaking grin.

"How awake are you?" she asked.

"Why?" Kora gave her a suspicious look back.

Then Hunter abruptly sat up and turned on a light. Before Kora could adjust, she had gone to the closet and tossed a denim jacket over Kora's legs, still under the covers.

"Come on," she said with a wicked smile. "We're going for a drive."

Kora put the jacket over the henley and slipped on the sleep shorts Hunter had offered her earlier. She pulled on her sneakers and followed Hunter out the door and down the stairs. It was then that her sleep-deprived brain registered that by drive Hunter meant on the motorcycle.

She shuddered in the cool night air outside Hunter's apartment. The bike was parked behind the tattoo shop, and Hunter pulled out an extra helmet from a seat bag and held it out. Kora realized that her curls were probably still unruly from sleeping on wet hair. She looked down at the sleep shorts Hunter had let her borrow, which had pictures of sleeping cartoon bears and said "Bearly Awake."

This is a terrible idea, she thought. But then she looked up at Hunter, who had slipped on a pair of sweatpants that rode low on her hips, exposing a strip of stomach and the elastic of her boxers. She wore a leather jacket and had one leg slung over the bike with an easy confidence. Kora grinned as she took the helmet. She hopped on the bike and wrapped her arms around Hunter's waist.

They started off slow, cruising through the empty streets of downtown and passing closed nail salons and tourist boutiques. When they got off the main road, they passed a 24-hour laundromat where a group of guys turned their heads. Kora smiled. She felt invincible.

Hunter drove them up the mountain, taking the curves slowly and checking for cars coming around the bend. The roads were pitch black, but Hunter's headlight was bright and wide, flooding the road ahead of them. The breeze got chillier the higher they went, so Kora wrapped her arms tighter around Hunter and stuck her hands under the leather jacket.

After a few miles, Hunter slowed down and turned off the parkway onto a small dirt road. Kora realized she knew where they were. This was the spot where they threw the graduation bonfire every year. Where she and Hunter met.

The dark blinded her once the headlight cut off, and her ears were ringing without the loud roar of the engine. As she took a moment to adjust, Hunter hopped off the bike and took Kora's hand.

Once her eyes were working, she could see the little path leading toward the bonfire pit, but Hunter led them around another bend to an overlook. A small fence lined the outside. Hunter leaned against it, rested her arms on the top rail, and looked out into the distance.

Down below, lights dotted the valley, sparse by the foot of the mountain and then crowded together toward downtown. It was close to a full moon, and they could see the outline of looming mountains that lined the horizon in the distance. The forest was loud and alive here, crickets and cicadas and owls making themselves heard. Kora leaned against Hunter and rested her cheek on the leather jacket-clad shoulder.

"I can't believe we have Amber to thank for meeting at that party," said Kora, speaking softly so she wouldn't interrupt the cacophony.

Hunter laughed. "What's your deal with her, anyway? Seemed like you knew her."

"Well, everyone knows everyone at Oakcrest," said Kora. "But yeah, she and I dated sophomore year."

Hunter looked intrigued. "Tell me more."

"There's not much more to say," Kora said, avoiding eye contact. "It was sort of obligatory. We were the only two girls who had come out in our grade, but other than that, we had nothing in common."

"Yeah, she didn't seem like your type," Hunter teased.

"Oh, and what's my type?" Kora asked, poking Hunter in the ribs.

"You know, tall, dark, and handsome."

Kora giggled. "Mysterious, beautiful tattoo apprentices who drive motorcycles and are really good kissers?"

"You think I'm a good kisser?" Hunter said.

"I didn't say I was talking about you," she said, grinning slyly.

"Oh, I forgot about all the other biker tattoo artists you've been kissing." Hunter playfully bumped Kora's shoulder with her own.

It was quiet for a moment. Kora breathed in the smell of pine mixed with an old campfire smell that was still coming from the bonfire pit.

"It's fine if you are kissing other people," said Hunter, quieter now.

Kora wished she could see her expression. The moonlight lit her cheekbones, the tip of her chin, and her hair shone in the dark, but that was about it.

"I'm leaving at the end of the summer," she said, her voice not much more than a whisper. "Kissing people... probably isn't a good idea."

"But you're kissing me."

"Yeah. That probably isn't a good idea either."

"But you're doing it anyway?"

"Yeah."

"Why?" Hunter turned to face her now, her nose only inches from Kora's. She saw the light flint in Hunter's dark eyes for a moment.

"I don't know," she breathed and leaned closer.

"Do you want to stop?"

The hairs on the back of Kora's neck stood up. She felt goosebumps feather her arms underneath the weight of the denim jacket. Hunter's scent surrounded her.

"No." And then they were kissing. Kora couldn't tell who had bridged the distance, but it didn't matter because they were both grabbing each other's hair and biting each other's lips.

A sharp breeze blew through the trees, and Kora shivered as Hunter's lips moved to her jaw. The dark made her touch more electric, the shock of each little movement sent chills to the back of her neck. Hunter's fingers skimmed along Kora's waist underneath the henley, her other hand buried in Kora's curls.

She wasn't sure how long they stood there, buried in each other's arms, leaning heavily on the sturdy fence railing. After a while, the owls stopped hooting and the crickets quieted. They kissed with only the humming of the cicadas for a soundtrack.

By the time Hunter drove them down the mountain again, the sky was beginning to lighten. Kora's eyelids were heavy as they walked through the door of Hunter's apartment. She dropped into Hunter's bed like she lived there, not even bothering to take off the jacket.

Hunter crawled in after her and pulled the denim off her, tossing it into the corner of the room. They bundled up under the covers, and Kora fell asleep as soon as her head hit the pillow. For once, she wasn't thinking about anything.

Chapter 12

Sage's dad found her asleep with her head on the kitchen counter. There was a plate next to her with a half-eaten sandwich.

"Didn't hear you come in," he said.

The voice startled Sage awake. She felt drowsy and disoriented, outside of time and space. She wasn't sure how much time had passed; the light coming through the window looked like mid-afternoon.

She didn't remember falling asleep. Connor had dropped her off that morning and she hadn't made it more than a few steps inside before crashing. Luckily, she seemed to have gotten some food first, but she was covered in many layers of dirt and sweat and wood-smell. She had never wanted to take a shower more.

"Just got home," she said, voice rough and scratchy. Her dad gave her a concerned look. She realized there were tears on her face.

"What's wrong?" he asked as he stepped closer to comfort her. She noticed that he was about to put his hand on her head and then, noting how dirty her hair was, chose her shoulder instead.

Sam was still gone. Her efforts so far had failed. The panic had become a deeper, more monotonous tone of dread and desperation. The notebook was an inscrutable jumble of myths and legends that she was no closer to deciphering. And while they were busy wasting time, he was out there somewhere, probably getting more lost by the day. He could be hungry, starving. Or worse. She refused to let that thought consume her.

She had good reasons for not involving her dad, she thought. He would worry. He would jump to the worst-case scenario and panic. He would call the cops, which Sage was still sure would help no one. But the weight of everything collapsed under that hand on her shoulder. She realized she was scared and wanted to hand this off to someone older, more in charge. She needed her dad.

"Sam was supposed to be back by now," she said, fresh tears spilling. "I don't know where he is. I think something is wrong."

Her dad moved his hand to her back and began rubbing small circles. It reminded her of when she would have temper tantrums when she was little and he would attempt to calm her down. It was soothing.

"I'm sure he's okay," he said. "You know how he is, always running off on his little trips. He always surfaces eventually."

"But he's been gone too long," she said. "He was supposed to be home over a week ago. Anything could have happened to him out there." She thought again of the bears. How stupid humans were to go out where bears lived.

Her dad sighed, looking old. She had never thought of him as being old before. She did not like it.

"He's probably just absorbed in whatever he's doing," he said, sounding defeated. "You know he gets obsessive about these things."

"He's never disappeared like this before," said Sage, feeling unbalanced. This wasn't how this conversation was supposed to go. She was supposed to be talking her dad away from the ledge, not the other way around. "He always tells me when he's going to be back."

"Really?" her dad asked. It seemed rhetorical, not like he didn't believe her, but like it didn't matter. "He's never told me. He just gets in his car and drives off, and eventually he comes home again."

Her dad crossed his arms and leaned back against the counter.

"You know, honey, I want your brother to stop this ghost stuff as much as you do," he said with a heavy sigh. In the afternoon light, Sage could see that his face was more worn than she imagined it to be. "At a certain point, you just have to let people make their own mistakes."

Sage could see she was getting nowhere. For a moment, she remembered the way the cops looked at her brother when they arrested him. Like their empathy for his grief had run out when he had chosen to express it in a way they didn't like. She knew her dad didn't see Sam that way, but the echo made her feel unsteady.

Rage was filling her up. It crowded her throat, quickened her pulse. But she knew it wouldn't do any good. Her father was barely here, barely conscious enough to really know Sam. It was going to be her responsibility, and anger wouldn't change that.

She swallowed the feeling down.

"You're right," she said, voice even. "I'm gonna go take a shower."

When she got to her room, she pressed a pillow to her face and screamed.

———— ◆ ————

The park looked different during the day.

Kora and Sage had spent countless nights parking the car in a hidden alcove of the parking lot and hopping the fence after the park was closed. Park employees came by every day at dusk to padlock the fence, but it was old wood only a few feet high. More of a suggestion, really.

Sage couldn't remember the last time she'd been there as a law-abiding citizen in broad daylight. There were kids climbing the wrong way up the slide, parents and nannies pushing strollers and holding onto dog leashes, joggers sweating their way around the hiking trail.

It turned out the creatures they sometimes heard ominously splashing in the lake at night were ducks. She and Kora had convinced themselves they were some kind of mutant beavers that had escaped from a nearby laboratory. The reality was disappointing, but the ducks were nice.

When Sage had fled her house, she didn't know where to go. She knew when Kora was feeling this way she usually came over, but she couldn't show up at Kora's house. It was being packed to move.

She wanted to call Sam. She wanted him to pick up and explain himself, and then she would yell at him and complain about their father, and then she would find him in real life, shake him by the shoulders, and demand to know why he was so obsessed with ghosts. She wanted to make their life look a little bit closer to the way it used to, or at least different than it did now. She wanted a big brother who would hold her and protect her and explain things about the world she didn't understand.

But even when Sam was there, he wasn't really there. He was a bundle of secrets and lies and grief. She realized she wasn't sure if she really knew him anymore, and the thought made the grief flare up in her chest.

Her phone buzzed in her pocket. She looked at the caller ID and saw that it was her swim coach. She groaned.

Sage liked Coach Cameron. She was young and nice and cursed just the right amount at practice for Sage to respect her. But she wouldn't buy the mono story for much longer, and she wasn't even done skipping practice. They were going back on the road in a couple of days.

"Hello?" she picked up.

"Hey, Sage," said Coach. "How are you feeling?"

"Fine," Sage responded automatically before she remembered she was supposed to be recovering from mono. "Much better."

"That's great. Can we expect you at practice tomorrow?"

The answer was no. But how could she explain it? Would Coach accept the truth—a family emergency? She knew the story of Sage's mother, everyone did. Maybe that would be enough. But Sage hated the idea of involving anyone else, especially after how her father had just reacted. The truth felt heavy and clogged her throat.

"Sage?"

The simpler truth was, she didn't want to do it anymore.

"No," she said. "I'm sorry, Coach. I don't think I can swim for the team anymore."

Coach was quiet for a long moment.

"I'm sorry to hear that, Sage," she said finally. "Can I ask why the change of heart?"

"I just don't want to anymore," said Sage, choosing honesty for once.

"I see," said Coach. In the background, Sage could hear the distant sounds of swimmers jumping into the pool and the assistant coaches barking orders. "I have to say, I don't understand why you would give up swimming now after you've invested so much time in it. You're one of our fastest swimmers. If you keep your times up through senior year, you could probably get a scholarship out of this."

"I know," said Sage.

And she did. It was the only reason she had stuck with swimming this long. It was a sport that she could get better at just by training more and working harder, which used to appeal to her as an overachiever with too much time on her hands. But things had changed.

"Honestly, coach," she said, relaxing back onto the bench, "with my family the way it is right now, I just can't afford to think about anything else."

There was another long pause.

"I'm sorry, Sage," Coach said again, sounding more earnest that time. "I really am. What your family has gone through is unimaginable."

Sage didn't really like when people said that. It was imaginable, she was more than imagining it, she was living it. But she understood that most people had no idea what to say. And there wasn't really anything she wanted to hear.

"Thank you," she said.

She heard Coach sigh on the other side of the line.

"You know I'll have to discuss this with your father," said Coach.

"Go ahead," said Sage. "I don't think he'll object." That part wasn't necessarily true, but she wasn't planning on listening to him. They didn't seem to agree on much anymore.

"All right, well, you take care," said Coach. "Call me if you change your mind."

"Okay," said Sage. She hung up the phone.

Around her, families continued playing and walking and running and swimming. For a moment, she hated all of them.

"Sorry," she heard. She looked up. A young boy was running toward her. She realized he had thrown his Frisbie right by her feet.

She picked it up and tossed it back to him. He grinned and turned around to throw it to his friend. She had to get out of here.

Time was running out until they needed to get back on the road, and she currently had zero leads. Without swimming to distract her, it was time to dig into the research.

There were a lot of things she didn't know, many of which were about Sam. It occurred to her that there was a place you were supposed to go when you wanted to know things, and a person who knew Sam possibly better than she did right now, and that person happened to work at that place. Very convenient.

She texted Noah on her way to the library.

On her way, she picked up coffees for both of them at the place down the street where Hunter worked, though she wasn't on shift. When she got to the library, she found Noah sitting next to a stack of books, some of which Sage recognized from Sam's room.

"I found all the books he's checked out that he either returned or we have extra copies of," said Noah.

He was freshly showered and looked much more put-together than he had when they had gotten home. He wore dark jeans and a navy blue henley. Sage wasn't really one for fashion, but she noticed that he dressed nicer than Sam, definitely nicer than Connor.

Sage pulled out the notebook and dropped it heavily on the table. They worked mostly in silence, occasionally jotting down notes from the books and exchanging theories. When Sage finished skimming a book, she set it aside and studied Noah for a second. He was intensely focused on the book in front of him and used his finger to guide his sight like it was braille. Sometimes he murmured something to himself. She wondered if he always looked like this when he was studying or if he was as obsessed with finding Sam as Sam was with finding ghosts. For the second time that day, she wished she could talk to her brother, and ask him why he befriended this nerdy, well-dressed librarian.

"Can you tell me about my brother?" she asked without really meaning to.

Noah looked up at her, tilted his head and squinted. "What about him?"

"Anything."

"He's your brother. What could I tell you that you don't already know?"

Plenty, she thought. But she tried a different angle. "What has he told you about me?"

Noah thought about this for a long time. His fingers traced the letters of the book in front of him, and he took long sips of his coffee.

"He said you were complicated," said Noah. "That you were different since your mom died, and he didn't know how different. But you were always funny and smart and a little bit mean in a way that's discerning instead of cruel."

"That's all stuff you could have figured out by now," Sage pointed out.

Noah nodded and continued. "He also said you were angry a lot when you were a kid. You had a lot of temper tantrums, but instead of screaming and crying you would just storm off to your room and quietly seethe by yourself until you calmed down."

Sage couldn't meet his eyes. She didn't totally remember what she had been like as a kid, but she could remember crying angry tears in her room, wanting someone to come check on her but being too proud to ask for it.

"That never really stopped," she said.

"He said that, too," Noah added quietly.

Sage looked up at the ceiling, a strategy she had read somewhere that could keep you from crying. She hadn't expected that Sam would have told Noah so much about her.

"He followed all your playlists from a burner account," Noah said with a grin. "He really liked your music taste but didn't want you to know that he liked it. He thought you were too pretentious already."

Sage hadn't known that. The music she could usually hear coming from Sam's room was nothing like the songs on her playlists.

"And he said you looked a lot like your mom," said Noah, "and he sometimes thought you looked nothing like him, but people could always tell you were siblings when you went out in public. He thinks you drink too much espresso for your own good. And he told me you have ADHD, but that's another thing I could have figured out on my own."

Sage laughed. Her fingers played with the edge of one of the notebook pages. Always moving.

"He thought he had it, too, for the record," said Noah.

"That's definitely true."

"Totally."

Sage's chest felt a little lighter than it had before. Another thing she hadn't expected—for Noah to make her feel better.

Noah was still thinking, tapping his pencil on the table.

"You fondly remember your family camping trips, but you don't like to be outside if you can help it," he said. "Again, I could have figured that out. You're at the top of your class, even though you get bad grades in classes you don't like. And he said he had no idea what you would be when you grew up, but that whatever it was, you would be excellent at it."

Sage had no idea what to say to all of that. She really thought Sam wasn't paying any attention to her. She thought they had nothing in common anymore, that their mom had taken all the joy and comfort they got from family with her when she died.

She realized in that moment that she had thought Sam didn't like her very much, and she desperately wanted him to. But she never reached out to him. Just like with her temper tantrums.

"He said all that to you about me?" she asked. "Did he ever talk about anything else?"

Noah looked down at his coffee again. He seemed a little embarrassed.

"You forget," he said, "I've known him for a year."

"So tell me about him," she said again, thinking he would say yes this time. "Like I'm not his sister. Like I'm some nobody."

"I wouldn't tell just anybody about him," said Noah, suddenly solemn. "He takes his privacy really seriously."

That just made Sage more curious. Why was Sam so secretive? What was he trying to hide? He watched and watched and apparently knew everything there was to know about his sister. Sage thought all their secrets were kind of on the outside now. Everyone knew they had a dead mom. What else was there to know?

"Okay, then tell me like I'm not nobody," she said. "Like I'm a friend. We're friends now, right? I mean, you already know all about me. I know he was hiding you for some reason, but maybe we would have been friends anyway eventually."

Noah smiled at that. "Yeah," he said. "I'm sure we would have."

He took another sip of his coffee.

"Okay, he's constantly alternating between hot and cold," said Noah. As he talked, he was looking off in the distance, contemplative and removed. "Literally, I mean. He always has a cardigan, and he's always putting it on, taking it off, putting it on. Like he can never get comfortable with the temperature."

Sage nodded, encouraging him to continue. She knew that already, but this was good.

"He likes mocha lattes, but if it's an older woman barista, he feels embarrassed about the sugar and orders a green tea instead," said Noah.

Sage laughed. That would be their mom's influence. She wasn't very strict, but when she encouraged them to eat better, her suggestion was hard to deny.

"He's very afraid of most bugs but refuses to call it fear," said Noah. "He says he just prefers not to be around them. But then he jumps up on a table if he sees a spider. Let's see, he almost never smiles but when he does, it's usually over something stupid or something brilliant."

Sage would have been satisfied with one or two things, but Noah kept going and she didn't stop him.

"One time, he came in with his shirt inside out and backwards, and when I asked him how long it had been like that, he told me he had slept in it the night before," said Noah. "He smells like aftershave, and he said he uses the same one your dad does because it makes him feel grown up."

Noah kept going, counting things out on his fingers as he thought of them.

"He likes animals, but he talks to them in this weirdly formal way, like he's trying to be respectful," he said. "He's incredibly smart, he makes connections I never would have thought of in a million years. But he doesn't know how to tie a tie or change a tire. He doesn't admit to liking Taylor Swift, but if pressed, he'll say his favorite album is *reputation*. He's funny, but almost no one notices because he's never smiling. When he's tired, he talks with his hands. I tell him he's probably Italian. And he wants to be a professor one day, like your parents."

Sage had been so captivated by these things that the last one caught her by surprise. Sam dropped out of college to become a full-time ghost hunter. She figured he had given up all his academic ambition or maybe had given up on the future in general. But she could see it—Sam wearing bulky sweaters and glasses and teaching a bunch of kids about folklore and legends, turning all the notes in his room into a book or two. She was distracted for a while, thinking about that, and when she looked up, Noah wasn't looking at her. He was leaning his chin on his hand, looking melancholy.

"Oh," she said, realization dawning on her. "You like my brother."

Maybe she should have noticed it earlier, but she had never been quick to notice romantic feelings. Perhaps because she had never really had them. But now it seemed obvious.

Noah didn't answer, just kept looking over her shoulder.

"He must like you too," she said. "He never tells anyone that much stuff about himself, much less about me."

"You don't have to say that," said Noah, finishing off his latte. "It's fine."

Sage rolled her eyes.

"Dude, I'm serious," she said. "I'm not exactly one for the reassuring lies. Surely Sam must have told you that."

Noah laughed. "That's another one I could have figured out by myself," he said.

He tried to take a sip of coffee, realized it was empty, and set it farther away.

Noah shook his head and said, "I don't even know if he likes guys. Surely that would have come up by now if he did."

"Did he ever talk about girls?" Sage asked.

"No," said Noah. "I guess not."

"He didn't tell me, either," said Sage. This also seemed like something she should have known. But Sam had always kept his secrets. "One time, my mom caught him with a hickey and when she asked how he got it, he said he fell down the stairs."

Noah's eyes went wide, and then he was really laughing, and Sage was too. They had to keep quiet because there were other people in the library, but tears started to well up in her eyes. It felt good.

They got back to work. Sage wanted to understand every page of Sam's notebook. Somehow it was easier now that she felt like she knew more about Sam. He liked her music. He had a secret maybe-crush. It didn't explain why he wanted to find ghosts so bad, but she felt like maybe knowing him better would help her find him.

She was glad for Noah's help. Sam had so much to come back for.

CHAPTER 13

When the five of them met up again to get back on the road, things felt much more solemn than the first time.

Kora had stayed with Hunter the last couple nights to avoid her mom. She would have gone over to the Riveras', but Sage was fighting with her dad, and Kora didn't want to get in the middle of it. Noah seemed sadder and more distant than before, less interested in the folklore and more concerned for Sam. Connor was withdrawn, trying to keep his distance from Kora and Hunter, but seemingly still committed to the cause. Hunter was the only one who kept a level head, though for once, she didn't try to crack jokes or lighten the mood.

Connor was less hesitant this time when he handed the keys over to Kora. Sage took her spot in the front seat and navigated them to their next destination.

This lead didn't seem promising, so morale was low. Sam had lots of notes on the Brown Mountain Lights—mysterious lights that appear over the mountains at night that you can only see from a distance—but there was no clear guidance on how he planned to investigate. All they had to go on was a printed-out list of scenic overlooks along the Blue Ridge Parkway where believers reported they could see the lights. They didn't have an exact plan, but they knew the lights were only visible at night, so they set up camp and waited until dusk.

The campsite was bare bones, just a spot of dirt in the woods, but it was enough. They set up a tent and snacked unenthusiastically, unwilling to put in the effort for a real lunch. By now, the sun had risen over the trees and beat down on them relentlessly. It was too hot to do much of anything, so Kora lay down under some trees and rested her head on her arms. They passed the afternoon playing card games and reading and using their shirts to wipe the sweat from their faces.

Connor went for a walk and came back with news of a nearby creek, so they all put on their boots and followed him. The creek was shallow and narrow but quick, and the water was cold, so it must have come from higher up the mountain. Kora stripped until she was just wearing her underwear and t-shirt, and she lay on the shallow rocks, letting the water run over her shoulders and down her legs. It felt so good she thought she might fall asleep.

She felt water splash on her face and looked up, holding her hand over her eyes to shield them from the sun. Hunter stood over her, backlit, dark hair gleaming. She stood ankle-deep in the water, her hiking boots stowed on a dry rock.

Kora splashed back, managing to wet the bottom of Hunter's shorts. Hunter examined the wet spot, shrugged, and sat down in the river next to Kora.

They sat in silence for a while, listening to the creek roll over rocks and cicadas shriek in the trees. As she closed her eyes and basked in the warm sun and cool water, she could feel Hunter's eyes on her, but every time Kora looked, they were trained on a smooth rock Hunter was turning over in her hands.

Once the sun began to dip, Sage called them all back to the campsite. They took turns changing out of their wet clothes, and

Hunter tied a length of rope between two trees so they could hang them up to dry.

Dinner was bags of chips and jelly sandwiches, which they messily assembled and ate without plates or napkins.

As the sun started to set, the gang left most of their things at the campsite. They climbed into the Jeep and set out on the Parkway.

"So, what's the plan?" Connor asked.

Kora looked at Sage. Her ponytail was so tight it looked like she had no hair on the top of her head. Her fingernails were chewed to the nub. She was in no shape to take the lead.

"Well, we have all these overlooks on a map," she said, pulling out the large gas station map of North Carolina where they had dotted a few spots along the Parkway with a Sharpie. "I guess we'll just go to each one and see if we can find anything to indicate that Sam was there."

The others were quiet in the backseat. It was a flimsy plan, she knew, but there was nothing else to do but search. She identified the first one on the map and pulled out of the campsite parking lot.

———— ◆ ————

Driving along the Parkway at dusk was beautiful, even if it felt a little futile. The sun was setting in the West over the valley below.

At their first stop, they found a small platform where travelers could admire the view. Linville Gorge dropped beneath them and stretched for miles in every direction, bright blue sky arcing above. A river carved its way through, rocky and subtle. Kora could see tiny hawks swoop over the trees in the distance, but she knew up close, their wingspan was impressive.

The myth of the Brown Mountain Lights said that small glowing orbs were supposed to appear over the mountains in the distance after dark. But at the moment, the whole valley was lit up with the last vestiges of the summer sun, the tops of the trees illuminated.

They found nothing at the first overlook, so they headed for the next. By the time the last sunlight dropped below the horizon, they had searched through five different stops along the Parkway, all of them beautiful, and all of them empty. Occasionally they saw tourists passing through, looking through binoculars and taking pictures with their phones. They walked along the perimeter of each one, hoping for a sign to appear in front of them, like the watch at Helen's Bridge.

No such luck.

The sixth overlook on their list was the biggest and most mentioned in the notebook—Wiseman's View. It was said to be the best vantage point from which to see the lights.

As soon as they drove around the bend and saw the parking lot for the spot, they saw that it was much more popular than the others. The parking area was almost full with cars. As they drove in and found a place to park, they saw license plates from all around the area: Tennessee, Kentucky, Georgia. One from New Mexico.

As they got out of the Jeep, the light was just turning from dusk to dark. They followed a dirt path from the parking lot to some stone steps that led down to a small outcropping. They passed a few people who were there to see the view, but not nearly as many as there were cars in the parking lot. Kora and Sage looked at each other. Something felt unnerving. Where were the rest of the tourists?

They continued walking down the steps until they reached the overlook. It was difficult to see now that it was darker, but the view was obviously stunning. Kora could see the dim outline of the mountains where they carved out of the sky in the distance, a small swipe of pink still hovering over the horizon. A few small lights dotted the mountainscape from remote vacation homes, but most of the valley was dark.

Kora had yet to see anything on their journey that she felt was undeniably magical, but something about the stars giving way to endless swaths of black where the forest continued uninterrupted made her feel calm and still. It had been a long day of nothing, and she felt her exhaustion and hopelessness quiet. Crickets chirped and cicadas hummed, and somewhere in the distance, another river tumbled over rocks.

Hunter stood next to her, taking in the same view. Kora bumped her shoulder against Hunter's and gave her a little smile. She got nothing in return. Hunter continued to look out into the darkness.

She was about to ask if everything was okay, but then she heard a noise.

It came from over her left shoulder, back up toward the parking lot. She glanced at the others and saw that they heard it too. It sounded like a person talking. They filed back up the narrow stone steps and went in search of the sound.

Halfway up the path, they saw light through the trees to their right. The voices were soft, but there were obviously multiple people talking. Kora's heart was in her throat. For one second, she allowed improbable hope to seep in. Maybe Sam had been right here the whole time, camping with some new friends. Maybe he got distracted and forgot to come home. Maybe he was just trying to see the lights.

Hunter and Connor went to get flashlights from the car. Kora led the rest of them into the forest. The people were not far off the path. Kora made sure her footfalls could be heard as they approached—she didn't want to startle them.

Five or so people gathered around a makeshift campsite with a single tent, a gas burner, food, blankets, and old-fashioned oil lamps. On the other side of the site, Kora could see that the forest thinned out so that this area had roughly the same view of the valley as the overlook. Large, expensive-looking telescopes and long-lens cameras were set up pointing at the mountains.

"Um, hi," she said. Everyone, most of whom had been moving around doing some kind of task, looked up and stared at her. In the dark, with only flames to see by, they looked like a bunch of large owls peering at her from between the trees.

"We have this area reserved," said a man in glasses who sat cross-legged on one of the blankets. His tone was unnecessarily aggressive for the situation, in Kora's opinion.

"Oh, sorry to bother you," she said, trying her best to sound charming even though she was mostly confused. "We weren't trying to—we were actually just curious what you were doing out here."

"Listen," said a woman in a large, bulky sweater and wildly tangled hair. "If you're not from the city you can't tell us to move. We're not bothering anybody. Nobody tries to use the overlook after dark."

Kora stared at the woman, uncertain what to say. She was taken aback by how immediately defensive they were.

"We're not from the city," Sage said aggressively. Kora did not think matching their energy was a good idea.

"We're just... tourists," said Kora. "We came to see the view, but we got here too late."

"Well," said the man who had spoken before, "lucky for you, you've arrived just in time for the real view."

Kora relaxed, as the man seemed to believe them. Noah stepped forward to speak.

"Excuse me, sir, are you talking about the lights?" he asked politely. "The Brown Mountain lights?"

Now, several pairs of eyes focused on him.

"They know about the lights," said one voice.

"Maybe they're from the message boards," said another.

"We know everybody from the message boards."

"Well, maybe they're converts. We did put up those ads online."

Kora raised her hand to get their attention.

"Um, we're not from online," she said. "We're looking for someone."

A woman who was previously gathering sticks in the woods approached. She had a more relaxed energy than the others, which might have been because she was a little bit older. She wore a practical sweatshirt and athletic pants and had short gray hair pulled back with a headband.

"Stop it, you're scaring them," she scolded. The rest of the group went back to the tasks they had been working on before.

The lady approached Kora and held out her hand.

"Irene Goldman, nice to meet you," she said. She had a nice scratchy voice, like a smoker, and some kind of Northeastern accent. Kora and Noah shook her hand. She moved to shake Sage's hand, but seemed to think better of it. "Can I help you kids with something? You said you're looking for someone?"

"Yes, ma'am," said Kora. "Our brother was researching the lights, and we haven't seen him in a little while."

Irene gestured to invite them to sit on the blankets they had placed around the small clearing.

"If he knows anything about the lights, he probably knows us," said Irene. She sat down in a folding chair across from them. "We're a group of like-minded individuals that come together online and in real life to discuss and witness the magical phenomenon of the Brown Mountain lights."

It seemed like something she had rehearsed and regularly recited.

"Great," said Kora with fake enthusiasm. "Do you know a boy named Sam Rivera?"

For a third time, everyone looked at her. Irene's calm demeanor was a little shaken.

Just then, Hunter and Connor entered from another direction, carrying several small flashlights.

"Oh no," said the woman with the sweater, standing up to stop them. "Please put those away. LED bulbs leave a faint trace of light behind even after they're turned off. It makes it harder to see the lights. We only use natural light here."

Hunter and Connor seemed alarmed and confused, but obeyed the woman and sat the flashlights down in the woods behind them, turned off.

Kora turned back to Irene. "Sam Rivera?" she prompted.

"Yes," said Irene. "We know him. Why? Is he all right?"

Kora's heart leapt into her throat.

"That's what we're trying to find out, ma'am," she said. "How do you know him?"

"He used to post on the message boards," said the man on the blanket, his tone disdainful. "But then he decided he was too good for us."

"That's not true, Albert," said Irene. "He just wasn't as interested in the lights as we are. He had other interests that he felt were more pressing."

"So you've met him, then?" asked Kora.

"Sure," said Irene. "He came around a few times, but then he stopped coming."

"When was the last time you saw him?" asked Sage.

"Over a month ago now," said Irene.

The growing bubble of hope that had been rising in Kora's chest popped and deflated. She felt worse than before. They were sitting with these weirdos in the woods and they were no closer to finding Sam. Sage seemed to be thinking the same thing. She got up and walked back toward the path. Kora decided to leave her alone for now.

"Do you know anything about where he might be?" she asked, desperation obvious in her voice.

"I'm sorry, honey," she said earnestly. "We only meet up in person like this occasionally. The rest of the time, we just talk on the message board. To my knowledge, he hasn't posted anything recently."

"Okay," said Kora, defeated. "Thank you for your time."

"I'm sorry we couldn't help more," said Irene.

Kora stood up and walked back toward the car, the others following behind. Sage was waiting for them, leaning against the Jeep, smoking a cigarette. Kora felt that her stress smoking habit was quickly becoming a regular smoking habit, but she decided it was not the time to point that out.

"We still have Valle Crucis," said Noah. He hunched down to look Sage in the eye, putting a hand on her shoulder. "We haven't run out of leads. That notebook is chock full of random notes we could chase down. We just have to figure out what they mean."

Sage didn't seem to react to what he said, but she stubbed out the cigarette and got back in the car.

Kora didn't know what Valle Crucis was, but she figured she would probably find that out in the morning. She climbed into the driver's seat and headed back for their campsite.

◆◆◆

Kora woke from a rare dreamless sleep in the back of the Jeep, Sage unconscious next to her. It was always so scary to watch Sage sleep, because she didn't move at all, like a vampire in a coffin.

Next to her where Hunter had been laying, the blankets were empty and warm. Their campsite only had room for one tent, and Connor and Noah had claimed it, so the girls had pushed down the backseat of the Jeep and squeezed in together. Sage's legs were wrapped around hers at the ankle, so she had to unhook herself to get out of the car.

It felt like she had only been asleep for moments, but an early morning gray pressed in on the windows of the Jeep, condensation blooming on the glass. Quietly, so as not to wake Sage, she wrapped a flannel shirt around her shoulders and snuck out the back of the Jeep.

The campsite was empty, and Kora could hear gentle sleeping sounds coming from the boys' tent. She walked along the trail and looked up and down the creek, but it was silent and still. She cut back to the road and headed for the nearest overlook.

As she descended the stairs, she could see a dark figure outlined against the brightening sky, sitting on the stone ledge. Hunter's legs hung over the side of the steep cliff. Kora sat down gently next to her and tried not to disturb the quiet of the morning. She looked out over the jagged drop and onto the sea of low-lying hills.

"It's early," she said softly. She propped her knee up and leaned her cheek against it, turning to face Hunter.

"Actually, it's late," Hunter said.

"You didn't sleep?" Kora asked. She could still hear crickets chirping in the underbrush. The sky was turning a diluted shade of pink and warmed Hunter's cheeks with a gentle glow. Hunter's silence answered the question. "Why not?" she whispered.

Again, silence. Hunter turned to face Kora. Her fingers just barely skimmed the curved line of Kora's cheekbone, eliciting a shiver down her back. Hunter's hands slipped into the hair just over her ear. Kora lifted her head from her knee so Hunter could run her hand down to the back of Kora's neck.

The dewy morning air raised the hairs on her arms, her shoulders, her neck. A cloud shifted, and one of the first rays of sun pierced through. Hunter's dark hair shone like obsidian. Kora felt like she could be anywhere in the world and still want to come back to this moment.

"Casual," Hunter whispered. "You told me you didn't want any more than that. Something quick, easy. Nothing to worry about."

Kora nodded. She closed her eyes as Hunter's finger twirled circles on the back of her neck, her thumb grazing Kora's earlobe.

"If I keep lying next to you at night and listening to you breathe, I'm going to want more than that," said Hunter. "It doesn't feel casual anymore. For me."

Kora let the words float between them, her eyes still closed. When she opened them, the sky had lightened a bit more, and she could hear the sound of birds beginning to call to each other in the dappled light under the branches. Soon the mountain would wake up and shake its leaves. Animals would skitter across the dirt.

"Is that still what you want?" Hunter asked. She was trying to make her face look neutral, Kora noticed, but apprehension was peaking through.

Kora took a moment to consider. She looked out over the pinpricks of sunlit treetops.

Connor had been comfortable, easy. He knew her completely—her family, her past, her fears. Spending time with his family was safer than spending time with her own.

Hunter was anything but easy. Every time Kora looked too long in her eyes, her breath caught, and the hairs on the back of her neck stood up. She was exciting, fearless, exacting. Even now, she was brave enough to ask the question. But the more she got to know her, the more Kora saw the tender parts.

She was leaving, she reminded herself. Art school, a distant dream, far away from the deep, persistent magic of her home. With the kind of passion Hunter elicited from her, she knew the heartbreak could be even worse. The prospect felt a little like when her mother first put the For Sale sign outside Kora's childhood home. Like if she thought about it too much, it had the power to break her.

Her mind raced with worry and doubt. Her skin sparked. But more than anything else, she felt warm, even in the chilly pre-dawn air. Her fingers twitched toward Hunter's thigh. Pulling away felt impossible.

She looked back at Hunter, whose eyes were burning.

"No," she said. "That's not what I want. I want more."

Hunter's breath caught. Her hand stilled on the back of Kora's neck, and she pulled their faces together.

As they kissed, the forest began to come alive with sound and color. The rays of sun burned off the mist that clung to the mountainside. Squirrels chased each other from branch to branch. Birds called louder and louder, echoing through the valley. Kora ran her hand over Hunter's jaw and felt the sun begin to warm her from the inside. She could smell wood fire and cedar and honeysuckle. She breathed it in and held it in her lungs.

When they pulled away, it felt like a new day.

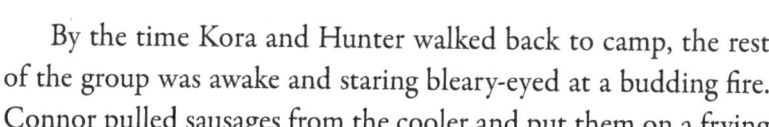

By the time Kora and Hunter walked back to camp, the rest of the group was awake and staring bleary-eyed at a budding fire. Connor pulled sausages from the cooler and put them on a frying pan. He looked up when he heard their footsteps and quickly looked back down at the pan when he saw them holding hands.

Kora wanted to feel guilty, but she couldn't. Her insides were full of sunlight and birdsong.

Sage was making instant coffee. Kora dropped Hunter's hand and went over to share.

"What's the plan for today?" she asked, grabbing cream from the cooler.

"Well, I think we've done all we can here," she said. "There's a bit more of the parkway I want to check, but then we can head north."

"What's north?"

"Valle Crucis. Supposedly there's a demon dog who follows people's cars." She held up a photo that was glued into Sam's notebook: a giant, black dog that looked more like a wolf the size of a bear.

"Yikes."

Once everyone had fully woken up and eaten some of Connor's sausage, they broke down the tents and then piled back in the car.

After stopping at a few more fruitless lookouts, Connor drove them to Valle Crucis. It was only about ten miles down the road from their campsite.

Their first stop was Mast General Store. There was a chain of them in the mountains—old, rustic stores that sold old, rustic Southern novelties—but this one was the first. Valle Crucis was a tiny town, and this was one of its only claims to fame.

The other was the demon dog, a creature who came out of the dark at night to follow cars down the road. Sage asked at the counter for directions to the stretch of road he was said to occupy.

Kora picked up a jar of pickles. She stood in front of rows and rows of them, stacked on old wooden shelves. When she turned around, she saw that candy was stored in buckets and sold by the weight. She put down the pickles and picked up a chocolate bar, dropping it into a green wooden bucket. Everything there was wooden.

Kora stood in line to pay for the candy behind Sage, who was talking to the sales clerk about local legends.

"Oh my goodness, I forgot about that old myth," said the girl. She couldn't have been much older than Kora, with light brown hair pulled into a quick ponytail and a simple white t-shirt under her work apron. Her name tag said her name was Eliza.

"So no one has been in here to ask about it?" asked Sage.

"Not that I've heard about, and I'm here almost every day," said Eliza. She gave Sage a sincere expression of apology. Sage brushed it off.

"Can you tell me where the demon dog is supposed to be seen?"

Eliza tapped her chin a moment and then called out for someone named Randy. An older man, in his mid-fifties, appeared from somewhere else in the store. He stepped behind the counter.

"This girl wants to know where the demon dog is," said Eliza and gestured toward Sage.

Randy let out a loud, obnoxious chuckle and clutched at his stomach. "Ain't no such thing as a demon dog, girlie," he said.

"I know that," said Sage tightly. "I just want to know where it's rumored to be."

After a moment, Randy stopped laughing long enough to give them directions. Sage thanked him curtly and went outside to wait by the car while Kora bought the chocolate.

"Do you know that girl?" asked Randy as Eliza rang her up.

"Yes, sir," said Kora. "I'm helping her look for her brother. He's missing."

Randy's expression sobered. "I'm sorry," he said, frowning. "I guess I shouldn't have laughed at her."

"No," said Kora, taking her bag. "You probably shouldn't have."

When everyone was back in the car, Sage repeated the instructions to Kora, and they started off down the road. The white siding and antique sign of Mast General Store faded into the distance.

Randy had told them to drive to the edge of town—which wasn't very far—on a thin, backwoods road he called a highway. They were to look for an old stone church. On their way out of town, they passed church after church after church, but none of them were made of stone.

"Welcome to the South," muttered Connor under his breath. "Churches freakin' everywhere."

Finally, after rounding a bend with a view of the whole valley, they pulled into the parking lot for the Church of the Holy Cross. It was made of stone, as promised. The main church building was followed by an inn and a rec room, and a log cabin sat across the parking lot. Kora wondered why they had so much space when so few people lived in this town.

Noah and Connor wandered across the graveyard out front, Sage and Kora went inside the church, and Hunter explored the grounds.

The inside looked like any other church. The aisle was red carpet, and the pews were polished wood. The altar held just a small, white cross and an ornate organ. The walls were lined with drawings that depicted the crucifixion of Jesus.

One of the drawings seemed out of place. It showed a man-like creature with gnarled hands holding up a cross covered with vines. He wore a black cloak and sandals and was much taller than any man. Next to him was a black dog.

"Is Jesus hulking out in this one?" Sage asked.

"Don't be disrespectful," said Kora. "Maybe it's the demon dog."

"Now who's being disrespectful?" said Sage with a laugh.

"I meant the dog, not Jesus," said Kora. Sage laughed again. Kora pulled out her sketchbook and did a very quick, rudimentary sketch of the weird image.

The two of them turned around to leave. When they looked back toward the door, they saw an old woman sitting in one of the back pews.

Kora jumped.

They hadn't passed anyone on the way in and hadn't heard her enter.

"I'm so sorry to disturb you," she whispered to the old woman. "We're leaving now."

The woman looked up from her prayer and smiled at Kora, but something about it was unsettling. Her face was wrinkled, but Kora couldn't tell how old she was. She wore a light blue dress and matching jacket that looked worn and faded.

"Y'all are not from around here, are you?" Asked the woman.

"No ma'am," said Kora. "We're from Pinebrook."

The woman made a humming sound, but Kora wasn't sure what it meant. "What brings you to the old Holy Cross?"

"We're looking for the demon dog," said Sage.

The woman chuckled. "No one's seen the dog in years," she said.

Kora raised an eyebrow. "So you believe in it," she said.

The woman rocked back and forth in the pew, like a complicated nod. "I saw him when I was a girl, driving through to get to Blowing Rock," she said. "That's why I moved here when I retired. Figured any place that lives in company with demons must be fiercely protected."

Sage sent Kora a look that said she disagreed with the woman's choice in residence. "Well, we won't bother you anymore," she said, and pulled Kora's wrist.

The air was several degrees warmer outside than in the stone confines of the church. They found Hunter, Connor, and Noah all sitting on the ground in the cemetery.

"Somehow, I think we had a creepier experience than you," said Sage, shivering.

"I doubt that," said Hunter. "We found a headstone with Kora's last name on it over there." She pointed down the hill.

They all frowned in the direction of the headstone, which read MASON in big block letters.

Kora shrugged. "My name is really common in this area," she said, unphased. Everyone relaxed.

"What'd you find about the demon dog?" Hunter asked.

"Only that it hasn't been seen recently," said Sage.

"We walked around the rest of the property," said Connor. "No sign of Sam or his car."

Sage crossed her arms and sighed. "Let's get out of here," she said. "This place is giving me the creeps, and there's no way Sam would have stayed for this B-list ghost."

As they walked back to the car, Connor glanced back at the road. "If we drive the rest of the way on this road, is the demon dog going to come after us?" he asked.

Kora laughed. "Only at night."

Connor walked a little faster toward the car. "Still," he said, "you can drive."

CHAPTER 14

"Where to now?" Kora prompted as she pulled onto the highway.

The sun was dipping below the horizon. Sage could have sworn they weren't in Valle Crucis that long, but the overcast weather made it hard to tell time. She pulled the notebook out of her backpack and frowned at it as she tapped a pen against the page.

"It's gonna be dark soon," she said. "We should probably find somewhere around here to spend the night. In the morning we can head home."

"That's it?" said Kora. Sage could feel her worried glance without looking up.

Sage frowned and tightened her ponytail.

"We can regroup again, take a giant collective shower, go back through the notebook, and come back out when we know more," she said.

She didn't like the idea of wasting more time going home either. But they were running out of leads. Sam's notebook was difficult to decipher without a hundred obscure books to reference. She and Noah needed time to figure out their next moves.

Plus, the weather was making her feel claustrophobic. It seemed like a storm might be coming. Her anxiety about finding Sam had become more and more pressing until it had leveled out, and now she just felt hollow.

It was starting to dawn on her that something really could have happened to him. Maybe not even something ghost related. Maybe he got in a car accident. Maybe he fell off a cliff. Maybe he got mugged somewhere. It could be anything. She might already be too late.

"Connor, can you look up nearby campsites on your phone?" Sage asked.

"Actually, I have a better idea," said Kora.

"You know somewhere else we can crash tonight?" Sage asked.

"Well, I know someone we can crash with," Kora said. Her expression was careful. Sage racked her brain for people Kora knew that lived nearby.

"No," she said. "We are not staying with Eris."

"Who's Eris?" asked Hunter.

"My cousin," said Kora. "She's a junior at Appalachian State, and she has an apartment in Boone."

"She's also an unreliable hippie who can't pay her rent and never wears deodorant," said Sage.

"She's not that bad," Kora objected, trying to keep her eyes on the road while she pulled her phone out of her back pocket. "You just don't like her because she treats you like a baby."

Sage scowled. She heard a giggle from Connor and turned around to glare at him. "As if that weren't reason enough," she growled, "she also gave pretty much the entire App rugby team chlamydia, including my friend from band camp."

Hunter laughed. "You went to band camp?" Sage's frown deepened, and she pointedly ignored the question.

Kora sighed. "Yeah, I told her she should be getting tested regularly. She said she didn't know where the campus health building was."

Sage grumbled "Public health hazard," under her breath.

"Hey," Hunter called from the backseat. "No slut shaming."

"I have no problem with her sleeping with them," Sage whined. "But it's irresponsible not to use protection." Hunter seemed satisfied with that answer.

"It's just for one night," Kora said. Sage grimaced, but she couldn't really argue with free housing for a night.

Kora got out her phone and dialed her cousin's number.

"Hey, E. I have a favor to ask," she said.

Eris Mason was not an organized person. Her apartment reminded Sage of Kora's bedroom, multiplied by ten. Art supplies littered desks and tables, clothes were strewn across the floor, and empty cereal boxes were stacked on the counter. Sage examined a glass that had been left in the sink for far too long and suppressed the urge to clean it.

Kora had used the spare key to let them in, and Eris had yet to come home. The apartment was small, but her roommate was miraculously out of town, so they had access to an empty bedroom. Kora and Hunter set up camp in there, Connor and Noah in the living room, and Sage on a hammock that hung from wall to wall in what could have been a small dining room.

When Eris arrived, she kicked open the door and stumbled in holding several bags—some Sage could tell were filled with produce from the farmer's market, others she had no idea. In between setting down her various bags around the room in no particular pattern Sage could discern, Eris kissed Kora on the cheek, shook hands with Hunter politely, and then mussed Sage's hair.

"Sagey baby!" she cooed. Sage grimaced and silently wished both of their extended families would forget she had ever been a child. She liked to pretend she had emerged fully formed as an adult from her father's head, like Athena.

Hunter ruined it. "I'm so glad you're reunited at last, Sagey baby," she said. Eris wasn't picking up on her sarcasm, which was endlessly infuriating to Sage.

"Me too," Eris sighed. "Connor, good to see you, too." Connor waved jovially. "And who is this?" she said, drawing out the "who" like an owl. Noah stared off into the distance for a second before he realized she was talking about him.

"I'm Noah," he said. "I'm a friend."

The corner of her mouth quivered in a half-smile. "Enchantée," said Eris and shifted her long, light brown hair over her shoulder. She held her hand out like he was supposed to kiss it, but he just shook it instead.

"Nice to meet you." Noah's voice was flat, unaware of Eris's blatant flirting. Sage couldn't help but giggle. Noah glanced at her inquisitively, which just made it worse. She covered her mouth with her hand while Eris made doe eyes at him.

"I think you're the first man to resist Eris's charms," she whispered. Noah's eyebrows shot up above his hair. He looked back and forth between Sage and Eris. Then, he laughed.

"Oh, no, I'm becoming a lady's man," he said miserably.

They both had to cover their mouths to keep from laughing. Eris frowned, but she pretended she couldn't hear them and went to put her produce away in the kitchen. As soon as she was out of range, they cracked up again.

Sage was laughing in the satisfying, full-body way that wasn't so common for her anymore. Noah's face was much more embarrassed than she had ever seen it.

"Could you not mock my cousin when she's letting us stay at her place for free?" said Kora. Sage and Noah tried to stifle their giddiness without much success.

"I'll make us some dinner," Eris called from the kitchen.

Despite the messy kitchen, Eris managed to put together quite the meal, including pasta with homemade sauce using fresh herbs and a robust salad. When it was ready, she began clearing space for them at her kitchen table, which seemed to be where she kept her important files, schoolwork, dirty dishes, socks with no pairs, and bras with the underwire poking out the side. She divided these items into various piles and moved them into different rooms.

Sage stepped closer to Hunter. "Have you ever been to Kora's house?" she asked, affecting an innocent tone.

"No," said Hunter, frowning down at Sage. "Why?"

Sage swept a hand in front of her at the mess that Eris was removing with the air of someone who did it frequently and without much guilt.

"Oh, you know," she said, a smirk spreading across her face, "just that this is pretty much your future if you and Kora ever move in together."

Hunter seemed to take in the words, and her eyes drifted from the table to around the room, where the mess was widespread and, in some places, exceeded charming and went straight to grotesque. Then she seemed to come back to herself.

"No one said anything about moving in together," she said. "We barely know each other. And Kora's going to art school."

Sage thought she heard something a little sad in Hunter's tone, but she decided not to push. Kora was helping Eris by collecting important-looking papers and moving them to the bedroom. When she came back in the room, she caught Hunter's eye and smiled a little as she fidgeted with the ends of her long curls. Sage recognized the tell. The girl was in deep.

But none of that was her problem, so she stayed out of it.

"Is she really this bad?" Hunter whispered, looking fearfully at a moldy plate on the counter next to her.

Sage only laughed.

◆ ◆ ◆

After dinner, the small house full of people was starting to grate on Sage. Eris had dragged Connor into some kind of drinking game that he was desperately losing. He was also flushed. Connor turned bright red at the first sip of alcohol. Sage checked to see if Kora minded this development, but of course she was distracted watching Hunter absolutely destroy Noah in chess. That couldn't be good for his nerd cred.

Sage slipped out the door without anyone noticing. Or so she thought, but she was only a few puffs into her cigarette when Kora joined her.

"I'm not going to object to your smoking," she said, "but we're at least going to get some exercise in while you do it."

Eris's apartment complex was in a small residential neighborhood just off one of the main streets. They walked through the back roads that butted up against the forest, and Sage smoked her cigarette while Kora unbraided and rebraided her hair. The air was dense and humid and the sky felt close. Sage definitely felt a storm coming.

"I can't believe you manage to swim so fast when your lungs are full of gunk," said Kora. Her tone was gently mocking, and Sage knew she wasn't really judging. But the comment reminded her that she hadn't told Kora yet.

"I quit the swim team," she said quietly on an exhale of smoke, hoping to come across casual.

Kora stopped in her tracks, hair halfway braided. She let it fall to her shoulder.

"Why?" she asked, face full of that big sisterly concern Sage tried so hard to avoid.

"Didn't want to do it anymore," she said. It really was that simple. Had she ever wanted to do it? She thought so. There was a time when the early mornings and the chlorine smell made her excited. Swim meets were a chance for her to release her competitiveness without any remorse. But now it just seemed like swimming in circles. What was she achieving with those trophies?

"What did your dad say?" Kora asked, walking again.

"I haven't told him," said Sage. "Coach said she was going to talk to him, so I guess he'll know when we get back."

"What do you think he'll say?"

"Honestly?" Sage looked over at Kora, who nodded as if to say, *obviously*. "I don't really care. He's not around enough to get a say in what I do."

Kora leaned over and pressed her shoulder to Sage's.

"You know what I think?" she said, voice soft. She had that Kora face, the one that said she wanted to sit around a bonfire and hold hands and talk about their feelings until everyone cried.

"What?" she asked, trying not to sound wary.

"Fuck 'em." Kora's face broke into a shit-eating grin, and she shook Sage by the shoulders. "You have talent coming out of your ass. You could set world records in pole vaulting or solving a Rubik's cube or making a million paper cranes. If you don't want to swim, you'll find something else to be excellent at."

Sage didn't know she needed to hear that until Kora had said it. Her shoulders suddenly felt heavy with her father's absence, with Sam's absence, with her mother's absence, everyone who should have been there to tell her it was okay to quit. Her chest tightened, and she leaned into Kora.

"You're going to kick ass at whatever you do," said Kora. "And if you don't, you can always come crash with me."

"In New York?" Sage asked, trying to picture it. Kora leaving. The thought was a dark cloud she had desperately been hoping would stay on the horizon.

"Or wherever," said Kora and pulled back so they could start on their walk again, still undoing the half braid and restarting it.

Wherever. Kora could be half a world away, and she would still be family. Sage would always have a safe place to land. For the first time since she had realized Sam was gone, she felt a little safer.

* * *

Sage woke up, predictably, before everyone else. The door to the bedroom where Kora and Hunter were sleeping was closed. Noah was on the couch, Connor was on the floor, both snoring.

She felt the throaty rumble of thunder rattle Eris's apartment. A light rain struck the windows and the house was chilly. Sage found a blanket that wasn't being used, wrapped it around herself, and started making coffee. A note on the counter told them that Eris had already left for class.

The boys woke up at the next crack of thunder. They startled awake at the same time, looking disoriented. As they stretched and slumped into the kitchen, rain began pounding the roof and lashed at the windows.

She wasn't sure if it was the weather or the fact that they were once again headed home with nothing, but the morning felt somber and strained. Sage silently poured the boys some coffee and they started quietly drinking it.

Hunter was the next one to wake up. She came out of the bedroom without Kora, which was not surprising to Sage, since they usually had to drag Kora out of bed. Hunter yawned and shivered, pulling a sweatshirt over her head.

Sage looked up when Hunter stopped and looked around.

"Where's Kora?" she asked.

"Was she not just in bed with you?" Sage asked.

"No," said Hunter. "She got up before me. I thought she was in the bathroom or something."

The four of them briefly looked around the apartment, but she wasn't in the bathroom and she wasn't in Eris's room. There weren't many places she could be hiding.

Sage glanced at the window, where the rain was now pouring at a slant. She had no interest in going outside, and she had no idea why Kora would be out there, but there seemed to be no other option.

"Maybe she sleepwalked," said Connor. He was still half-asleep and holding his chin with his elbow propped on the kitchen counter.

"Does she do that?" asked Hunter, alarmed.

"Yeah, sometimes," said Connor with a yawn. "She usually doesn't go very far."

Suddenly, they all heard the sound of the Jeep's engine starting up. Connor jumped up and ran outside, not stopping to put on a rain jacket or shoes. The other three looked at each other for a brief, startled moment and then ran after him.

Connor had jumped into the passenger seat of the Jeep. Sage climbed into the back with the other two behind her. Kora was sitting in the driver's seat, staring blankly ahead with her hand still resting on the keys.

Sage didn't see the problem until Connor waved his hand in front of her face, and she had no reaction.

"Oh my God," said Hunter. "She's sleepwalking? She started the car. She could have driven off a cliff."

Connor gently moved Kora's hand and turned the car back off, taking the keys away from her. Sage took a beat to try and get her heart rate back down to a normal level.

"Has this ever happened before?" Sage asked, feeling a little faint.

"One time I found her in the front yard with my keys," Connor said. "She's never made it this far, though. She was just standing there, nowhere near the car."

"How can I possibly not know about this?" Sage demanded. "I've slept in the same bed as her a lot more often than you have, Connor."

Connor shrugged, looking chastened, even though Sage could admit it wasn't his fault.

"I don't know," he said. "She usually gets back in bed and falls back asleep after a while. Maybe you just slept through it?"

Sage felt like she was having a heart attack. She leaned back against the car seat, which was now soaking wet.

"What do we do now?" asked Hunter. She was looking at Kora's blank, sleeping face with a disturbed expression that reflected how Sage was feeling.

"Nothing," said Connor. "I have the keys, so she's not going anywhere. You're not supposed to wake someone who's sleepwalking. I Googled it a bunch after the first time it happened at my house."

"Nothing?" Sage demanded. "She's in the driver's seat of your car!"

"Again, I have the keys," said Connor, jungling them in front of his face. "What do you th—"

Just then, Kora startled awake, her hands jumping up in front of her like she was going to take the wheel.

She made an undignified startled noise that sounded kind of like "Blagh."

Everyone stared at her, unsure what to do. Sage expected her to ask where she was and what happened, maybe freak out and demand to know why she was in the car.

Instead, she continued staring straight ahead like she had when she was asleep, only this time she was sitting up ramrod straight.

"I had the weirdest dream," she said. "Sage, I think we have to go to the place where your mom died."

Sage felt the blood drain out of her face. Of all the things Kora could have said upon waking, this one was the most unsettling.

Kora settled down then and looked around her.

"What are we all doing in the car?" she asked.

Chapter 15

Sam wasn't sure how long he'd been in this forest. It could have been days or weeks. He knew if it had been weeks without water he should be dead by now, but time seemed to be speeding up and slowing down as he walked.

Something was wrong about this forest. He knew his way around these mountains. He could close his eyes and know which direction was North just by instinct. He could navigate by the stars. He could start a fire with kindling and a pile of leaves. He was not capable of getting lost.

And yet, he was. He was very lost. He didn't know how far he had traveled from his campsite. His sat phone was only putting out weird static.

For months, he had been returning to the forest that was bifurcated by Town Mountain Road, where his mom's car had suddenly run off the road. He knew there must be something about this place that was different. It had a stronger spiritual energy than anywhere else he'd been so far. That couldn't be a coincidence.

He had brought his backpack, which contained copies of his relevant notes—he wouldn't risk bringing his journal, his Holy Bible, out to the woods, where anything could happen to it—and objects he hoped to use to better understand this place.

An old deck of tarot cards, well-worn from years of use, that he had bought from a witch in Blowing Rock.

A dowsing rod, used to find water underground. It never worked for him, which he suspected was because he didn't have the right skills.

Stones from the French Broad River. Only the ones that called out to him the most.

The feather of a Carolina wren that he had tracked in this same forest.

None of them had given him the answers he wanted. It had been so long since he started looking into ghost stories in the mountains, and sometimes he felt no closer to finding the truth than he was when he started.

He was walking back toward his car, ready to go home, when he found the forest shifting in front of him. And now, he was lost. The sky was still wheeling overhead, the stars impossible to place.

He knew he could not have gotten lost like this on his own. Something was leading him away from his path. And he had yet to determine if that force was leading him toward danger or answers.

He tripped over a loose root and stumbled. Frustrated, he sat on the ground. Moving forward wasn't getting him anywhere. He couldn't even tell if he was moving out of the forest or deeper into it.

If whatever unseen force wanted him to go somewhere, it could tell him itself. Until then, he was going to sit on the ground and go through the contents of his backpack, hoping something could help him.

He found some loose notes that he had taken on this area: old maps and records from the county clerk's office, stories that he had collected, the topography of the valley he hiked through. All things he had memorized.

Sam pulled out his tarot deck and began to shuffle it the way he had been taught. His knowledge of the tarot cards' meaning was rudimentary, but he was hoping if he pulled a card, whatever was guiding him would send him a message. His deck was unique—the witch who gave it to him had drawn the illustrations herself.

He split the deck and pulled the first card from the bottom pile. The Hermit.

Sam rolled his eyes. That wasn't helpful. He knew he was a hermit. Researching ghosts was a pretty lonely endeavor, and most of the people he met through this work were strange and difficult to get along with. But this work had to be kept secret.

Whatever it was that lived in this forest, his mother had died because of it.

Sometimes he wished he could tell Sage. But he couldn't put her in harm's way like that. And he knew she would be resistant to the ideas laid out in the notes. She was a scientist, and skeptical of the arcane. He didn't blame her. He used to be a skeptic, too.

He examined the illustration of the Hermit. It was an old man carrying a staff and a lantern. His face was hidden by a hooded cloak. The image made him seem more like a shepherd than a hermit. He was holding the lantern out in front of him, as if it were guiding him.

Sam thought he understood the message: look for guidance. Open himself up to communication. The psychics he had talked to were always talking about opening up channels for spirits to flow through, but he never really understood.

He closed his eyes and pictured himself as the old man, holding a lantern in front of him, following it without question. When nothing happened, he opened his eyes.

The forest had moved. Or maybe he had been moved, it wasn't clear. Now, he was close enough to the road that he could hear cars driving by.

He scrambled up to his feet and threw his things into his backpack. Knowing this forest, he couldn't rely on it to stay put. He sprinted toward the road.

When he got there, he saw his car, right where he left it. He had emerged from the woods right next to a bridge that stretched over a ravine. There was a small shoulder just before the bridge that was a convenient access point for the forest.

This was where his mom died. So this was where he always started his investigation.

As he left the thick coverage of the trees, he realized it was raining. He gave himself a moment to catch his breath before he dashed through the rain to his car.

After pulling him in all directions, the forest had led him where he needed to go. He wasn't exactly comforted by that, but at least he had his car back. And he knew better now for next time. The spirits were getting stronger, and he couldn't rely on the methods of navigation he had been using before. Once he got home, he could regroup, maybe ask Noah for his thoughts on spiritual navigation.

He opened the passenger door and was about to duck into it.

All of a sudden, the rain stopped. Not like it stopped raining, but the raindrops paused in the sky, suspended above the ground. Sam looked around. He had never seen anything like this. In his research, he had heard of rain going in the opposite direction—ground to sky—but he had never heard of it stopping mid-air.

Further up the road, a car was paused in the middle of a downward slope. Sam realized he couldn't hear the animals, even without the sound of rainfall to drown them out.

When he looked down, he saw that his dad's old watch was on his wrist. He had lost it weeks ago. It was stuck at 2:47.

Then, a force hit him.

It was like a wall of sound that had a physical weight to it. Sam was barreled over by it as the rain and the car and the animals all started up again. The force pushed him over the guardrail.

Sam had a split second to realize that he was falling before he hit the ground. As the wave of sound had hit him, he had heard a voice. He was sure of it—it was his mom.

CHAPTER 16

Kora's dream started, like many of her dreams, in Sage's house.

She couldn't find Sam and thought he might be on the roof. The second floor was completely dark. As she climbed the stairs, the light from downstairs faded and she was guided only by the familiar feel of the banister beneath her left hand, the wall beneath her right.

When she got to the top, her foot fell straight through where the step should have been. The feeling of falling swept through her stomach.

Once she steadied herself, she looked up to find that she was on the side of a road. A car she recognized was on the road, but she couldn't place it. At first she thought the car was parked in the middle of the road, but then she realized it was frozen in time. She tried to look through the windows but they were all black.

"Kora," she heard her name get louder as the person's voice zoomed toward her. She placed the voice and the car at the same time. It was Sage's mom.

The car. The sharp curve of the road.

Realization came to her in the way of dreams, like the knowledge was always there.

This was the place Sage's mom had died. And Sage's mom wanted her to go there.

After Kora woke up and announced her dream to the group, she and her friends climbed out of the Jeep and went back inside. They were all soaking wet, so it took a while for them all to change into dry clothes. When they were done they gathered back in the living room.

"Okay, I'll start," said Sage. "What the fuck, Kor?"

"Yeah," said Hunter. "What she said."

Kora shrugged. "Sometimes I sleepwalk."

"Since when?" Sage insisted.

"Just the last couple of years, I guess," she said. Kora was still stuck in a half-dreaming space, and she was overwhelmed by the interrogation.

"Why don't I know about this?"

"I didn't think it was a big deal," Kora said helplessly. "It's never happened at your house."

"How could that possibly be?" Sage asked. "You spend the most time at my house."

"I don't sleep very well at your house," said Kora, feeling embarrassed. "I only sleepwalk when I'm sleeping really deeply."

Everyone took a moment to digest that answer, and Kora relaxed a little. She didn't like feeling on the spot.

"Okay, let's table the sleepwalking thing for now," said Sage.

There were some noises of consternation that Sage waved away.

"We have something more urgent to attend to," said Sage. "Kora, do you remember what you said when you woke up?"

She did. And even more vividly, she remembered her dream. She was used to having nightmares and all sorts of dreams, really, but they didn't usually feel this close to her waking life. It wasn't that the dream felt real, it was that she felt less real when she woke up.

"Yeah," she said. "I think we should go."

"Why?" Sage asked. She had her fingers templed in front of her lips, and Kora could tell she was one flippant answer away from a total meltdown.

"I can't explain it," said Kora. "Just in my dream, it felt like we should go there. It seemed urgent."

Sage stared at her for a long moment. They could read each other's expressions so easily it was like she shared a secret, silent language. She felt Sage trying to discern more information from her face, but she didn't know what there was to find. She couldn't explain it any better than that.

"Okay," said Sage after the longest pause in history. Kora heard everyone else let out a held breath. "Let's go."

❖ ◆ ❖

Mist clung to the mountainside as Connor drove them out of Boone. Everyone else had agreed that since Kora had sleepwalked into the driver's seat of the car, she shouldn't be allowed to drive anymore, which she thought was unfair.

They passed little roadside markets and boutiques before they turned onto the Blue Ridge Parkway. It was ordinarily a beautiful drive, even on rainy days, the green of the distant trees blurry and lush under the fog. But with the rain, the tall pine trees lining the road seemed to press in above them, closing the strip of visible sky.

Kora watched Sage tap her thumb repetitively against her thigh. She didn't know how to reassure her, or even if that was the right thing to do. The engine of the Jeep thrummed, and the wish-wash of the wipers echoed their heartbeats.

Even though she had never been there, Kora somehow recognized the exit for Town Mountain Road as they approached it. Her chest tightened.

Sage was silent as they took the exit, only speaking to give Connor directions. Connor was driving five miles under the speed limit like there was a cop behind him. The rain was still coming down in big splats on the window.

Kora counted the mile markers. She knew where the accident had happened: mile marker fifteen. She had heard the cops telling Sage's dad.

"Slow down," Kora told Connor. He complied, and Sage became more twitchy.

Kora looked at Sage and had the sickening feeling of not knowing what Sage was thinking. Since the dream and the sleepwalking, it felt like there was some invisible distance between them. Sage was a reserved person, a private person, but Kora knew her inside and out. And right now, she had no idea what was going on inside her head.

The mile markers passed by.

Eight, nine, ten.

Kora's heart raced, and her hands were shaking. She wished she could hold Sage's hand. She didn't understand why she was so afraid. It was just a brief stretch of a long, winding road through the mountains. She didn't know what her dream meant. What could possibly be left that could hurt them there?

Thirteen, fourteen.

As they got closer, realization was a rising pool of darkness in Kora's stomach. A car was parked on the side of the road, just by the mile marker. It was like her dream, but not. Time was not stopped. It was speeding forward at a sickening pace.

Looking at what could only be Sam Rivera's beat-up old Chevy, with the dented fender from running into the magnolia tree at the farmhouse, Kora had the striking feeling of seeing strange things in the woods, like cans of energy drinks and abandoned chairs at the old bridge in Asheville. She could see that it was real and obviously there, but she couldn't fathom how it had appeared in such an unlikely place. It was like the car had been dropped there through a portal from another time, another place. Her dream suddenly seemed very dreamlike. This was real life.

Kora felt tension seeping up her throat and clawing its way into her lungs. An infinite, aching moment bridged between her and the car like the stretch of a rubber band, but then she blinked, and time snapped forward.

Connor pulled over behind Sam's car.

Kora couldn't hear anything as she followed Sage out of the car. Rain was pouring down, and her ears were ringing. It was hard to see the ground in front of her.

They passed the car; its passenger door was open. It didn't seem to be damaged.

The stretch of road in front of them was clear, just a grassy shoulder and tall trees lining both sides. The car was pulled over right in front of the bridge that Kora remembered from her dream, just a brief shift from asphalt to concrete with short guardrails lining the edge. Below, a ravine carved beneath the parkway.

Kora saw Sage lean forward to look over the edge.

Everything ceased to blur and became startlingly, mercilessly clear. She followed Sage and looked for herself.

Time had snapped again.

Kora was staring at a body on the ground below, a twenty-foot drop. Though it was covered with dirt and wet leaves and debris, the sprout of coal-black hair and the ripped Dirty Projectors t-shirt were unmistakable.

The body of Sam Rivera.

From their vantage point at the top of the drop, Kora could see a mess of blood, maybe a bone sticking out where it wasn't supposed to be, everything out of place like a Picasso piece. Like someone had tried to make a puzzle out of Sam and had shoved pieces in spots they didn't fit. Rain batted against his back, and her back, and everyone's backs as they each braced themselves against the storm.

Kora caught one glance at Sage's face, just as broken as the body below. Then her vision went fuzzy. The next thing she knew, she was toppling over the railing and into the ravine with Sam.

CHAPTER 17

Sage was sitting in the front seat of a cop car with a shock blanket wrapped around her shoulders. She wasn't sure how long she had been sitting there, only that darkness and hot rain were pressing in on the windshield.

She couldn't hear anything, but she knew by the fuzzy, swimming lights outside that an ambulance had arrived. She wondered vaguely why they had bothered to call one. He was clearly dead. Connor called, she remembered. She tried to imagine what he might have said to the 911 operator and shook her head to dismiss the thought.

Then she remembered that Kora was the one in the ambulance. She felt a pang of guilt for forgetting, but time kept skipping forward at odd moments.

Numbly, she recalled that morning, when Kora had woken from her sleepwalking. It seemed like an eternity ago. The uncertainty of how her dream had led them to the truth ate at her, but she put it in a little box in her mind and put it away. It didn't matter anymore. Sam was gone.

She couldn't focus on anything outside. A few cops were walking around, but when she looked through the dark window, all she could see was the memory of Sam's broken arm, stuck at an odd angle.

The door opened, and rain spattered against the side of her face. She didn't turn to face it or turn away. Someone pulled on her arm, and she stumbled out of the car. She found herself wrapped around someone's torso. Breathing in, she realized it was her dad.

His shoulders were shaking. The wind and thunder were loud, and sirens were somewhere very close so she couldn't hear if he was crying. She closed her eyes and pressed her cheek into his chest.

They stood like that for what felt like a very long time, getting soaked to the bone with every minute. *The blanket is probably ruined,* she thought.

———— ◆ ◆ ————

That night was a jumble of confusing moments that bled into the following morning. Sage wasn't sure if she had slept at all or if she had blinked and time had jumped forward again.

She watched from her perch on the couch as a parade of people came in and out. First there were the cops, who asked them more questions and offered their sympathy. And then Hunter and Connor had stopped by to let them know how Kora was doing (beaten up but fine, sedated). And then there were neighbors and family friends, who came bearing casseroles and more sympathy. Sage watched them all pass by with affected boredom.

Sage waited patiently for everyone to leave before she lost it.

By the time the sun set, she was jumping out of her skin. Everyone's words grated on her nerves. She wanted to smoke. She wanted to swim. She wanted to jump off a bridge.

Instead, she cleaned. The urge to move her body and do something with all the extra energy pushed her through meaningless tasks. She did the dishes by hand and set them out to dry. She scrubbed the already near-spotless countertop. She took the trash out and put a new bag in the can.

When she finished dusting in the den, she moved on to the dining room. She carefully opened the door to the china cabinet and stared at the dishware. It was a very old set, family heirlooms on her mom's side. They hadn't used them in years. Her mom was always the one to cart them out at Thanksgiving. She said there wasn't any point in having nice dishware if you weren't going to use it sometimes. Sage remembered once when Sam had dropped one of the crystal goblets, and it shattered on the floor. Their mom just laughed and picked him up, passing him to their dad so Sam wouldn't walk over the broken glass with his bare feet. And then she had swept it up and handed him another glass like it was nothing. Like it wasn't over a hundred years of family history brushed into a pan. She never made them feel guilty for their mistakes.

The restlessness that had kept her moving all morning turned into unbridled rage. She wasn't sure what had sparked it, and she didn't care. This was a familiar feeling, and Sage ached with relief. This was a feeling she understood, that she knew what to do with. It flowed through her as she stared at the dainty, intricate designs on the china.

The first dish could have been an accident. One second, she was reaching into the cabinet, and the next, it was shattering on the ground. But it was so satisfying. There was a permanence to it, of breaking something into so many pieces it could never be put back together. She remembered her mother's gentle smile as she poured apple juice into Sam's new, unbroken glass, and her insides burned. How patient their mother had been, how kind. She had cared about her children more than any objects.

The second plate was definitely on purpose. She threw it against the wall and closed her eyes in the split second it made contact in case any splinters of glass ricocheted toward her face. She was surprised to feel tears slide down her cheeks. Next, she grabbed a goblet, just like that one Sam had dropped. It had a chipped rim, she realized. That just made her angrier. She threw it onto the table.

By the time her dad found her, she was almost finished with the china. She didn't want any evidence left of their Thanksgiving traditions. The rage pulsed through her veins and provided a nice distraction for anything else she might have been feeling, and the smashing glass was satisfying to her restless hands. Her dad slammed the cabinet door closed, and she could see that he was yelling at her, but she couldn't hear him.

She knew she should feel guilty for destroying a priceless family heirloom, especially one with so much sentimental value, but all she could feel was rage. Breaking the dishes had helped, but it wasn't enough.

When her hearing finally clued in to her father's yelling, it only swelled. Her sneakers crunched over the broken glass as she walked away from him, striding toward the kitchen. He was barefoot and had to go the long way to meet her there.

"What were you thinking?" he was screaming. She noted with some distance that she hadn't seen him yell like that in a long time. Part of her was satisfied with pushing his buttons. She wanted him to yell, to do something. As her father stepped into her way and blocked her path to the door, the rage still simmered away. She itched for some other way to release the feeling, to move and strike her way through emotion.

Her dad opened his mouth to yell again, and she screamed. It was long and high-pitched, and she would think it was lame if she were watching a horror movie, but when she did it, it felt bloodthirsty and effective.

But it wasn't enough, she could still feel that anger pumping away inside her. In a quick movement, she turned around and smashed her fist into the wall.

There was a sickening crack in the drywall.

She heard more than felt herself stop screaming. The rage melted away, and all she felt was pain.

As the nurse wrapped up her hand, Sage could feel the sensation of her skin biting into the wall again and again. It wasn't helping the adrenaline that still buzzed under her skin. Her mouth was hot beneath her tongue, and her forehead was sweaty.

Every time she thought of Sam, she saw his crumpled body at the bottom of the ravine. She remembered the sticky notes he would leave before his trips, how succinct and empty they were. Nausea roiled in her stomach, and she clenched it with her uninjured hand. The nurse seemed to notice.

"Rough night?" she asked, her Carolina accent pleasant and kind. She had pretty brown eyes and auburn hair that was pulled back in a neat ponytail. It was unfortunate that she looked so nice. Sage didn't want to hurt her feelings, but no Southern charm in the world was going to work on her.

"You could say that," she said. Sam's twisted arm flashed through her mind again.

"How does the other guy look?" the nurse asked. She gestured toward Sage's bloody knuckles with a knowing smile.

"Like a two hundred dollar drywall repair," said Sage and stared at her fist as she turned it over so she didn't have to look at the reddening gauze. She prided herself on being able to see other people's blood without a second thought, but she got a little more squeamish when it was her own.

"What'd it do to you?" the nurse asked, looking Sage up and down like she was trying to determine how violent she was. Sage sat up straight to make herself look taller.

"It was asking for it," said Sage. She attempted a joking smile, but her hand was aching, so she suspected it came across as a grimace.

"Well, it looks like you showed it who's boss," said the nurse, seeming unconvinced. They fell back into silence as she finished wrapping gauze around Sage's hand and began fitting her with a brace. The bone wasn't broken, but she would need to wear the brace for the next few weeks.

She felt the sluggish lethargy that came from being on pain medication, but it did nothing to curb the wrongness she felt. Her emotions were raw and jagged, and she couldn't stuff them back in. All she wanted to do was go home and attempt to sleep herself into oblivion.

Once they were done, Sage walked to the elevator. Her dad had dropped her off, needing to "start making arrangements." The thought of that phrase brought up a fresh wave of nausea.

She knew she could get a ride home with one of the others. They were around somewhere, fetching ice chips for Kora.

She sighed and pressed the up button. She still had one more stop to make.

Chapter 18

When Kora woke up, she kept her eyes shut for a while. The fluorescents were too bright, and her head was pounding. The longer she was awake, the more pain she became aware of. Her chest burned, and her toes were tingling like her foot had fallen asleep. When she felt a hand in hers, she opened her eyes.

Her mom was sitting next to her, grasping her hand like it might fly away at any moment. Kora wasn't quite ready to have the full weight of her attention yet, so she said nothing. She just studied the look of worry on her mother's face and then looked around the room. The last time she had been in the hospital was when Sage had her appendix out. The room looked different from the bed.

Thinking of Sage brought back a brief flash of memory. She saw Sam's crumpled body lying at the bottom of the ravine. The pain in her chest seared, and she winced. She felt her mother look at her.

"Hi, honey," said her mom. Her voice was fragile, and it looked like she might cry. Kora didn't want that. She felt bad enough already.

Kora tried to sit up, and a ripple of fire ran up her chest. Her vision went black for a second. She laid back down, and her mother pressed the button on the side of the bed to raise it into a sitting position.

"You bruised your spleen and broke a couple of ribs," her mom said. "And you've got a concussion. You're gonna have to stay here for a couple more days at least."

Kora tried to nod and immediately felt the effects of the concussion. Her head was spinning.

Memories of Sam were threatening to flood her. Not just his body or the long search for him. Good ones too, from a long time ago. She remembered picking blackberries with him in the summer, pushing each other off the trampoline, the way he always bumped her elbow when she sat next to him at Thanksgiving because he ate with his left hand. She remembered getting angry at him for trying to scare her, the time he let her paint his nails, when she dared him to eat dog food. Moments where he was silly and annoying and funny and cruel and sweet. An entire lifetime of this boy who had been her family.

Her stomach turned, and she heard her heart rate increase on the monitor. She wanted to turn over and hide her face under the covers, but it was hard to move around in this bed.

It didn't feel real, and yet the gruesome image would never leave her. She wished she hadn't seen him like that.

"Sage?" she whispered, her voice hoarse.

"She's at home with her dad."

Kora closed her eyes. She understood that. This was not about her. Sage was going through hell. But she still wished she could see her, hold her. Try and understand this horrible thing that had happened to them. Try and explain the unexplainable.

The sharp pain in her ribs returned. It was hard to keep from audibly wincing.

"Are you in pain?" her mother asked. "It's been a while since they've given you medicine, let me get a nurse." She got up and pressed a button on the wall. A nurse came in a few minutes later and asked her a question, but Kora had a hard time paying attention. Her head was still pounding.

"Would you like some more pain medicine?" the nurse repeated. Kora nodded. The nurse pushed a syringe into her IV, and she watched the tube as her vision began to swim.

———— ◆◆◆ ————

The next time Kora woke up, her mother was gone, and Hunter sat in the chair next to her bed. Her hair was pulled up into a ponytail, but most of it was too short, so lots of pieces fell around her face and on her neck. She wore a muscle tee that had clearly been a crew neck before she had cut the sleeves off. Kora watched for a moment as Hunter picked at her fingernails, her eyebrows pulled together in a dark expression. Even through the haziness from the drugs and the dull ache from her injuries, she was glad to see Hunter. When her mom was there, the room felt claustrophobic, too heavy with worry. With Hunter, she could breathe a little bit better.

"Hey," said Kora. Her voice was still hoarse, and she wondered how long she had been asleep this time.

Hunter looked up from her nails and smiled. "There she is."

"Here I am," Kora smiled back. "All beat up."

"Yeah, you took a spill." Hunter's tone was lighthearted, but her face contorted as she said it.

"I won't be doing any hiking any time soon." She looked down at the bandages that wrapped around her torso.

"Sure, you will," said Hunter. "I'll just have to carry you."

Kora smiled. "I believe you could." She reached out her hand, and Hunter took it, careful not to mess with the IV sticking out of it. Kora cringed. She hated needles.

"Where did Mom go?" she asked.

"Downstairs," said Hunter. "She had to take a phone call from the realtor."

"And Sage?" she asked.

"Still at home," said Hunter. "We told her you're okay. I'm sure she'll be here as soon as she can."

Another wave of grief rocked through Kora's aching chest. She felt like she couldn't breathe, but she could see on the monitor that her oxygen levels were normal. She focused on the air coming in and out.

Sage and her dad. The only surviving members of their family, living in a half-empty house. Staring down the barrel of even more grief casseroles and awkward conversations with distant relatives, everything Sage hated about her mother's death coming around again.

Kora wanted to get out of bed and drive across town, show up at the Rivera house with a box of donuts, like she had done after every loss, big or small. But she was trapped for at least a couple of days. And deep down, she knew she should probably give them their space.

"Are Connor and Noah okay?" she asked.

"They're still in shock, I think," said Hunter. She looked down at Kora's hand, her voice melancholy. "And confused. No one is really talking about what happened. I guess he probably fell like you did. It's just... not what any of us expected." She looked up at Kora, and she was surprised to see tears in Hunter's eyes. "They've been hanging around the waiting room. It feels weird for any of us to go home. I can go get them if you want to see them."

Kora reached her other hand, the one that had no wires attached, and pushed some of the pieces of hair out of Hunter's face. "Later," she said. "I just want to be here with you for a while."

"Okay," Hunter whispered. She leaned down and pressed a gentle kiss to Kora's knuckles.

The two of them turned on the hospital TV and watched the home shopping network. Kora's mom came back, and Hunter moved to give her the chair, but Kora squeezed her hand and shook her head. Her mom raised an eyebrow as she took the seat in the corner that Hunter had been sitting in. She was obviously looking for an introduction, but Kora didn't have it in her. The nice ladies on TV held up pretty jewelry, and she watched as the price dropped. Their voices were soft and gentle.

◆ ◆ ◆

Eventually, Kora's mom went home to get some sleep. She kissed Kora on the forehead and told her she would be back before bedtime. Hunter yawned, and Kora sent her away, too.

"Tell the boys they can come up," she said. Hunter nodded and kissed her lips, being very careful not to touch any other part of her so she didn't hurt her.

"Thanks for being here," said Kora. Hunter swiped a small piece of hair from her forehead.

"I wouldn't be anywhere else," Hunter whispered.

Soon after Hunter slipped out the door, Kora heard it open again. She assumed it was Connor and Noah, but when she looked up, she saw Sage's small outline in the doorway.

Even backlit by the hallway light, her face in shadow, seeing Sage made Kora wince. It hurt worse than the broken ribs. She wanted to be strong for her friend, but it felt impossible, like holding up the world on her broken bones.

They stayed like that for a while in silence with Sage leaning on the doorframe. Kora let her wait until she was ready to come in.

"I thought you were at home," Kora said softly when Sage sat in the chair next to the bed.

Sage held up her right hand, which was bandaged with gauze and a brace. Kora gasped and tried to sit up, but there were too many wires.

"What happened?" she said, scrambling to find the remote so she could elevate her bed.

Sage was looking down at the floor. She was quiet for a while.

"Punched a wall," she said, finally. Kora opened her mouth to say something, but Sage cut her off. "I don't want to talk about it."

Instead, Sage leaned forward and rested her head on the blanket that covered Kora's legs.

For a moment, Kora wasn't sure what to do. Sage had never been a very physically affectionate person. Sometimes she would allow Kora to snuggle her when they watched movies on the couch, but otherwise, she generally preferred not to be touched. This was an expression of vulnerability Kora wasn't used to.

Slowly, she reached out her hand and began to stroke Sage's hair. When she got no pushback, she relaxed and continued, pulling the fine golden hair to the side. She was grateful to have something to do to help.

"I don't think I'm supposed to be mad at him," Sage all but whispered, "but I am."

Kora's hand stopped for a moment, and then continued.

"That's okay," she said. "You can be mad."

Sage turned her face toward Kora, head still resting on the bed. "Yeah?" she asked.

"Yeah."

Sage gave her a small smile. "You look like shit."

Kora laughed. She gestured between her bandages and Sage's brace. "Aren't we a pair?"

After that, Sage sat up and crawled into bed beside Kora. They turned on the hospital TV again and watched part of a telenovela. Kora didn't speak Spanish, so Sage was the only one who knew what was going on, but she didn't mind. She reached out and took Sage's good hand, and they stayed like that in the quiet until the lights in the hallway went out and the whole room was dark except for the soft blue glow of the TV.

Miraculously, she fell asleep.

CHAPTER 19

Sage knew the funeral was important, but if you asked her afterward how it went, she wouldn't have been able to tell you anything. It passed by in a haze of bad catering and speeches she half-listened to and small plastic cups she filled with cheap red wine.

Kora and her mom and stepdad were there in the front row with Sage and her dad. Somewhere in the pews behind them were Connor and his whole family, Hunter, and Noah. There were tons of kids from school, but Sage didn't particularly want to see them. She held Kora's hand and managed to get through the day.

There was an endless line of people to greet them and most of them Sage had never seen before. She found that distasteful. If she had never met them, surely they couldn't be that important to Sam. As soon as she could get away with it, she bailed.

Lots of people came back to the house with them. Kora's mom cooked spaghetti in the kitchen even though dozens of casseroles and baked goods covered the kitchen counter. Sage pulled her friends away from the mourners and into the living room. She put on a movie for them, and Kora made them popcorn.

They stayed like that for a while. The mourners got the hint that the teenagers in the living room were not to be disturbed. After the second movie ended, the house was quiet. Her dad had gone to bed, and Ronnie had left the spaghetti on the stove. Hunter brought a few bowls of it out to them.

Without much discussion, Kora started pulling pillows and blankets from all the other rooms in the house, and Connor got up to help her. It was something they had done with Sam when they were little, piling it all in front of the T.V. and falling asleep watching movies.

As they moved the blankets around and got comfortable, she noticed that Hunter and Noah were staying, too. They had barely been to her house before. It was funny how short a time she had known them, and yet they were her closest friends. She had always been standoffish, not willing to put in the time or effort to meet new people. Why bother when she had known her two best friends since birth? She had Kora and Sam, and that was enough. But she found that she didn't want the others to leave.

Sage was on the end next to the couch with Kora on her other side. If she lifted her head, she could see Hunter sitting up with her back propped on the adjacent couch, Noah wrapping himself around a large stuffed bear that had been Sam's, and Connor's eyes drooping on the other end. What a strange group they were. Strange to come together over something so gruesome. Stranger still that it all felt comfortable and familiar.

Sage wasn't sure what the first two movies were. She had been somewhere else. But once all the lights turned out and the world condensed to the soft blue glow of the TV, curled up with her friends in a large pile of pillows and blankets, she started to watch. It was *Spirited Away*. They had owned it on VHS when she was young and had watched it over and over again, rewinding the tape each time it ended. She looked over at Kora and watched the way the blue light flickered over her face. Back then, Kora had been afraid of this movie. It wasn't No-Face that scared her, the creature most people found spooky, but the scene where the main character's parents turned into pigs.

Sage had never found the movie scary when they were kids, but this time when they got to that scene, it was more unnerving than before. She nudged her shoulder against Kora's.

———— ◆ ————

The weeks that followed were very different from the period after her mother died. That had been during the school year, and there was only so much time she and Sam could take off from school before they had to go back.

Their dad was determined for things to go back to normal as quickly as possible. He had always found little sense in wallowing. It wasn't that he was unemotional, he just liked to keep busy. So he threw himself into projects at work, Sage became a more committed swimmer, and Sam looked for his ghosts. It took a long time for them to notice that none of them were coping particularly well, even with all the distractions.

Now it was different. Even after everything that had happened, the summer was only half over. She had quit the swim team. Her father had taken to staring at his computer for long periods of time, though she wasn't sure he was doing anything. Clearly, if Sam was any indication, obsession was not the solution to the grief they had wanted it to be. So Sage decided she was allowed to stay in bed as long as she wanted. Two deaths in the family in as many years entitled her to do nothing as long as she could stand it.

Kora followed her lead. Most of the time, they slept in Sage's bed, watching TV on Sage's laptop.

Sometimes it was almost fun, a break from her frantic school life. Then sometimes she passed hours at a time without moving or thinking. Other times sobs ripped from her chest so hard she felt like she was dying. And sometimes she slept peacefully with her head in Kora's lap. She knew from experience that there was no fighting against the current of these waves, so she just rode them out until the harder feelings dulled.

◆ ◆ ◆

Her first outing was to Hunter's house.

Her friends had noticed Sage's "stay in bed" approach to grief and showed concern—even Kora, who had also spent the last several weeks in bed next to her, was starting to rejoin the outside world and tried to pull Sage with her. Everyone banded together to get Sage out of the house, and Hunter finally convinced her by offering her a ride on the motorcycle.

Sage had always liked going fast, and the motorcycle felt like flying. She clung to Hunter's torso and imagined driving it herself. She thought that might be her next coping mechanism, after doing nothing got boring. Hunter would teach her, she was sure. She had plenty of time on her hands now that she had quit swimming and Sam—

The thought hit her like a brick wall. She sucked in a painful breath and tried to keep from crying. As she got her breathing under control, she focused on the feeling of the wind that whipped past her helmet. Even as she dealt with the pain and grief, sometimes Sam's absence caught her by surprise.

Sage liked Hunter's place. It was clean and messy at the same time, organized in a chaotic way. It was easier for Sage to handle than Kora's room, which was just messy, with no kind of system whatsoever. Sage hoped that Hunter would rub off on her and not the other way around.

Kora arrived with the others in tow a few minutes later, her car much slower than the bike. Sage briefly wondered if Connor was comfortable hanging out at Hunter's place since last she checked he was still pining for Kora, but he seemed normal. Maybe Sam's death had put things in perspective a little.

Everyone spread out and put their stuff down, claiming every couch and chair and bit of floor of Hunter's small living room. Once they were settled, Hunter pulled out boxes of cereal and crackers and bags of chips and laid them out on the counter.

"Dig in," she said. "You've been eating too many casseroles."

Kora immediately picked up a bag of gummy bears and tossed a handful into her mouth.

They gathered on the rug in the living room and passed around a bottle of cheap wine Hunter had in her cabinet.

They could have put on a movie or a TV show or anything, really. But Sage had been doing too much of that lately. Sage didn't feel like talking out loud, but she thought it might be nice if other people were talking around her.

Hunter opened a cabinet beneath her TV and pulled out a small collection of board games. She skipped past the more intellectual ones, like Scrabble and Monopoly, and suggested the ones that involved communication, like Charades and Pictionary. They settled on Cards Against Humanity. Sage felt guilty whenever she caught herself laughing, because her brother was gone and she was having fun with her friends, but she tried to cut herself some slack.

Kora and Noah began constructing an elaborate house of cards that kept falling, and the more wine they drank, the faster it would crumble. This inspired Hunter to pull out Jenga, and they played several rounds of it. Sage won two out of three with Connor as the runner-up. He was red-faced and sunny as always, tears leaking out of the corner of his eyes as the tower tumbled onto Kora. She stuck her tongue out at him, and he laughed even harder.

They had nothing to worry about from Connor, she realized. He seemed perfectly at ease in Hunter's apartment, even as the night got later and Kora wrapped her arms and legs around Hunter and leaned her face against Hunter's back. He just chatted amiably to Hunter and Noah. They really were friends now.

That night they all slept at Hunter's place. For the first time since they had come home from finding Sam's body, she found it hard to sleep. Lethargy had been a powerful drug, and most days, she found it hard to stay awake. But that night, she kept looking around, taking in the unfamiliar sights and sounds and smells of Hunter's apartment. She wondered if she would be spending more time there now. If she and Hunter would still be friends after Kora left for school. And the biggest question: the dream. How did Kora know? That thought sent a pulse of anxiety through her veins, and she decided not to think about it.

Her brother was dead. Dead dead dead. The worst had already happened. There was nothing left to worry about.

CHAPTER 20

Kora couldn't tell how many days had passed since Sam had died.

After the fall, she had been in the hospital for three days and nine hours, of that, she was excruciatingly sure. And then the funeral. And then a whole lot of nothing.

She knew her mother was being very gracious by not asking Kora to come home and pack the rest of her things. They probably had a buyer lined up, and she had no idea how long it would be before she would be expected to vacate the premises. Would she have to stay with Sage for a while before leaving for school? She didn't mind spending extra time at the Riveras'. She'd been there for an uncertain amount of time already, but the sense of limbo that stretched between her and New York gave her stress hives. The idea of getting an education and moving far away and making paintings of skyscrapers and bridges seemed impossible and unimportant.

But she made herself go home, for her mom's sake. The house was much more packed than the last time she had been there. Piles of boxes were taped shut, labeled with Sharpie, and stacked against the wall of the living room. The kitchen cabinets were all open, and half-full boxes of dishes sat waiting for more bubble wrap to finish the job. Holes in the walls where photos had been removed were spackled over.

She realized with some small amount of guilt that a lot of her room had already been packed by someone else. The bedding had already been stripped, like her mother assumed she wouldn't be spending any more nights there. It made her sad. She thought it was weird she could even still be sad about things that weren't Sam. But everything else was still there. It felt unfair that so many things could suck at the same time.

Her mom found her trying to decide which of her knick-knacks to give away. Ronnie's hair was tied up in a loose clip at the back of her head, and she wore a cotton t-shirt from an old band tour. She smelled like the perfume that Kora had always loved. When she was little, she used to spray it on her stuffed giraffe whenever she was leaving for summer camp or sleepovers so she would have her mom's smell with her. It made her miss her mom, even while she was right there.

"I'm making another run to the Goodwill tomorrow so put everything you want donated in the front hall, okay?" her mom asked, looking around the room like she was calculating the moving costs. Kora nodded and wrapped her arms around her mom's waist. She rested her cheek on her mom's stomach. Ronnie patted the top of her head and then, when Kora didn't move, stroked her hair. It felt nice.

"I keep thinking if Sam comes back in a couple months so many things will be different," said Kora. "He could walk out of his grave and not recognize me because I got a haircut and a whole new outfit. And he could come here looking for me and find a whole new family."

She expected her mom to point out that Sam wasn't coming back, but she didn't. She just kept stroking Kora's hair.

After a while, Kora had to sit up straight because her ribs were starting to ache where she had broken them. The bruises had faded to an ugly yellow and purple, and she didn't like looking at them. She avoided the mirror because a dark splotch colored one of her cheekbones. If she was leaving the house much, she was sure it would draw attention, but she wasn't.

"Do you want some aspirin?" her mom asked, using her softer mom voice, like when Kora was sick.

"I'm okay," said Kora. "Some morphine would be nice though. Or some cocaine. Ecstasy. PCP."

"Ha-ha," her mom fake laughed. "You know I can tell you've never done any of those things by the way you say it."

"Whatever," said Kora, grinning. "I could be a secret drug kingpin, and you would have no idea."

Her mom's eyes went sad for a second. She thought maybe she had gone too far, worried her over nothing.

"I just remembered when Sam got in trouble for selling some of Sage's Adderall," she said, her voice quieter than before. "Weird, what becomes a funny memory once someone is gone, huh? I thought I would be mad about that forever."

"I don't think he's off the hook for everything," said Kora, patting her mom's arm. "Like the time he put gum in my hair. Or when he let my fish die. He still has some amends to make for that one."

Ronnie attempted a wet smile, some of the hair falling out of her clip. She stepped away and took another glance at Kora's walls.

"I should have taken a picture before I took down all your art," she said. "You'd built up quite the collection. But you'll always have it to put up again when you have a house someday."

Kora remembered how mad she had been that the art was a little crumpled in the bin. Part of her felt like it was a small thing now, and part of her wanted those perfect preserved prints even more. She wanted to feel like she belonged somewhere permanently, that she would leave behind something important when she was gone. The future was big and scary, and she wanted to layer everything with the past as long as she could.

Kora looked out the window at the garden. The late afternoon light illuminated the gold of the sunflowers.

"Maybe I'll take some with me," she said.

—◆—

Hours later, Kora's room was almost entirely packed up. She laid on the bare mattress that had been her bed for the last several years since it had been upgraded from a twin. Now she would be going back to the smaller frame in her dorm room.

The sun had gone below the trees, and the room was dim without her lamps, which were stuffed into boxes. She felt hollow. The idea of driving back to the Riveras was impossible. So she called Hunter instead.

"What's up?" Hunter said when she answered, sounding out of breath. The background noise sounded like she was outside.

"I'm sad," said Kora. "What are you doing?"

"I just parked at home," she said. "About to head up."

"Hot."

"Why is me walking up a flight of stairs hot?"

"Don't know. Just is."

Kora listened to the sound of Hunter's footsteps on the metal stairs, her keys clicking into the lock, the creak of the door as she opened and closed it.

"You okay?" Hunter asked.

"Oh, you know," said Kora. "The future is scary. Everything changes. Life is unknowable. Existence is suffering."

"So the usual?"

"Pretty much."

Hunter hummed. For a moment, Kora enjoyed the silence. She listened to the electric hum of the phone and Hunter's quiet breathing on the other line. She imagined those sounds traveling through airwaves and power lines, crossing town and coming out of the speaker. In her mind, they collected leaves and mountain air and the nighttime humidity on their way to her. Hunter and everything she loved in one soft, grainy sound.

"Want to come over?" Hunter asked.

"Yeah."

— ◆ —

Hunter's apartment had become more familiar than Kora's childhood home, since the latter had been stripped bare, and that was both comforting and disconcerting. Kora wore one of Hunter's big sleep t-shirts and lay in her bed while Hunter made them ramen in the kitchen. She watched, distracted by Hunter's tight crop top and old sweatpants.

They ate in bed with Kora sitting against the wall with her feet in Hunter's lap. Like before on the phone, the silence was soothing. Kora had that feeling she got whenever she looked out over the mountains, like all her problems were very small and far away.

The shirt she wore was soft, faded cotton and felt cool on her skin. It fell to her thighs, and she liked the sight of her bare legs draped across Hunter's sweatpants. Hunter was reading while she ate, her brow furrowed slightly.

"I don't want to go to New York," said Kora. It was like the words were water in a bucket that had just spilled over.

Hunter glanced up at her, book still in hand. She carefully dog-eared her page and sat it down in her lap.

"You know I would never ask you to stay," Hunter said carefully, finger fidgeting with the page edges.

"I know," said Kora. "It's not about that. I like you, but I wouldn't stay for one person. I just don't want to. I think I knew that when I applied."

"Then why did you decide to go?"

"I thought it was my only chance to be a real artist," Kora said softly as she looked into her ramen bowl. The heat on her palms calmed her. "That's all I've ever wanted. Getting into art school felt like I got handed everything I was supposed to want wrapped in a bow. How could I turn that down?"

Hunter was quiet for a long time. She ran her finger back and forth over the edges of her book's pages, ruffling them gently. Even as she waited for some kind of response, the silence felt easy and warm. She didn't worry about what Hunter would say, though she wanted to hear it. It was enough just to have said the words out loud. The pressure slowly leaked out of her, and she felt herself deflate.

"I never applied to college," said Hunter after a while. Kora could see the wheels in her mind turning. She liked that Hunter was thinking about this, about what to say to her. "It just wasn't something I considered. I knew what I wanted to do, and I knew it didn't require a degree."

Hunter half-smiled and absentmindedly traced little circles into Kora's leg with her finger. Her eyes were unfocused as she sifted through her thoughts.

Kora remembered that moment by the fire, the first time Hunter told her about her family, her past. It was such a privilege to get to see her like this, so open and thoughtful.

"I don't know what it's like to have an opportunity and have to turn it down. I imagine it's scary." Hunter looked at her, and Kora was filled with gratitude. "What I can say is that you don't owe your future to anyone but yourself. Not your mom, not Sage, not me, not even Sam. It's your life. You're the one who's actually going to live it. And if anyone tries to tell you otherwise, I'll run them over with my bike."

Kora laughed. Hunter smiled at her. Her chest felt light and warm. Something like music was singing under her skin.

"My mom is leaving," she said, stacking up the rest of the obstacles that had been turning over in her head all summer, hoping Hunter would help her knock them down. "I won't have a place to stay here anymore. I could live with Sage, but she and her dad have so much stuff to work out. I don't want to distract them from it. And I don't have a job, so I can't get my own place. My mom put down a deposit on art school. I don't know what to do."

"None of those is a good reason to go to college," said Hunter. It seemed very reasonable when she said it. "You can stay with me until you get a job. And you can tell your mom you'll pay her back for the deposit. If she wants it right now, I'll steal it from the cafe. Then you won't have to worry about finding a place to live because we'll have to go on the run."

Kora leaned her forehead onto Hunter's shoulder. "I would run away with you," she said softly.

"Me too."

"You'd really let me stay here?" She looked around at the carefully decorated walls and clutter-free rug on the floor. At least since most of her stuff was currently being stuffed into boxes it would be harder for her to make a mess of Hunter's apartment.

"I think it's too soon for us to move in together," said Hunter. "And I don't want to be the only reason you choose not to go to school. But you can stay here until you find a place. I'll help you find a job. You can apprentice with Jeb, or we can talk to Noah, maybe the library is hiring."

She looked down and pulled Kora's chin with her hand so they were face to face again.

"You have options," she said. "And I will make sure you're the only one deciding."

Kora closed her eyes and breathed in Hunter's scent. For the first time since that acceptance letter arrived at her house, since her mother had put up the For Sale sign, since finding Sam's body, and all the way back to his mother dying, she could see a new future. It was very fragile and uncertain, but it was hers. And the feeling that had been constricting her chest for months loosened just enough that she could breathe.

"Okay," she said, and it was.

When they had finished their ramen, they sat out on the landing together, feet resting on the top step. Everything was closed downtown, but a few stragglers walked back to their cars, and the streetlights bathed everything in fluorescent light. The night was humid and loud. Kora felt awake.

CHAPTER 21

For the first time since Sam died, Sage was alone.

She didn't know where her father was, but that wasn't new. Kora had spent the night at Hunter's. Noah had a shift at the library. Connor was picking his brother up from basketball practice.

It made sense. They all had lives they had to get back to, jobs, families. The search was over. She knew they would leave eventually. But she didn't expect to feel so totally alone.

She hadn't been alone when she had fallen asleep. Kora had stayed late enough to make sure of that. At the time, she had been pushing Kora out the door, insisting she didn't need to be babysat. Now she didn't know how she was supposed to get through a whole day alone, much less fall asleep that night.

The morning passed in a blur. Afternoon? She wasn't sure. She ate a bowl of cereal and then a portion of leftover grief casserole. She checked their DVD collection to see if there was anything she hadn't watched and rewatched recently. She tried to sleep some more.

She really, really didn't want to ask anyone to come back over after they had been here near-constantly for days. Weeks? She wasn't sure.

She made it another hour before she broke down and texted the group chat, but she refused to admit that she was lonely.

Who wants to go for a drive?

⸻ ◆ ⸻

Sage rode shotgun to Town Mountain Road. Her shoes were lofted on the dashboard, making prints where the rubber soles touched the glass. Kora chatted with the others from the driver's seat about anything but what was in front of them. Connor picked music from his phone, and Hunter made fun of his choices. Noah told Kora about the classes he would be taking once the semester started. It was like before. So much that it chafed at her.

It wasn't really her thing, talking. It was never Sam's thing either. They had always been content to sit in silence together. If he were still alive, she would never stop talking to him. There were so many questions she wanted answers to. The sound of the rain on the windshield and Connor's weird annoyingly upbeat music distracted her from the endless stream of inquisitive thoughts.

Sage had been thinking since the funeral. As the shock faded and reality set in, the question of Kora's dream kept nagging at her. It was taking up headspace that she needed for grieving. So, she thought about it.

She had come to the conclusion that Sam must have gotten a message to Kora somehow. He must have known he was in danger and sent Kora some kind of psychic wavelength. She had no idea the spiritual mechanics of it, but she had no rational explanation. Her cold, calculating scientist's heart was forced to confront the unknowable. She was feeling very put out about it.

When they slowed alongside the railing, fog clung to the trees in wisps and clouds and made the forest next to the road look far more intimidating than it usually did.

The five of them filed out. The rain had subsided to a mist, but the mud was soaking into Sage's canvas-topped shoes.

She led the way to the side of the road. Over the metal rail, she could see the part of the ravine where they found Sam. It was a different kind of day, hotter with more mist. It felt the way all days felt after Sam, dazed and not quite real.

Kora stood next to her, their shoulders only an inch apart. She could hear Kora breathing. To anyone else, it would have seemed steady and calm, but Sage knew that Kora only breathed so deeply when she was trying not to cry.

The others hung back and let them have their moment. The wind picked up through the trees, blowing leaves around. Even in the summer, long before they turned yellow and fell off, leaves gathered on the ground in the mountains. They stuck to Sage's legs and the muddy tops of her shoes.

"Do you want to say anything?" said Kora.

Sage nodded. Historically, she had not believed in talking to the dead. But now she was forced to consider the idea that he might actually be listening.

It took her another second to find what she wanted to say. Rain spat on her face. The weather felt gross. She was tired, despite having slept for most of the last week. Two weeks? She wasn't sure. She wanted to go home. But the idea of going home without him was a new punch to the stomach every time.

"I'm sorry I didn't find you sooner," she said. Her voice was being carried away by the wind, but she was glad. She didn't want to hear it anyway. "I knew something was wrong. I knew you were lost. But I convinced myself I was overreacting."

She felt Kora grab her hand.

"I'm sorry I called you an asshole," she continued, and Kora let out a wet little laugh. "And sorry I broke mom's china. I would offer to pay for it, but it's, like, a hundred years old or something, and I don't have any money. And it would have gone to you, and you're dead. So it would be mine now anyway.

"A bunch of stuff has happened since you left. I quit the swim team. Kora has a new girlfriend. Connor almost bought us a room at that fancy haunted hotel. I met Austin and Noah. I see why you liked them."

She looked around, wondering what exactly she was doing.

"If you have anything to say to us, now would be the time," she said.

They heard nothing but the sound of the wind blowing through the wet leaves.

"Okay, well, that's it," she said, aiming for nonchalant but her voice broke. "Goodbye, I guess."

Kora turned back to the others. Hunter hugged her, and they held each other for a long minute. Sage stayed and looked at the forest. Noah stepped up beside her and said nothing. Sage leaned her head against his shoulder, and he put his arm around her.

"You should probably tell him you have a crush on him," said Sage. "Just in case he can hear you. It might be your last chance."

"I'm sure he knew already," said Noah. "I'm not that good at hiding things."

Sage laughed a little and found her throat hurt.

"Sage," said a voice from her other side. She turned, but Kora and Hunter were still hugging. She kept turning, and Connor raised an eyebrow at her.

"What?" she asked, frowning.

"I didn't say anything," he said.

"Well someone did," she said. "Someone said my name."

Connor shrugged. "Wasn't me," he said.

"Sage," she heard again, louder this time. It was familiar, but she couldn't let herself think it. She had been hearing him in everyone's voices, especially her father's. Her grieving brain wasn't trustworthy. She shook her head.

"Sage!" the voice screamed this time. There was no avoiding it; it sounded exactly like Sam.

The sound rang in her ears, and she wished she could believe that he was there, that he was back, but she refused to let herself tumble into that hole. She closed her eyes, hoping the sound would go away. Of course she would hallucinate him, just when she was starting to feel like she could breathe again. *I should never have come back here*, she thought. She opened her eyes.

Sam was standing in the middle of the road.

Kora screamed.

Sage couldn't tear her eyes away from Sam's face to look at her, but she knew from the sound that they were seeing the same thing. That was the only way Sage knew it was real. She was looking at him. His whole body was darker than normal, and his face was white and bloody, but it was him. He wore his black hoodie over a Dirty Projector's t-shirt. His hair was a mess of leaves and branches. It was Sam. It was Sam.

His face was struck with shock. She imagined her face looked the same.

The voice came again. His lips were moving, but the voice didn't sound like it was coming from his direction.

"Sage," it said again. She wished it would stop. Every time she heard it her chest ached. "I've been looking for you. I couldn't find you. I was so scared."

He started shaking violently. Not like he was shivering, but like the image of him was vibrating in the air, like static. She couldn't keep her eyes directly on him.

"I'm here," she said, though she wasn't sure if anyone could hear her. She couldn't hear her own voice. She couldn't hear anything but Sam and the terrible wind.

"I don't know where I am," he shouted. "I don't know what happened."

His body darted to the other side of the road and back without really moving. She was sure she imagined it. She was sure she was imagining all of this. Everything that had happened since Sam left for his trip was some kind of awful fever dream.

Sam's head tilted to the side at an uncomfortable angle.

"I want to go home, Sage." His voice sounded so broken. All she wanted to do was touch him, be sure he was really there.

She stepped forward an inch from the blacktop.

Wind filled her ears, and she couldn't hear the car, only saw its lights as it navigated the curve. It passed through where Sam was standing, like it would hit him, but it didn't. Sage screamed, but when the car was gone, so was Sam. Like he had never been there.

The wind died down, and the silence was deafening. In that moment, nothing could have convinced Sage that what she had witnessed really happened. Nothing at all, except that when she turned to her friends, they all wore expressions that exactly matched hers.

Kora's face was stained with tears, but her expression didn't look like she was crying. Her jaw was hanging open in shock. Her entire body was still. Sage couldn't take it.

"Kora?" she asked. Her voice was empty of force, like quiet screaming, but carried easily without the noise of the wind.

Kora's hand moved before her face did. She grabbed Sage's shoulder, and her eyes moved to Sage but looked like they were seeing right through her.

"Sam," Kora said. "It was Sam."

CHAPTER 22

"I'm sorry, are we supposed to just accept that ghosts are a thing now?" Sage's voice was significantly higher-pitched than usual, and she moved her arms emphatically as she talked.

It was after dark, and the five of them had hopped the fence at the park so they could process what they had just seen without onlookers. Kora and Noah sat on the swings while the other three stood in a semi-circle around them. Sage paced back and forth across the playground, kicking up mulch with her Converses.

Kora didn't know what to say. The sound of Sam's voice felt less and less real by the minute, but she couldn't deny the evidence. On the drive here, Kora had asked Hunter to describe exactly what she saw, and it matched up to a tee. Hunter had never met Sam before, never even seen a picture of him.

She had wanted to see Sam again, of course she had. But that was not what she had in mind.

"He was looking for ghosts," said Noah. His voice was scary in the dark. "He must have known this was a possibility. He must have seen something. There has to be—" he stopped and rested his forehead on the swing's chain.

"I thought we would find him in the woods, hypothermic and dying of starvation, having broken his sat phone," said Sage, "not dead. And definitely not undead."

"We knew it didn't make sense," said Kora. "All the things we saw, my dream, your mom. It didn't make sense, but now it does."

Sage looked murderous for a second. "How does any of this make sense?" she didn't scream, but it was close.

"There's something about these mountains," said Kora. "Some kind of energy here, I don't know. But think about that railing. It was so easy for me to fall over the side just from seeing something that scared me. What if Sam fell for the same reason? What if he saw something that scared him, and it made him fall too?"

Sage let out a long, exasperated sound. She went back to pacing. Despite being the youngest and shortest of them, Sage had a way of looking years older than everyone else. Kora tried to remember when that had happened but couldn't picture what she had looked like before. Photographs of baby Sage frowning at the camera found their way into her mind, and she thought maybe she was always that way.

"I thought—" Sage started, then stopped. "I thought he was just looking for my mom. Some kind of closure thing."

"Maybe he was," said Hunter. "But that doesn't mean he was wrong."

Sage dropped her head in one hand. "I can't believe we're actually talking about ghosts," she said. "I keep expecting one of you to tell me it was you wearing a sheet trying to scare the shit out of me."

"That did not look like a person in a sheet," said Kora. A distant streetlight was all that illuminated them.

"If it was somebody trying to scare us, it worked," said Noah, his voice shaky. "I'm scared. Aren't you?"

Sage glared at him. "I'm incredulous," she said.

"Well then get credulous," said Hunter. "If you want your brother back—and I'm pretty sure you do because we've spent half the summer trying to find him—we need to figure out why he's a ghost and how to find him again."

Sage's eyes widened. Kora looked over at her girlfriend, who was almost impossible to see in the dark. The park had no streetlights, so it was nearly pitch black except for the moon. Hunter wore a black shirt and pants and blended in with the trees, but her eyes were shining bright, arms crossed. She looked the definition of a leader. Kora remembered how Hunter had taken charge that first night camping, lighting the fire for them. It was a relief that one of them at least appeared to know what to do.

"At least now we know where to look," said Noah. "I don't think it's a coincidence that we saw him the same place he died."

Sage looked like she was going to be sick. Hunter wordlessly handed her a water bottle, and she took a sip, but it didn't seem to help.

"Okay," she said finally. "Okay, what's our next move, then?" She looked back and forth between the two of them, searching for an answer.

"I guess," said Hunter, "we go back."

Connor appeared in the darkness, having stowed the car somewhere private.

"We're going back," Sage filled him in. "Can we take the Jeep?"

"Of course," he said. "Why wouldn't we?"

"I wasn't sure if you would need to pack," she said as she stopped pacing to look at him. Kora did too. She had forgotten he was supposed to leave soon for college. And so was she, as far as anyone knew. But his school started much earlier than hers.

He shook his head. "I'm helping with the search until the day I leave," he said.

"Thank God," said Sage. "Kora's car still sucks."

No one said anything, but they all looked like they were thinking the same thing: they would do anything for Sam, now. They were all in.

After the others left, Kora and Sage stayed at the playground until well past midnight. Kora was positive she wouldn't be sleeping anyway.

The night was dewy and humid in the way that only a mountain night could be. The stars were sharp and still, a dusting of freckles on the deep midnight sky. The two of them lay on their backs on the dock, the sky stretching from one side to the other.

"What did you think we would be doing this summer?" Kora asked.

Sage ran a hand through her ash blonde hair, which was colored gray by the darkness.

"I thought there would be a lot more movie nights and a lot fewer ghost brothers," she said.

Kora thought of Sam's face, pale white but just the same as when he was six and had been caught pointing a BB gun at her. He was sullen and pitiful, long eyelashes casting shadows on his cheeks. Terrifying and wistful. She wanted to see him again. She wanted to go back and tell him she forgave him for the BB gun.

"Well, we did end up watching a lot of movies," Kora whispered. Sage huffed a laugh. "How the hell did we get here?"

"You drove," said Sage with a smirk.

Kora play-shoved her and then checked to make sure Sage was nowhere close to the edge of the dock.

"Jerk," she said, though she was laughing.

"You know what I mean," said Kora, a smile dancing on the edge of her lips.

Sage sighed. It was more dolorous and colorful than her usual expressions. "I don't know," she said honestly. "I thought he was invincible." It wasn't the sort of admission Kora was used to getting from her. She patted the top of Sage's hand with her own.

"Me too," she said. "And, I mean, he kind of is. He survived death, that's pretty hardcore."

Sage laughed. "Imagine how badass he would seem to those metalhead guys he used to hang out with in high school," she said.

"We should tell him that," Kora agreed.

"We have to find him first."

"We need to find out why he's back and why he's there, specifically," said Kora. "Maybe then we can figure out how to see him here, too." She gestured vaguely in the direction of Sage's house. "Here as in Pinebrook, not this park specifically. Though I'm not picky, wherever is fine, as long as he's with us."

Sage tapped her fingers against her stomach and hummed to herself. She took a deep breath and let it out.

"At least we saw him," she said. "All that matters is that we found him. He's still here, and we'll bring him home."

Kora lay back, too. The stars seemed close and oversaturated. She thought of Hunter, sleeping soundly only a few miles away. It was a comforting thought.

In less than a month, she was supposed to fly far away from these magical hills, these dusty stars, these friends of hers who made everything still inside her. She hadn't told anyone yet that she was staying. It wouldn't be real until she talked to her mom. She still felt like she wouldn't be allowed. But she gave herself a second to feel the relief. She was staying, she was staying. These stars would always be above her. She was staying where she belonged.

When exhaustion started to seep into their bones and they shivered in the wind, they walked back off the dock and headed to Sage's house.

Kora turned off all the lights in the house one by one. They folded up the blankets they had been sleeping on from the living room floor and packed them away into the linen closet. She crawled into bed next to Sage.

———— ◆ ————

Kora's dream was as simple as it was frustrating. She wandered through the woods looking for Sam, but when she opened her mouth to call out for him, no sound came out. It was dark, and her phone was dead, no flashlight. Every time she walked around another tree, everything looked the same, like it had reset. She could feel herself getting more and more lost.

She woke up sweaty and confused, still a little outside of time and space. It was pitch black outside the window. She wasn't sure what to make of her dreams now, and she found it unsettling. She slipped out of the bed, trying not to jostle Sage.

Kora crept down the old wooden stairs, careful not to step on the creaky ones. When she got to the bottom, she noticed a blue glow coming from the living room. Had they left the TV on? Or had Leo been watching something after they had gone to bed? There was no sound. Just in case it was him, she didn't go any further, just sat on the bottom step. From there, she could see the moving lights over the wall. The reflection was soothing, like ocean waves or clouds moving overhead.

She closed her eyes. She knew this place inside and out. No matter what happened with her mother and school and Sam, she would always have a home.

CHAPTER 23

Sam's room was not big enough for the five of them, but they managed. Connor sat on the bed and leaned back against the headboard. Hunter sat in the open window, half her body out on the roof. Kora, Sage, and Noah were sprawled out on the floor. Sam's books and notes and loose pages of research covered every inch of available space.

Sage had called them all there to look deeper into his notes, try and make sense of what they had seen. So far, it wasn't working. In the light of day, the memory of Sam's ghost felt foggy and distant, and if they hadn't all experienced it together, she was sure they would have dismissed it by now. But they hadn't ruled out group psychosis, like that theory about the Salem witches that they were all eating moldy bread and hallucinating.

Kora frowned at a book on spiritual energies and squinted to read Sam's minuscule margin notes.

"I can't tell if this says 'trees' or 'tires,'" she said.

"What's the context?" asked Noah.

"He's written it next to a list of energy conductors."

"I don't see how tires would conduct energy, considering they're made of rubber. Must be trees."

Kora frowned but copied the note to her own list.

"Anybody know what rhabdomancy means?" asked Connor and frowned at a very tattered book. No one answered, so he made a note and kept reading.

"This book is pretty useless," said Hunter, tossing it aside. She picked up a new one and leafed through the table of contents. "And kinda racist. Sage, what are we looking for here?"

Sage didn't know. Books were supposed to have all the answers, but she was still pretty shell-shocked and couldn't really even formulate a question yet.

"Anything that can explain why my brother is a ghost would be great," she said. "Extra points if it can tell us how to find him again."

"Noted," said Hunter, flipping to a chapter she had evidently deemed worthy of exploring.

It was still unsettling to be in Sam's room without him, even more so to bring friends here. It felt like trespassing. But their research had to extend beyond magic and spirits to Sam himself, to retrace his path to ghosthood. Anything could be a clue, not just in his books or notes but in the strange and confusing catalog of his mind that spread across all surfaces of his room.

And it provided good context for Hunter, who didn't know Sam, and Connor and Noah, who had only ever seen one side to him.

Even Sage, his sister, and Kora, who had spent more time in this house than she had her own, had never spent much time in this room. Sam was private, secretive, guarded with his personal space.

His room was darkly lit and sparsely decorated. It was cluttered but not disorganized. Unlike Sage's room, which was meticulously curated, and Kora's room, which was covered in bits of her personality and suspicious crumbs, it was hard to find evidence of him there other than the small library of obsession.

Sage returned her attention to the book in front of her, which was a recounting of interviews with locals who had experienced ghost encounters in Johnson County. That hadn't even been on their list of places to search, but there it was, hidden away under a huge, teetering pile of similarly opaque literature. It didn't have much to offer in the way of spiritual magic or processes, just good old-fashioned storytelling. She found it compelling but unhelpful. Setting it to the side, she looked around for her next target.

She returned to the section of Sam's notebook she was trying to decipher. There were quotes from some of the books and other texts they didn't have, some printed off and glued in, and ubiquitous margin notes written in frantic and near-illegible handwriting. She found a page on Valle Crucis and saw that Sam had dismissed it as unimportant. She remembered the creepy church and had to agree.

It struck her that they had been to the same place months apart in almost the same search.

She noticed that his notes were rarely about whether or not there was merit to the ghost stories, and more about what the stories could tell him about magic and ghosts. All this time, she had assumed he had been searching through all these texts to find evidence that they were real, but this idea seemed almost inconsequential to him. What really drove these notes was a need to understand them. He analyzed why certain areas might be considered haunted while other sites of tragedy and death were virtually unaffected. Underneath these stories was a throughline of something more, something ancient and undefined. She could easily understand how Sam became caught up in this. There was no end, no definitive answer, only more questions.

"There's a lot in this book about how to talk to spirits," said Kora. "Beyond your garden-variety ouija board approach and finding a legit medium. Maybe one of these rituals could work."

"What would we need for the ritual?"

Kora stared at it for a long time without answering. "Hmm. Human sacrifice."

"Maybe put that one away."

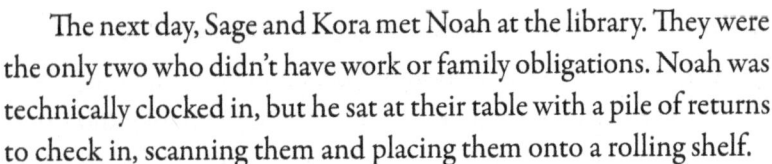

The next day, Sage and Kora met Noah at the library. They were the only two who didn't have work or family obligations. Noah was technically clocked in, but he sat at their table with a pile of returns to check in, scanning them and placing them onto a rolling shelf.

"Noah, do you know anything about Richard Sharp Smith?" asked Kora. "He's mentioned in the endnotes for this story about Helen's Bridge, but I don't recognize the name."

"He was the architect who designed the bridge," said Noah, without looking up from his stack of books. "He worked on the Biltmore Estate and some other famous buildings in Asheville. And he was a Freemason. That's why there are Masonic symbols on the side of the bridge."

"Oh," said Sage. "I guess we wouldn't have seen those since we went at night. Freemasonry is sort of ritualistic, right? Is that why people think Satanic worshippers hang out there?"

"I doubt it," said Noah. "More likely, teenagers get drunk up there and parents glommed onto it during the Satanic Panic. Better to believe there are cultists trying to corrupt your children than accept that your kids like to get drunk and make out in the woods, I guess."

Sage hummed, looked down at her notes, and jotted down a reminder to look up the Freemasons.

"When do your classes start, Noah?" asked Kora.

He pulled open his phone and looked at his calendar. "I still have a couple weeks," he said. "What about you, Sage?"

She wasn't sure. She hadn't thought much about school starting. Was it that soon already? She looked down at the date. They were already well into August.

There they were, the last days of summer, sitting in the library reading dusty old books. She should have been savoring her last days of no school. Her last days with Kora too, though she was vehemently refusing to think about that until she absolutely had to. They could have spent the day making magazine collages or driving around town or swimming in the river, the way they used to every summer before this one.

But that restless feeling under her skin she'd had since she first realized Sam was missing hadn't gone away. Not when he died, not when they found him again. She couldn't shake the feeling that he wasn't really gone, that he was in trouble somehow. And the idea of sitting around while he was out there somewhere was just as intolerable as it had been weeks ago.

She glanced at Kora, who was leaning her head on her hand, propped up by her elbow, taking slow slips of her latte. She was leafing through yet another book on the occult, and Sage could tell just by looking at her that the words were starting to blur together. They had been at this awhile and things weren't getting any clearer.

"No idea," Sage said, realizing that Noah was still waiting for her response. "Guess I should look that up."

"What about you, Kora?" he asked. "When are you leaving for New York?"

Sage did not look up from her book. Truthfully, she didn't want to know.

"I haven't bought my plane ticket yet," said Kora.

"Don't you have to do that soon?" asked Noah, frowning and looking up from his books.

"Yeah," said Kora vaguely. "I have to talk to my mom about it."

"You don't seem excited," Noah noted.

"Yeah, you know," said Kora, though they didn't, in fact, know. "Just feels weird to leave right now."

Sage looked up. Kora's wild curls were pulled up into a loose bun on top of her head, which meant she hadn't showered recently. She only ever pulled it up when it was too dirty to hang around her face. The corners of her eyes crinkled when she talked. The glitter on her cheeks had been there for days. Her nails were bitten down to the nubs.

"It's okay to go," Sage said reluctantly. "I'll be okay. I mean, I'll miss you, but I'll call you all the time. And I have more help now." She gestured to Noah, who nodded.

"I know," said Kora, still not looking at her. "It's just really far away."

As much as she had been avoiding the thought of Kora moving away, the idea that she would give up on her art school dreams just because Sage's life was a disaster was unbearable. Kora was too talented to turn down something like that.

"It's not your job to take care of me," Sage said, stealing Kora's coffee and taking a sip. "It's your job to go become a crazy-successful artist and eventually pay for me to go to grad school."

Kora laughed. "I see," she said. "So really I'm just your future sugar daddy, and you want to make sure I can provide for you."

"Exactly," said Sage, hoping she had convinced Kora to stop martyring herself.

She looked down at the sea of papers in front of them. She felt guilty for pushing her friends to keep moving forward in a frantic search like their lives depended on it. Sam was already dead. She was determined to find him again, but she was also sure things couldn't get any worse. They could afford to take a break.

"Let's get out of here," she said. "What do you want to do today?"

"What do you mean?" asked Kora.

"We should probably see the sunlight at least once this week," said Sage. "We could go shopping. Or to the park. Maybe bother Hunter at work."

Kora lay her head down on her open book, cradled by her arms. She took a deep sigh and closed her eyes.

"You're probably right," she said, the sound muffled by the book. "I'm too tired to go shopping." She opened her eyes and glanced up at Sage through her crossed arms. "We could go to my house."

Sage hesitated. As far as she knew, the Mason house was mostly packed into boxes, and Kora had been avoiding it like the plague. She couldn't remember the last time Kora had spent the night there.

"You want to?" she asked. Kora sighed again.

"I should probably spend some time there before it's too late."

Sage nodded and started closing books, shoving loose pages into folders and notebooks, and piling up their research. Noah was almost done scanning his pile of books.

She wouldn't let Kora leave with her most recent memories of their hometown being ones of death and grief and endless, frustrating mystery. Pinebrook had a reputation to maintain.

— ❖ ❖ —

When they pulled up at Kora's small bungalow, Sage realized how long it had been since she had last been there. When they were little, Kora, Sam and Sage were shuttled back and forth between their two houses almost every day of the week. Because of their parents' work schedule, the Riveras often relied on Ronnie for pickup and dropoff while Kora stayed over when her mom was working nights. This house was as much a part of Sage's childhood memories as her own house was for Kora.

Once they had gotten old enough to coordinate their own carpools and stay home by themselves, Sage had stopped coming over as much. Kora always came over to her house. She hadn't really thought about why.

Sage noticed that the wooden porch had been freshly painted. The planters were overflowing with begonias. The old wooden porch swing was reattached to the porch ceiling and drifted slightly in the breeze. She remembered the day the chain had snapped off after Sam had jumped onto it at a running start. He had busted his head open on the brick corner of the house's foundation. The scar was faded but still visible over his eyebrow. At least, it was the last time she had looked closely at him, which she realized had been a while.

Ronnie was out for the night, probably working or running errands for the house. Kora turned on all the lights and opened the refrigerator.

"Not much in here," she said. "Mom hasn't been cooking much."

Sage rifled through the pantry and pulled out a bag of tortilla chips and an unopened jar of salsa. She and Kora shared them, dipping the salsa straight from the jar. They sat on the couch, and Kora turned on the TV.

"What do you want to watch?" she asked.

"I guess we lost track of whose turn it is," said Sage. Kora chewed her way through a very large mouthful.

"I think," she tried, finished swallowing, then started again. "I think we may have watched every movie ever made."

"At least once," said Sage. She put the chips and salsa on the couch between them and rested her feet on the coffee table. She wasn't really supposed to do this at home, but Kora's house had always had more lax rules.

Kora put on some baking show that neither of them had ever seen. It was really aggressive and high-pressure, and Sage started making scathing commentary about their choices, as if she had ever baked anything that hadn't come from a box. Kora grabbed a couple of beers from the fridge and handed her one. They drank and watched and laughed and inevitably spilled the salsa on the couch. Kora cleaned it up with a wet rag and then tossed it into the sink. Sage had forgotten how much she liked it there.

"I still can't believe your mom is selling this house," she said quietly while Kora queued up the next episode.

"Yeah," said Kora, "me neither."

Kora looked around the living room, and Sage followed. The walls used to be covered in eclectic art and every surface scattered with knick-knacks, but now most of that had been packed away. They still had the old leather couch, the same ratty blankets, the small dent in the wall where Sage had thrown a video game controller in frustration.

"You know you can stay with me whenever you want, right?" asked Sage. It should have been a given, but she had to be sure. "You don't have to ask. I don't know if you're planning to go to Santa Fe for the holidays, but you can always come here."

She hadn't even thought about the prospect of Thanksgiving and Christmas without Kora and her mom. She couldn't remember the last time they had spent the holidays apart. Kora smiled at her and nodded.

"Remember that year your uncle got drunk and tried to carve the turkey with the electric carver and your mom had to put him in a headlock?" Kora asked, laughing into the mouth of her beer.

"God, that was a good one," said Sage. "Remember when Sam cheated at Spoons by stealing one from the kitchen and hiding it under his butt?"

"Still mad about that. What about when we slid down the stairs in the duvet cover and Sam broke a finger grabbing the banister to slow us down."

"Or the first year Sam drank wine in front of our mom."

"I really thought she was going to have a meltdown."

"So did he," Sage said, grinning. "He was sweating all through dinner. But I knew she wouldn't. She was way too cool for that."

Kora smiled and sat her beer on the coffee table. "I miss them a lot," she said.

"Me too," said Sage.

Once it got late enough for Sage to leave, she borrowed a sweater from Kora's room because the temperature had dropped enough to be chilly. She looked around the empty house. It seemed darker than she remembered it, even with all the lights on.

"You gonna be okay here by yourself?" she asked.

Kora scoffed. "I've done it plenty of times."

"Yeah but that was before we knew ghosts existed. And before you almost sleep-drove Connor's car off a cliff."

Kora laughed and then stopped, looking around the house. Apparently, she deemed it safe because she smiled a little and said, "I'll be okay. I have some more packing to do."

Sage walked out to her car, but before she got in, she turned around and snapped a quick picture of the house. Soon, it would be totally empty, and she didn't want to remember it that way. She looked at the picture, dark in the front with the windows glowing. Probably not one she would frame and hang on the wall, but she'd take it.

———◆———

As soon as she got home, Sage headed for Sam's room. She was becoming more comfortable in there, but she wasn't sure if that was a good thing. As she dug through more piles of his books and notes, she thought it would be nice if there were more light, but the idea of changing up his furniture made her seize up, so she left it alone. She took out her contacts and wore her glasses instead to give her eyes a break.

They had already sorted through everything Sam had on top of his desk, which was a feat in and of itself. Now, they were working their way through the various piles around his room and the desk drawers, which were stuffed with papers. Some of them were irrelevant, like old school papers, a copy of his birth certificate, his Eagle Scout project binder.

When she got to the bottom drawer, it wouldn't open. She had forgotten that it was locked.

She remembered that they had Sam's keyring from when the cops dropped off his personal effects. It was downstairs in the bowl where they were all supposed to keep their keys, but no one ever did. She ran downstairs and grabbed it.

It was pretty sparse, just a keychain with his college's logo, a lanyard, and a few keys. She recognized the key to the Volvo, and there was their house key. A few more she didn't recognize.

One of them was smaller than the rest, the size of a padlock key. That had to be it. She brought it back upstairs and tried it. The bottom drawer unlocked.

Inside were stacks of manila folders, the same kind their mom had used in her file cabinet in the study. They weren't labeled, so she pulled them out and spread them out in front of her.

The top one was her mom's research for her last thesis on the witches in Macbeth, something about menstruation and witchcraft. Sage remembered getting into a fight with her dad about it because he made a face while her mom was talking about menstrual symbolism. She flipped through it, but it was all familiar.

The next one was notes from her PhD dissertation on Chaucer. Boring. Her mom had finished her degree before Sage was born, but she had heard her ramble on about early English lit so many times she could probably have recreated the thesis from memory.

The notes were nothing new, but it was nice to be reminded of her mom's impassioned speeches about iambic pentameter and dramatic irony. Sage used to be annoyed when her mom would probe her on every book she was reading for English class, even though she knew Sage barely skimmed them. Now, she wished she had paid closer attention.

Reading her mom's writing was as close as Sage had gotten to hearing her mom's voice again. She thought maybe that was why Sam had her notes.

Sage opened the last one and expected to find notes from another one of her mom's writing projects; maybe an early draft of one of her books, or graded student papers she had never given back to them.

Instead, the notes were unfamiliar. There was a bibliography of titles she mostly didn't recognize, but a few she did. It included books on folklore and ghost stories, like the ones surrounding her in piles—Sam's books. She kept reading.

The pages were out of order, so it was hard to follow, and it seemed incomplete. But from what she could understand, these were notes on the new research project she had started right before her death. Only it wasn't about early English literature, like all her other work.

It was about local ghost stories.

She combed through the files, trying to understand why her mom would have started this project, and how it connected to Sam. Were they working together? Was this why he had become so obsessed after she died?

The more she read, the more frustrated she became. It was obvious her mom was nowhere near done with this research when she died, there weren't even rough drafts of writing on it, just notes, lists of sources, and photocopied pages from books.

She leaned back against the desk and looked around Sam's room. Maybe this was a lead, or maybe this was just raising more questions that no one could answer. It all felt impossible. She thought she understood how Sam became so wrapped up in this, though. It wasn't just for fun. There was so much at stake, things she couldn't even begin to understand.

When she went back to her stack of books, she started focusing on the task at hand: finding ways to speak to Sam. If she could just ask him some questions, all of this would be easier.

Somewhere in these books was a way to see him again, and she couldn't sleep until she found it.

CHAPTER 24

"I don't think this is working," said Sage, wiping sweat from her forehead.

Kora agreed. It was hot, and they had been walking through the forest for over an hour. Sage was recording audio on her phone and periodically playing it back to see if she could hear anything mysterious. So far, it was just static, bird noises, and Sage making annoyed grunts whenever she swatted away a bug.

"Maybe we should get an actual tape recorder and leave it here overnight," said Kora.

"Then we'd have to spend 12 hours listening to it."

"I think you can listen to it sped up."

Sage appeared to be contemplating that. Eyebrows furrowed, she leaned over and spit into the grass.

It was late afternoon, and the forest was washed in orange and gold. Where direct sunlight came through the trees, the tall grass looked sallow. It was hard to believe it was the same misty, overcast forest where they had seen Sam.

"Do you think ghosts can feel this heat?" Sage asked, frowning.

"I'm guessing not," said Kora and wiped her face off with the front of her shirt. "Aren't the dead supposed to be eternally cold?"

"Jesus," said Sage. "Freaky. I can't believe my brother is a full-on specter."

"We don't really know what he is."

Kora sat down and leaned back against a tree trunk. It was the kind of unbearable summer heat and humidity that clouded her lungs and made it hard to breathe.

Sage sat down next to her, careful not to lean their shoulders together to avoid the extra body heat.

"What the fuck are we going to do, Kor?" she asked, her voice unusually melancholy.

Kora studied her best friend's profile: sweaty blonde hair pulled back in a tight pony, straight nose, sharp jaw, dark brown eyes. There was something fierce about Sage that made people who didn't know her a little unnerved. Sometimes, when she wasn't paying attention, Kora could easily be fooled into being intimidated. But then she remembered all of Sage's dorky haircuts and her struggle through braces, how she cried when Bambi died, her bad emo music playlists. It had gotten worse since her mom died. She couldn't really remember how Sage had been before, but she was harder now.

She thought about Sage's question. Sage always had the answer. And now she was asking.

"I'm not going to art school," said Kora. It wasn't an answer, but it was what she had to offer.

"Fuck off," said Sage, jutting her chin out.

"I'm serious," said Kora. "I'm not going."

Sage turned to face her, defiant anger twisting her features in a way that reminded Kora of childhood tantrums.

"Don't be a martyr," said Sage. "I didn't ask you to do this. I can find him on my own. You go live in New York and drink oat milk lattes and sketch statues at the Met and become some obnoxious art freak I can't stand to be around. Get out of here, Kor, I mean it."

Despite Sage's grimace, Kora had to smile. There was a reason they were friends, and it wasn't because they were raised together. Though that was a perk.

"I'm not doing it for you," said Kora. Sage started to speak again, but Kora continued. "Or anyone else. I just don't want to go, Sage. I know everyone thinks I should. Maybe at some point it was my dream, but it's not anymore. I don't want to get out. I belong here."

Sage was quiet for a long time. The cicadas buzzed around them, volume rising and falling in waves. The grass simmered. Kora felt a drop of sweat slide down her back.

"Let's get out of here," said Sage. "Get some AC going in the car."

Kora smiled. She knew Sage was glad she was staying. And she knew they had more time to come back again and again—as often as it took until they found him.

That night, Kora moved through the Rivera house, listening to the sounds of Sage and Noah playing a particularly cutthroat game of Jenga. Hunter egged them on, a little too drunk to risk playing with her shaky hands.

Kora was looking for Connor, who had disappeared after getting up for another drink, but she wasn't in a hurry. It was nice to hear laughter fill up the space again. This was supposed to be his going away party, after all.

When she rounded the corner, she saw a light on in the study. She peeked her head through the door and saw Sage's dad hunched at the computer, a fleece blanket wrapped loosely around his shoulders. He looked up as she hovered in the doorway.

"Hey, Kora," he said, his voice soft and unfocused. He turned back to the screen in front of him. Hunter's throaty laugh carried from the den.

"We're not bothering you, are we?" Kora asked.

"No, no," Leo said. "It's nice to hear you kids having fun. I'm not getting much done anyway."

"What are you working on?"

He sighed and swiveled in the desk chair to face her, crossing his arms over his chest and pulling the blanket tighter. "Someone dropped out of the speaker series at the university, and the dean asked me to fill in with one of my old presentations. I'm going through them, but I'm not sure I have anything worth talking about."

Kora was surprised they had asked him, considering he was supposed to be on sabbatical working on his next book. But she knew the dean liked Leo. She probably thought getting out of the house would be good for him.

"Maybe you could talk about something new," she said, leaning in the doorway. "Even if it's half-baked, you might get some good ideas out of it."

Leo frowned, but he didn't seem opposed to the idea. He swiveled back around and started clicking on tabs. "Yeah, you might be right." He peered back over his shoulder. "Thanks, Kora."

"No problem." She left him to his studies.

Connor wasn't in the living room, and the bathroom was empty, so she headed upstairs. There were no lights on, but she could hear the crickets chirping from outside and knew there must have been a window open. She stepped into Sam's room and saw Connor's dark silhouette sitting on the roof just outside the narrow window.

She remembered first bringing Connor up to the roof one night when he came to dinner at the Riveras. Sam was away at Boy Scout camp, so she didn't mind trespassing in his room for roof access. She and Connor snuck away for a few minutes to look at the stars.

But when she stepped through the window, thoughts of Connor faded. She remembered when she was small enough to easily fit through the frame, sliding out after Sam, their hands sticky against the rough slats. They would clamber around the sides of the house, up and down the roof's peaks, peering into the attic windows. She remembered Sam jumping down one time, plummeting fifteen feet and hitting the ground with a thud and a hard breath. He was fine, but he wasn't allowed to play video games for a week.

She tried to shake away the memories as she sat next to Connor. His eyes were distant as he methodically rolled his beer bottle between his hands. The roofing shingles dug into her thighs, and she listened to the cicadas shriek.

"I'm surprised you remembered how to get up here," she said. She held out her hand in a silent question, and he passed over the beer.

"It's a nice view," he said. She followed his gaze over the dense, overgrown bushes that crowded the driveway, past the old barn that used to house chickens, on to the tall grass and woods in the distance. The sky was still light blue in the west, and fireflies blinked in between the trees. It was the kind of beauty she had gotten used to, but it made her heart race anyway, the landscape colored by familiarity. Her second home. Soon to be her only home. She felt her throat tighten, and she took another sip of his beer before handing it back.

"It is," she said. "I don't know why anybody would leave a place like this." She had been talking about herself, but when she glanced over, she realized how Connor would hear her words. "Oh, I didn't mean you. I'm sure you're excited to go to L.A."

"I am," he said, but his expression darkened. "It feels wrong, though. Like I'm leaving you and Sage behind when you need me most."

Kora considered that. Somewhere in the distance a bonfire was burning. The smell of smoke mixed with sharp pine and old wood.

Connor looked out at the horizon, and she studied his profile. The stubble on his chin had grown out a little. His hair was getting longer, the curls falling over his ears and into his face. She could hardly remember what his cheek felt like under the backs of her fingers. Relief made its way through her. There was nothing left of her old feelings except comfort and gratitude.

"We'll miss you," she said. "But we'll be okay. We have each other."

Connor glanced up at her, and his lips tilted in a sad smile. "And Hunter."

Kora looked down at her hands. "Her too."

"I like her, you know," Connor said. He huffed a laugh. "I don't think she likes me too much." Kora laughed at that. "She does, in her own way."

"I hope she helps you," he said. She stole a glance and saw nothing but honesty in his eyes.

"Thanks, Connor," she said. "I hope you love California. I hope it's everything you want it to be."

Connor frowned again, his brow furrowing. He took a long sip of his beer.

"I want to go, but it still hurts to leave." He glanced at her. "Why is everything so hard?"

"Because we're growing up," Kora said with a shrug.

The side of his mouth quirked up a little. "How do we make it stop?"

Kora laughed. "Let me know if you figure it out."

She leaned her head on his shoulder. The light blue of dusk melted into navy. Stars that had been hidden by the sun came into view. The forest became just a silhouette against the sky. Heat lightning struck in the clouds and brightened the leaves for a moment before returning to darkness.

Connor took the last sip of his beer and climbed back through the window one leg at a time. Kora followed him and stood still for a moment, letting her eyes adjust to the darkness in Sam's room, away from the moon and stars.

"Do you really think it's going to be okay?" he asked, his voice quiet in the dark. Kora groped around for a second before finding his shoulder and squeezing it.

"Yeah," she said. "I do."

They wandered back downstairs to where Sage was relentlessly bragging over the toppled Jenga pieces. Kora slid her arm around Hunter's waist and watched her full-belly laugh at Sage's trash talk. She glanced at Connor across the table, who grinned back at her.

After all summer trying to figure out what she wanted, afraid to hurt anyone, things finally felt settled. She felt something inside her slot into place.

CHAPTER 25

In the square, gilded mirror laid out in front of her, Sage could see the reflections of the treetops above, green and hyperreal. Surrounding the mirror, she had haphazardly placed her materials, everything her research called for that she could easily access. To her left, a bowl of water and a bundle of herbs. In front, above the mirror, assorted crystals and a flickering candle. She hoped any spirits lingering nearby would not be offended by the Bath and Body Works label. To her right, Sam's watch and some feathers she had found in her backyard where her father used to raise chickens. She had all the elements, something belonging to Sam, and his blood flowing from her veins.

"This better fucking work," she said to the trees. "You wouldn't believe how much mugwort costs around here."

She had no idea how to start. Her research had described a dizzying number of methods, from scrying to chanting to ritual sacrifice. This was a new world, and she wasn't sure she really belonged in it. She had the unsettling feeling the trees found her unwelcome.

She started by closing her eyes and listening. It was twilight, and the crickets were already chirping, the cicadas humming. Creatures darted in and out of bushes. Branches stretched for each other in the breeze.

When she opened her eyes, everything looked the same. She sighed, then remembered that breathing was important. She focused on her breath, in and out, in and out.

Once the mosquitos started eating her legs, she got frustrated and pulled Sam's small pocket knife from her back pocket. She didn't particularly want to injure herself, but blood was supposed to be important, and she was nothing if not practical. The cut she made was tiny, just a small slice to her thumb, and she squeezed a drop of blood onto the mirror. With her intact fingers, she smeared the blood across the top of the mirror and then dabbed a little onto Sam's watch for good measure.

This time when she closed her eyes, the sounds of the forest seemed farther away. She could hear the rushing of her own blood in her ears, could hear her hair moving in the wind. When she breathed in, she smelled lavender and clean sheets and old wood. She could almost hear Sam's laughter—not how it had been recently, but from when he was a kid, full-bodied and shameless.

When she opened her eyes, she was hopeful, but still there was no one there. Tears budded against her will. She was so tired of being sad. If he was gone, she wanted him to be gone. If he was there, she wanted him to be there.

"You dropped your stupid watch," she said to no one. She picked it up and clutched it in her hands. "Which looks terrible, by the way. It's been outside this whole time. Getting trampled by teenagers and possibly Satanists. Are you a Satanist teenager? Is that why you were there?"

No one answered. She put the watch back down and dipped her thumb in the water to clean off the little smudge of blood.

"I found mom's stuff," she said. "Were you looking for her? Or just carrying on her legacy?"

The wind picked up, and it almost sounded like a voice. She closed her eyes again, and tears dropped down her cheeks. She was so angry. She couldn't do this anymore. It felt pathetic to try and useless not to. All this hope was giving her a headache.

Something in the breeze whispered her name.

Her eyes snapped open and scanned the forest around her. It had gotten a shade darker while she had been there, but she couldn't see anything.

Then she caught some movement in front of her. Not in the forest, but in its reflection in the mirror.

She leaned over it and saw Sam's face. It was upside down, as if he were sitting across from her and leaning into the mirror just like she was. But when she looked up, he wasn't there.

In the mirror, Sam's mouth was moving, but she couldn't hear what he was saying. She watched him for a few seconds and then dug in her pocket for her notebook. She had jotted down things from Sam's notes and her own research, and she wondered if any of it could tell her how to talk to him.

None of the notes were helpful, but she had an idea. She laid the palm of her hand on the mirror next to the reflection of her face. Sam watched her with wary eyes and then did the same.

"Can you hear me?" he whispered. The sound didn't come from his reflection but from the trees. She looked around for a moment before looking back at his face.

"I can hear you," she said. A bubble of hysteria ran up her throat and she laughed. "God, it's like that cell phone commercial. Can you hear me now? Except you're..."

She usually had no problem calling a spade a spade, but it felt rude to point out that he was dead. In the mirror, he looked relieved.

"I'm so glad I found you," he said. "I've been wandering around here for so long, listening for your voice. Time is so weird here, I don't know how long I've been gone. I heard you talking about my watch."

She grinned and held it up for inspection, careful not to remove her other hand from the mirror and interrupt their connection.

"It's going to need some fine-tuning," she said.

"Keep it," he said. The strange tree-voice sounded stronger and lighter, almost like the laugh she had heard earlier. "I don't think watches would work here anyway."

For some reason, this made tears well up again, and she quickly brushed them away with the back of the hand holding the watch.

"I can't believe you're here," she said, her voice breaking. "We buried you."

"I'm so sorry, Sage," he said, his voice mournful, echoing through the leaves. "I never would have left you on purpose."

"That's bullshit," she said, her voice soft and not unkind. "I love you, and I forgive you, but you've been leaving me this whole time, Sam. While I was looking for you, I realized I don't even know you anymore."

"That's not true," said Sam. "You know me. I'm the same as I always was, I just know things now, things that are dangerous. But I guess I have to tell you."

"Tell me what?" Sage asked. "What were you looking for? Why were you so obsessed?"

Sam's face was pained in the mirror. It was strange to see his lips move and shoulders rise but not feel his breath or hear his voice.

"You said you found mom's notes," he said. "How much do you know about her last project?"

"I know she was looking into local folklore," said Sage. "I thought it was weird, since she used to only ever care about the classics. But that's pretty much it. Is that why you started looking into this stuff?"

The light dimmed further, and Sage realized she couldn't see Sam as clearly. His face was shrouded in shadow, the sky behind him a deeper blue. If she looked closely, she could see stars shimmering above him that were bright and clear above her.

"It's complicated," he said, "and I don't know how much time we have. I don't think I can stay for long."

Sage took a deep breath and pressed her other palm to the mirror so that both her hands framed either side of her face. She nodded for him to continue.

"Mom started working with someone from the folklore department on a whim, just wanted to check it out," he said. "But when she looked into it, a lot of the stories checked out. Sightings of ghosts across different groups and time periods that didn't know about each other but reported the same things. She decided to do some more research.

"I guess she decided books weren't enough, she needed to go into the field, talk to some people. She used ethnography and took oral histories. But then the notes say she saw some of the ghosts herself."

Sage's breathing quickened, and she had to focus to keep her hands from slipping off the mirror. She wanted to look around, hold her head, do something to shake off this nervous energy, but she kept her eyes on Sam's shadowed face. They didn't have much time, and she had to know more.

"She had her own sightings written down," he said. "And then there were more notes about spirits and energy, different from the oral history stuff. This was not about folklore, it was about magic, real magic, like she believed it. I had to know if she was right."

Sage almost laughed. "I guess you proved that theory correct," she almost whispered.

"It's not just me," he said, his voice growing louder and more urgent. "That's what I have to tell you. I didn't fall over that ledge, Sage. I was pushed by something. And I heard Mom's voice. She was trying to warn me, or save me, I don't know. But I know it was her."

Tears spilled over Sage's cheeks, but still she didn't lift her hands from the mirror or look away from him. Something clicked in her head: Kora's dream. The message wasn't from Sam, it was from her mom. She was trying to save Sam by letting them know he was in trouble, showing them where to find him.

"Have you seen her?" she asked, voice cracking. "Is she there with you? Can I talk to her?"

He shook his head, careful to keep his eyes on hers.

"I haven't seen her since I fell," he said. "I'll keep looking, I promise."

She nodded and sniffled. It was almost fully dark, and she remembered that she was in the woods, where bears and other dangerous animals came out in the night.

"But Sage," he said, "there are others here. Not like Mom. Like the thing that pushed me."

Sage could see the fear in his eyes, even upside down.

"Some of them are like people, but some of them are older, more distant," he said. "Some of them I can see, some I can just hear, some just show me signs. I hear languages I don't understand and see symbols in the rocks and the branches I don't recognize. I don't think they hurt me on purpose. I think they're trying to talk to me."

"What are they trying to tell you?"

"They're angry," he said, eyes wide. They were the only thing she could see of him now. Those blue, round eyes. She missed him so much, her back bent with the ache of it.

"Why?" she whispered, voice anguished.

"It's hard to tell," he said. "There's so many of them, and they don't all agree. But their power is massive, and it's everywhere. They say this land is old, much older than us. And we've done a lot to destroy it. So much violence and death. Their bones are lost."

"What do they want?"

"I don't know," said Sam. He was silent for a moment, eyes sharp in the navy sky. "To be put back where they belong. For the land to be right again. They all want different things, but they agree something's not right. I'm trying to listen so I can help. I think that's what Mom was trying to do."

"Did she die because of this?" Sage whispered.

"I don't know," he said, voice miserable. "I wish I knew. I'm going to try and find her, Sage. I promise. We have to help her."

She finally allowed herself to close her eyes as tears clouded her vision. They fell onto the mirror and mixed with her blood where it was smudged across the top.

"I have to help *you*, Sam," she said. "I'm going to find a way to keep you here."

When she opened her eyes again, he was gone.

The forest was dark and she was alone.

CHAPTER 26

The park was sparsely populated for a sunny day. Kora supposed it was a weekday, and some of the charter schools would have started classes already. The end of summer was rushing past them.

Kora sketched an outline of the jungle gym with two small figures climbing over it. Behind them, azalea bushes were in full bloom. The sun was high above them, casting everything in sharp contrast, bright colors and stark shadows.

Behind her, Hunter laid out on their picnic blanket, arms folded behind her head. She wore sunglasses, and her hair splayed around her. Beads of sweat dotted her upper lip.

Once she was satisfied with her sketch, Kora leaned back and rested her head on Hunter's stomach. She sighed as Hunter ran her fingers through Kora's hair.

"Ouch," she said, pulling her hand back. "Your hair is on fire."

"That happens."

"Does your scalp ever get sunburned?"

"Just by the part."

Hunter shook her head, but she flipped Kora's hair over and began playing with the cooler hair toward the back of her neck.

Kora closed her eyes. The sun warmed her cheeks, but a persistent breeze kept her cool. It was a rare day where the heat felt pleasant instead of stifling.

"You better be wearing sunscreen on that tat," said Hunter. "I'm not going to design something for you if it's just going to fade in ten years."

"Are you wearing sunscreen?" Kora snarked. She knew the answer.

"Do as I say, not as I do."

Kora turned to rest her cheek on Hunter's chest, moving a little to feel the soft cotton of her t-shirt. She could almost fall asleep like this.

"Uh oh," said Hunter. Kora opened one eye, squinting against the sun to look up at her.

"What?" said Kora.

"Sage texted the group chat: SOS, meet at diner."

Kora turned over and sat up on the blanket. She took Hunter's offered phone and read the text for herself. It couldn't be good. She started gathering everything they brought with them and putting on her shoes.

"Duty calls," said Hunter.

Sage was sitting in their regular booth at the diner, sipping Coke at an alarming rate. She was obviously amped up about something, her knee bouncing up and down and hitting the bottom of the table.

Kora and Hunter slid in across from her, but they didn't ask her anything until Noah pulled in, looking worried.

"Okay, Sage," said Kora. "Spill. What's the SOS?"

Sage took one more long sip of her Coke, then pushed it away, breathing heavily. She leaned in and they all followed suit.

"I saw Sam again," she said. Kora looked up and saw a manic excitement in Sage's eyes, but also the darker edge she had expected. This stuff was scaring both of them.

"Where?" asked Kora.

"Back in the woods," said Sage, playing with her straw wrapper. "I brought a bunch of stuff from the books, and I have no idea which one did it, but it worked. He was there in the mirror talking to me."

"Mirror?" asked Noah.

"Yeah, some of the books said mirrors were good conduits for the dead," said Sage.

Noah pulled a notebook seemingly from nowhere and wrote down what she had said. Kora leaned over and saw that the page was already half-full of scribbles.

"What did he say?" Hunter asked. She was eyeing Sage's bouncing leg and quickly moving fingers. Kora was pretty used to it at this point. This was not that far from Sage's norm before her anxiety and ADHD were medicated. But she knew it was a little nerve-wracking.

"A bunch," said Sage, leaning over to watch Noah add to his notes. "He said our mom was researching this stuff and that's why he got so invested in it. He thinks she saw a ghost before she died. And he said that's why he fell over the railing—he saw her or heard her. I'm not sure. Just like we saw him."

Kora realized that she had fallen in the same way Sam had, over the railing and into the ravine, but she had walked away with pretty minor injuries, and he had left the land of the living. She shuddered. Her ribs ached where they had been broken.

"But that's not even the most important part," said Sage, unusually theatrical. "He told me there are a bunch of spirits over there that are angry at humans for messing with their land and their bodies. He wants to help them."

"I mean, that doesn't surprise me," said Hunter. "This area has some messed up history to contend with. If I died on the Trail of Tears only for my bones to get blasted off the top of a mountain for coal, I'd be pretty pissed."

Sage nodded. "I think this might be why Sam is still around," she said. "And why he's able to talk to us. Maybe he's supposed to be a messenger."

"But why him?" asked Kora. "And why us?"

Sage's shrug was twitchy. "No idea. But I have to help him. He's all alone out there trying to make sense of these restless spirits and has no way of doing anything about it." She looked down at her hands where they were tearing apart a second straw wrapper. "And if he really did see Mom before she died, maybe I can find her, too."

Kora had to lay her head down on the table for a second. This was a lot for one summer. She needed a moment of disbelief. The table was quiet.

"All right," she said, voice muffled by her arms. "I'm in. Let's help these spirits, I guess." She turned her face to the side so she could see them. "I have nothing better to do. I'm an unemployed high school graduate with no job prospects and no future."

Sage threw the straw wrapper at her.

"Shut up," she said. "You're a talented artist with tons of time to figure things out. But also yes, thank you, I accept your help."

"I'm in too," said Hunter. "Not unemployed, but I love a challenge."

"Obviously," said Sage. Kora assumed she was talking about the trips to find Sam, but when she looked up, Sage was looking at her pointedly. Kora threw the straw wrapper back at her.

"I think we should start by looking into binding rituals," said Noah. "It sounds like whatever you did worked, and if we can find a way to contact him more consistently, we can figure out what he needs."

"Fuck yeah," said Sage. She slammed her hand down on the table. "We have a plan, gang. I daresay we're ghost whisperers now."

◆ ◆ ◆

When Kora got home, there was a Sold sign in front of her house.

She had the unexpected urge to cry. She had known the house was on the market. They had been staging it for months. Paul had already started his job out in Santa Fe, living in a hotel and looking at houses. It was just a matter of time. But now, she really had to say goodbye.

When she walked in, her mom was in the kitchen, cooking something in a skillet. Muddy Waters was playing from the speaker, and she was barefoot in old, ripped jeans and a peasant shirt. She hummed along while she shook the skillet, mixing what looked like stir fry. Her light brown hair was tied back in a loose braid, streaked with gray. Kora always forgot her mom was getting older until she looked at her.

When they were apart, she could only remember sitting on the bathroom counter while her mom applied her makeup, watching her with awe. There was a magic to it that Kora had never mastered.

Kora sat at the kitchen island across from her mom, watching her cook. Her mom smiled and pulled out an extra bowl for Kora.

"You sold the house," Kora said, attempting a smile.

"Yeah, we got an offer yesterday," her mom said. "We'll be in escrow for a month, but then it's official. Paul's going to put an offer on a place in a couple days."

"I'm happy for you, mom," said Kora, and she meant it. This house would always mean a lot to her, but she had a lot more holding her to Pinebrook than she had given due credit.

"Thanks, sweet pea." Her mom went back to humming and moving around the kitchen, pulling out spices and leaving the cabinets open.

Kora knew she had to tell her mom about New York. She didn't want to ruin the moment, but now that the house was sold, she wasn't sure how quickly her mom would be leaving. There might not be a better time. And there would never be a perfect time.

"Mom, I have to tell you something," she said.

Her mom turned the stove off and moved the skillet to a cool burner, then turned around to face her.

"Shoot," she said.

Anxiety spiked through Kora. Before now, her decision didn't mean anything. Telling her mom made it real.

"I don't want to go to art school," she said.

Her mom stared at her for a long moment with her shoulders hunched and arms crossed, like she was trying to figure out a complicated puzzle.

"What do you mean?" she asked.

"I just don't want to go," Kora said again. She pulled at the ends of her hair. "I know I'm supposed to want to. I thought going to art school was the only path for me. Painting is the only thing I've ever wanted to do, the only thing I'm good at."

"Honey," her mom interrupted, shoulders relaxing slightly. Kora let out a breath. "Painting is not the only thing you're good at. There are a thousand things you could do with your life. But I thought this was what you wanted."

"Art is still what I want to do," said Kora, sitting on one of the bar stools. "I just don't know if going to a big, fancy school in a big city is the only way to make that happen. I don't think that's me. Or maybe it used to be, but things changed. I've changed, I think."

Her mom leaned forward over the counter, resting on her elbows. She looked tired, suddenly. More tired than Kora had seen her in a long time. Kora's throat felt scratchy as she fought the urge to cry.

"Kora, sometimes you have to move on from things," her mom said. "I know you don't think you can live without Sage, but you can, I promise you. And Pinebrook will still be here when you come back."

Kora leaned back, surprised.

"You won't," she said, her tone accusatory. "You'll be in Santa Fe."

Her mom crossed her arms again, looking angry and hurt.

Kora was angry, too. She had been nervous about her mom's reaction, but if she was being honest with herself, she never really thought her mom would try to talk her out of it. Kora had always had free reign to make her own choices.

"That's not fair," her mom said. "I'm making the best decision I can for my future, and you should do the same. I've already paid the deposit. I understand that you feel nervous, but that's no reason not to go to college."

"I don't think this is the best decision for my future anymore," Kora insisted. She clenched her fists against the underside of the bar stool.

"You don't want to stay here," her mom said, bringing her hand down firmly on the countertop. "You're just scared to go somewhere else."

Kora was not a person who often got angry. With a best friend like Sage, she was always the calm one, the one who stepped in when emotions were running high. She usually had a joke or an anecdote or a word of advice to give everyone the chance to take a breath.

She realized that she had been angry at her mom for a long time. Maybe even before the house, before Sam, before any of it. She was a teenager, but she had never been treated like a teenager. She made her own decisions because she had the responsibility of taking care of herself. All summer, she had been off traipsing through the woods, and her mom never questioned it. But now she wanted to provide motherly input into Kora's future.

Rage bubbled up in her gut in a way that Kora didn't like. She didn't feel like she could control it.

"I'm not the one who's running away," Kora said. Her mom took an involuntary step back. "I'm not just going to leave and start a new life somewhere else because this one is hard. I have family here, and I'm not going anywhere. I would never abandon Sage like that."

"You can't make your decisions based on other people," her mom said.

"Of course you would say that," Kora scoffed. "You've always made your own decisions, whether or not they were right for me. You're selling the home I grew up in and moving across the country, and you didn't even ask me if it was okay."

"I don't have to ask your permission to sell this house, Kora," her mom said.

"Well, I don't have to ask your permission, either," said Kora. "You can't make me go to school."

Her mom turned around to face the stove and dropped her head into her hands.

"Things can't go back to the way they were, Kora," her mom said. "The life we had here is gone. It was hard enough to keep going without Liz, but now Sam—" her voice cut off as she covered her face in her hands.

Sometimes Kora forgot that when Sam and Sage had lost their mom, Kora's mom had lost her best friend. They had been like family since before Kora was born. Her mom didn't visit her own family much. She had lost the one person she relied on more than anyone else, the person who helped her raise a daughter by herself.

And Sam. Kora thought about Sam's ghost, the flickering outline of his black t-shirt, looking real and impossible at the same time. She was still figuring out how to grieve someone who might not be fully gone. Some part of her wished she could tell her mom that a part of Sam was still around, but she knew it wouldn't make enough sense to be comforting.

"All this sadness, all this grief, it's not good for me," her mom continued, her face still partially covered by her hands. "I need to go somewhere fresh, where I don't have to think about it all the time."

Kora felt sad for her mom and guilty that she had hurt her feelings, but it wasn't enough to take the heat out of her anger.

"I like it here," Kora said. Her throat ached and her eyes burned. "If you don't then fine, go. But you don't get to make my decisions for me."

She expected this to ignite more fighting, but instead, her mom laughed. Her shoulders slumped and she turned back around, leaning against the oven.

"You sound just like me," she said, "when I left the farm. Yelling at your grandparents that they couldn't stop me."

Kora was stunned by this response. She didn't know what to say. Her mom's laughter had taken the wind out of her sails.

"I love your grandparents, and some part of me still loves the farm," she said with a sigh. "But my childhood wasn't what I wanted it to be. And it wasn't what I wanted for you. I wanted you to have everything you needed for a good life."

"I do have that," said Kora. "I don't have to go to New York to find that."

Her mom nodded slowly, contemplative.

Kora was forced to confront her immense gratitude for the sweat and grit her mom had put into making their life in Pinebrook work, to provide for them both. Regardless of her anger and frustration with the way she grew up, she knew her mom was strong, and it made her feel like she could be strong, too.

"I'm sorry I sold the house without asking you," her mom said. "I just needed to get out of here. And once you decided to go to school, I felt like I didn't have to worry about you anymore."

"That's still true," said Kora. "I think I can have a good life here."

"I'm sure you can," her mom said with a watery smile. "You've got that Mason fire in you."

Kora stepped around the island and hugged her mom. She inhaled her perfume and rested her head on her mom's chest.

She realized with another wave of grief that the Pinebrook she was choosing to stay in was one without her mother in it. She wouldn't have her beautiful, quirky, old childhood home to come back to, or her mom's perfect garden.

She and her mom had their issues, and they hadn't figured them all out. It was probably going to be good for their relationship to be in different cities for a while. But still, she already missed her.

"Where are you gonna live?" her mom asked. Kora couldn't see her face but she knew she must be looking around at the house full of boxes. "And what are you going to do?"

"Get a job, I guess," said Kora. "I can pay you back for the deposit."

"I don't really care about that," her mom said, leaning her cheek on top of Kora's head. "I just want you to be happy. And I want to know that you're going to be okay here without me."

"I have Sage," said Kora. She would never be alone as long as she was with Sage. "I can stay with her until I find a job."

"I'm glad that she and Leo will have someone around to help them out," her mom said. "They need it."

They were both quiet for a moment as they remembered the unfair loss of Liz's ineffable presence in the Rivera family.

"Also," said Kora, pushing through the sadness to get all of the news out at once. "I'm sort of seeing someone. And she lives here, so."

Her mom gave her a sly look, and Kora knew what she was thinking.

"I didn't choose to stay because of her," Kora said, rolling her eyes. "I had already decided."

Her mom seemed satisfied with that. She turned around and tried to get the stir fry started again.

"Sit down," she said. "Let's have one last dinner in this house."

CHAPTER 27

It was still dark out when Sage woke up for her first day of her senior year. She wouldn't have to leave for another couple hours, but even after half a summer with no swim practice, she couldn't shake the habit of waking up early. She stretched slowly and went downstairs to make a coffee. She had time to kill.

Senior year. Soon, she would be in college, surpassing Sam's level of education. Or maybe she would have a mental breakdown, drop out of school, and look for ghosts like he did. Maybe they would become ghost siblings, haunting Pinebrook and never getting old. The thought overwhelmed her.

Her dad sat at the kitchen table with his tablet, eating a plate of toast and squinting through his glasses at the screen.

"What are you working on?" she asked. Her voice broke the morning quiet, and her dad jumped a little. "Sorry."

"Just catching up on emails," he sighed, closing the tablet and setting it aside. "I've decided to go back to teaching this semester. It's time to give up on my research project. I'm not getting anywhere."

"And the school will let you do that?" she asked, pouring herself some coffee and taking a seat beside him.

"They've been very lenient with me," he said, voice sad. "I don't have to wonder why that is."

Sage nodded. She thought back to her swim coach's concern when she quit the team. She could relate.

"What are you doing up this early?" he asked.

"First day of school."

His eyebrows shot up. He opened his tablet again and flicked through his calendar.

"Sage, I'm so sorry. I didn't even realize what day it was."

"It's fine," she shrugged. "I figured it out."

"It's not fine," he said. He took his glasses off and set them beside his plate on the table. "I know I've been a bit absent. Before Sam–I thought we would all lean on each other and it would be okay. But you both needed a father. I'm going to be here."

"You did your best," said Sage. "I'm sorry I freaked out on you. It's not your fault. We're all just figuring it out."

She felt an ache that was quickly becoming familiar as she thought of Sam's image flashing on the road in front of them. She couldn't tell her father, the physicist, that Sam's death was much more complicated than absent parenting. But she wished she could ease some of his guilt.

She figured letting him parent her might be the best solution.

"Let's make dinner tomorrow night," she said. "Kora can come over. Maybe Noah and Hunter, too. I don't think I told you, but Noah was friends with Sam. They met at the library."

Her dad raised his eyebrows. "Oh, I didn't realize. Sure, they can come over."

"Great," said Sage, finishing her coffee and getting up to put it in the sink. "I'll text them. I think they're going to be around a lot this year." She smiled as she thought of the four of them, crowding around her kitchen table, reading books and playing games, and figuring things out together.

She had made friends without really meaning to. They had just appeared in her life the way Kora had. She realized she was very ill-prepared for college, where she would actually have to try.

———— ◆ ————

She tried to pay attention to third-period chemistry, but the equations on the board all blurred together. Science had always been her favorite subject, but chemical equations seemed pointless at the moment. She was stuck in a dusty classroom with ten other students who were dutifully taking notes and asking the right questions, and all she wanted was to be outside in the woods, looking for Sam.

At lunch, she sat under an old birch tree outside and halfheartedly ate the salad she'd bought at the cafeteria. Now that she wasn't swimming, she could probably eat things that weren't green, but she had gotten used to rabbit food.

She pulled out a book she had been reading on tarot cards. It wasn't strictly relevant, but she thought understanding different theories and interpretations of magic would help her narrow down what was happening with Sam. The book had colorful illustrations of card designs. She stroked the glossy pages and tried to imagine what Sam could be trying to tell her with each card.

Her phone buzzed. It was a text from Noah to the group chat: *Library @ 5? Found something interesting.*

Connor texted back, *Guess I should leave the group chat :(miss you guys already!!*

Kora sent a heartfelt goodbye from all of them and then Connor removed his contact from the group. Hunter sent *RIP Connor* and a series of gravestone and skeleton emojis. Noah said, *Too soon.*

She grinned. Around her, fellow Oakcrest seniors were sitting at picnic tables, laughing with their friends. Some of them were inside practicing their instruments and performing scientific experiments for extra credit. Bunch of nerds. She was reading a book about tarot and joking with her friends about her dead brother's ghost.

But more than that, she had hope. For the first time all summer, reading Noah's text, she felt like she could breathe. She wasn't alone. They were as in this as she was. Sam was really out there, and they could find him again.

Will be there at 5, she texted back. *Send me your coffee orders.*

⬧◆⬧

After school, Sage stopped at the coffee shop downtown and picked up everyone's drinks: red eye for herself, iced lavender oat milk latte for Kora, dirty chai for Hunter, americano for Noah. She liked knowing their coffee orders. She liked the feeling of waiting for the tray full of cups to come out, evidence that she had somewhere to be and people to meet. She especially liked not devoting every waking moment outside of school to homework and beating her personal record for swim times.

She drove to the library with the windows down, careful to set the tray of drinks in the floorboard so it wouldn't topple. It had taken some convincing on her father's part for her to drive Sam's car to school, but he needed his own car to get to work on campus. She reminded herself that the car was always supposed to be hers eventually. It just came to her a different way than expected.

The radio was playing bluegrass, which she usually didn't care for, but it matched the windy September day outside. The weather was finally starting to cool.

This was a lot better than scrambling to get to practice. If something had to take its place—and something did, since even her medicated ADHD wouldn't allow her to sit idle for too long—driving around town, drinking coffee, and digging through hundred-year-old research with her friends wasn't a bad replacement.

Funneling her anxious energy into schoolwork and sports eventually hit a point of diminishing returns. What would success bring her? Entrance to an Ivy League school? Maybe a swim scholarship? She wasn't sure she even wanted those things. School had always been a means to an end, something to occupy her mind and prove her worth. She liked science, but she couldn't tell if that was because she was genuinely interested in the subject or because she found it the easiest to study—memorize facts, balance chemical equations, and follow exact instructions in labs. She knew she didn't feel the same way about physics as her dad did. He was obsessed with understanding everything he could, asking questions no one else thought to ask, working for the sake of knowledge itself. Sage doubted she would ever be that passionate about anything.

Except now. Now she had something that pulled her mind in strange and exciting directions. Since her mirror-talk with Sam, she had realized that even if Sam hadn't fallen down that ravine, this still would have become her fight. First their mother and then Sam had become wrapped up in this world, and it was inevitable that she would too.

She missed Sam like one of her lungs was gone, a fresher, sharper version of the ache she felt for her mother, but instead of reminding her of her grief, this research gave her a place to channel it. She felt closer to understanding them. And maybe she was learning something about herself.

Her disciplined, pragmatic approach to the world had been tossed out the window as soon as she saw Sam's face in the woods. Now, she was relearning everything from scratch. And it felt good.

She pulled into the library parking lot and noticed that Kora's ancient car and Hunter's motorcycle were already there, parked next to each other. She smiled to herself and walked up the front steps.

Noah had staked out a table for them, and she set down the coffee tray in the middle.

"My hero," said Kora, taking a long sip from her latte.

"Um, I'm sorry, which one of us just had to go to school for eight hours?" Sage scoffed. "How are you the tired one?"

"Give her a break," said Hunter with a smirk. "She didn't get much sleep last night."

"Gross," said Sage. "You're lucky I still hang out with you. Noah, you're currently my favorite."

"I'm about to become your permanent favorite," he said with a wide grin. Sage hesitated with his coffee in her hand, because he seemed a little over-caffeinated already, but he scooped up the americano and took a sip anyway. "I think I know how we can get Sam to stick around."

He pushed a book and a pile of notes in Sage's direction. Sam's notebook was open on the table in front of him. Sage had let Noah take the notebook so he could study it while she was at school. It took immense strength to let someone else have it, but she knew she could trust Noah.

Sage sat down and started flipping through the pages he had marked with sticky notes. The book was old, falling apart a little at the seams. She flipped it over to look at the cover: *Spells and Rituals.*

"Where did you find this?" asked Kora, looking over Sage's shoulder. "I'm pretty sure we would have seen this in the collection before."

"It was on loan to some special collection, and we just got it back," he said. "Technically, it's not supposed to be taken out of the reading room, so please do not spill anything on it."

She flipped back to the first page he had indicated. It was a binding ritual meant to ground a spirit to the waking world. Sage scanned the instructions. It was fairly straight-forward, though she would have to look up some of the materials.

"What makes you think it'll work?" she asked.

"I thought about what you said after you went to see Sam, about how he appeared in the mirror," said Noah. He looked as excited as she'd ever seen him, even more focused than when they had gone on the ghost tour and he had talked nonstop to the tour guide. "Mirror magic appears in folklore from all over, but when I focused on Appalachian folklore, I found repeated mentions of covering mirrors after someone dies to prevent the spirit from getting stuck."

"Stuck like in the mirror?" asked Hunter. Sage glanced over the illustrations on the yellowed page, mostly sketches of herbs and household objects.

"I think just stuck in this life," said Noah, taking another hurried sip of his coffee. "It's not very clear. But it made me think—Sam said the spirits are connected to the mountains somehow. I think our best bet is to look for local writings on magical practices. There might be something unique about Appalachia compared to other places that makes the magic here special."

Sage flipped the book to the front pages: published in 1847 in Asheville, North Carolina. Her heart leapt.

"So this could really work?" she asked, trying to keep the hope out of her voice. She didn't want the others to get their hopes up. It was too late for her.

"It's worth a try," said Noah.

Sage looked over the list again. The herbs were mostly things she could get at the specialty health foods store in Asheville. Some of them, she would have to research. But the ritual also called for specific celestial events: a full moon, a meteor shower, a lunar eclipse. She wasn't sure when the next ones would be.

"It might take us a while," she said, "but we have a plan." She looked up at Noah and grinned. Kora reached out and squeezed her hand. Noah finished off his coffee.

They spent the rest of the afternoon looking for books on the obscure herbs from the list and researching lunar cycles. The full moon had just passed, so it would be almost a month before they could try it, but that would give them time to secure everything they needed. Sage buzzed with anticipation already.

This was it, they were doing something.

The anxiety that had thrummed through her veins since the beginning of the summer had become a different, more pleasant kind of feeling. She was eager to see Sam again, eager to find out more about these ghosts.

Sam was dead, but it was all just beginning.

As they walked down the steps of the library toward their cars, Noah put his hand on her shoulder. She stopped and turned to face him.

"I keep thinking how psyched Sam would be about all this," he said quietly. "How he should be here with us, reading all this."

Sage looked up at him. The sun was starting to set, and the evening was going to be cool. She searched her own heart for signs of sadness but found only the familiar grief, old and steady.

"He will be," she said. "This is going to work. And then he'll be here to help us."

Noah grinned. He held out his fist for her to bump.

She got home after dark and started on her homework. It was senior year, and she had hours of work before she would be able to sleep. But for the first time, the work wasn't a disciplined chore she would diligently push herself through.

She had something to look forward to.

CHAPTER 28

A bead of sweat dripped down Kora's chin onto her chest. She was carrying a heavy box and couldn't put it down, so she wiped her face on her shoulder, which did little good since it was just bare skin. When she finally got to the car, she let out a loud huff as she pushed the box into the trunk.

Now that the house was sold, her mom was preparing to move everything to Santa Fe, which meant Kora had to take anything she wanted to keep and put it in storage. Leo had been kind enough to let her keep some boxes in their attic. Her furniture would be sold on Craigslist or donated. Everything she needed for now would be going to Hunter's place. It wasn't much, just clothes, toiletries, and as many art supplies as she could fit.

It felt strange that after eighteen years of all her stuff being under one roof, it would now be spread out across multiple houses in two different states. She felt like her soul was being kept in different places, like she was being put on one of those Medieval stretching torture devices.

Hunter came up behind her and put another box in the car. This one had all her childhood memorabilia: trophies and school awards, a few exemplary art projects, toys and trinkets. It made her smile to see Hunter holding it, like if she opened the box she could learn everything there was to know about Kora, every version of her there had been.

"I think that's it," said Hunter as she wiped her dusty hands off on her jeans. "Your mom said to come see her in the kitchen."

Kora left Hunter to shift the boxes around in the car so they would fit. She found her mom packing up the last of the dishware they had been using over the past month. When she heard Kora come in, she stood up and turned around. There was a wide, toothy smile on her face that Kora rarely got to see.

"We're almost done!" she said, pulling Kora into a hug. "Can you believe we're saying goodbye to this place?"

"You're saying goodbye," said Kora. "I'm still gonna have to pass by here and see interlopers occupying my room."

"Be nice to the interlopers," her mom said. "They gave me a good price for this old house."

"They better have," said Kora. "I'll accept nothing less than eight million dollars."

"Okay, maybe not that much."

They laughed and walked around the living room. The furniture was pushed up against the wall, ready to be hauled out to the truck. Everything else was in boxes stacked in rows in the hallway.

In many ways, Kora was more ready now to leave this place than she had been at the beginning of the summer. It was nice to step back and feel grateful that she had a consistent home for so long. This house had done her good. She would miss it a lot. But she wouldn't be lost without it. She had several homes waiting for her.

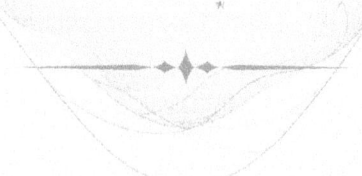

Once they had dropped off the boxes at the Riveras' and dragged Kora's suitcase up the stairs to Hunter's apartment, they hopped on the motorcycle and drove up the parkway. Hunter pulled over at one of the scenic overlooks. It was almost sunset, and there were families sitting at the different picnic tables.

"Are you glad you're staying here?" asked Hunter, sitting down on an old wooden bench and putting her arm around Kora. "You don't wish you were heading up to New York?"

"Definitely not," said Kora. "You don't get views like this in New York." In front of her, the clouds were a mix of deep orange and magenta, color streaking across the sky. Behind them, it was a deep blue, night creeping in. In between, the hills and valleys stretched in the distance. Everything she loved in one long range of green.

"Thanks for letting me stay with you," she said. To their left, a toddler screamed in delight as he ran around a small stretch of grass.

Hunter looked at her and smiled. The sunset lit up one side of her face in a gentle glow. One eye glittered in the light.

"I wasn't ready for this summer to end," she said.

"Me either," said Kora, leaning her head onto Hunter's shoulder.

Somewhere in the nearby forest, an owl hooted, awake early in the evening glow.

◆

Kora and Sage made it through a couple hours of quiet, with Sage working on homework and Kora drawing loose sketches, before Sage got restless. Kora had always possessed a sixth sense for these moments. She clocked the shaking of Sage's knee, the tapping of her pencil against the table, and quietly dug around for her keys. Sage caught on quickly, and they walked out to the car.

They had no destination in mind. The night was cool and crisp. It was the kind of false autumn air that September sometimes tricked them with before the heat surged again. Kora rolled the windows down and played some music, but she didn't listen to it. As she drove along winding mountain roads, she breathed in the air whipping past and felt alive with something intangible that burrowed under her skin.

Eventually, she found her way to a large empty field off the highway. It was too dark to see much of anything, but she pulled off and parked the car anyway. She and Sage climbed onto the hood and looked up at the stars.

She felt that same feeling that she had lying next to Sage on the ground that night at the campsite, like magic was pressing into her through the soil.

The mountains were ancient, worn down by time and eroded by water, bones, footsteps. The trees had long memories. Feeling it now, knowing what she did, it felt impossible that Kora had ever doubted there was magic here.

She could feel it when she drove through town with the windows down, breathing in the radiating heat air and listening to the radio. Sometimes the music cut out and through the static, and she could almost hear the humming of spirits, hiding between the dips and crags of the mountains. She could feel it when she let the shrieking of the cicadas beat in her chest, filling her with something warm and close and alive.

But most of all, she could feel it when she looked at the people she loved. They were children of the mountains, born here and brought up under the dark shadows and blinding sun. People moved in and out of town all the time, but somehow she had surrounded herself with others like her—friends who understood how it felt to be humbled by the vast landscape of their birthplace.

Maybe that was why she had been so reluctant to go to school in New York, far away from the vibrant greens and earthy scent of her hometown. When the magic that connected her to these mountains was stretched too far, it dimmed and dampened. She felt anxious and unmoored.

Of course Sam wanted to see this magic up close. It had shaped him, cradled him, whispered to him in his sleep. The oldest of them, he had been exposed to the magic the longest. Land this old with a history this deep, it could seep into their dreams. Kora found herself wanting to talk to him again, not just because his spirit was lost in the strange in-between of the woods, but because she wanted to understand what he had seen. She wanted to keep following the path they had found from the trails he had left behind.

She turned her head and looked at Sage. When it was just them, she could see Sage's face relax just a little. She remembered the little girl who was always frowning. Everyone had thought she was angry, but Kora knew better. Sage was always thinking, always looking closely at the world and taking nothing for granted. Inside there was a scientist plagued with curiosity. It was her favorite thing about her best friend and she could see it now.

They had so much to think about now, so much to figure out. The world had expanded rapidly around them and become so much bigger and stranger than they ever could have believed. But Kora couldn't find it in herself to be scared. She was born there, and she was sure she would die there. Everything in between she would do with help.

When she looked back up, the stars glittered in the vast midnight, and she smelled the sharp pine and rich earth. She was home.

EPILOGUE

Sam looked up and frowned at the stars. He was a Boy Scout, he knew how to navigate by their placement in the sky. But something was different about them here. Every time he looked up, they seemed to be in a different place. Constellations shifted and stirred. Stars zoomed in and out of focus. He was starting to realize he wasn't supposed to find his way out of these woods.

He thought it should be colder. Time was strange, but he thought it might be fall. Sometimes the leaves looked yellow and orange, but then he would look around a wide trunk, and they would be back to a vibrant green. He had mostly given up trying to figure it out.

Sometimes he could hear voices in the trees. Some of them were calm and helpful, some of them were tainted with disdain. Most of them spoke in long-dead languages he didn't understand. But he was starting to learn. He could feel their eyes on him as he continued to wander.

He supposed, if pressed, he would admit he wasn't really looking for the way out anymore. He knew he was tied to this forest, now, like it or not. He hadn't dared venture too close to the road because he didn't want to know if his car or—he forced himself to think it—his body was still there. He thought he remembered talking to Sage after they had found his body, so they must have moved it by now, but time was so strange. If he went in the wrong direction, he might end up back at the beginning.

The thought of Sage brought an ache to his chest. Or it would if he could feel his chest. Regardless, the grief still bowled over him. Sage, so stoic and full of bubbling rage, didn't deserve this. She didn't deserve a dead brother on top of a dead mother. She didn't deserve the weight of all this—the centuries-old feud of mountain spirits—any more than he did. He wished he could protect her from it. But without a body or a voice, he was useless. He supposed that was why he was still moving. Maybe she would come back. Maybe when he stepped around the next tree, she would be there, and he could talk to her. Tell her he was sorry. That he would help her however he could.

Instead, there were more trees. Sam sighed, but he wasn't sure he was really there. He didn't really have lungs anymore, probably. He chose not to think about it too hard.

The night sky shifted into a brilliant blue and the stars disappeared. The sun shone and the birds sang. He had stepped into the day.

Sam paused in his meandering path and looked around. The trees were moving again, restless in their distress. He recognized the instinct, even if he didn't feel it anymore. He thought of Sage's nervous tics, bouncing her knee and sneaking cigarettes when she thought no one was looking. It made him feel a little closer to real, to a particular place and moment in time.

He started walking again. Sage would come back. His mom would, too. This had to have happened to their family for a reason, and Sam was determined to find it.

Far above his head, a bird call pierced the sky. Sam closed his eyes and continued walking, trusting that the forest would guide him. He was at its mercy, now.

Somehow, for some reason, the mountains had chosen to speak to him. He knew in his bones that he needed their help.

He just had to find a way to listen.

ACKNOWLEDGMENTS

First of all, I want to thank my best friend Rachel Henley for inspiring the friendship between Kora and Sage. Even when we lived in different countries, you were my biggest champion, and I wouldn't have had the courage to keep writing without your faith in my skills.

Thank you also to my sisters Kendyl and Harleigh. You're eternally my target audience and my measuring sticks for what's interesting and cool.

To my parents, for gifting me with their creativity, providing me with all the resources they could manage, and allowing me to go to the most expensive college in the country, only to support me when I said I wanted to come home. And for never telling me to get a real major.

To my Aunt Cindy for keeping my first ever book, *The Blue Butterfly*, which I wrote when I was six. To Meredith Neal and Audrey Shafer, my two grandmothers, who unfortunately were unable to see this book be published but who I know are proud of me.

To every teacher who has made me feel special and talented and seen—especially Margie Baker, who not only fostered my love for reading, but also showed me a queer future I could aspire to.

To Lisa Kastner at Running Wild Press for saying yes. To Aimee Hardy for approaching this book with kindness and enthusiasm.

Eight years ago when I started writing this book, LGBTQ+ young adult fiction was a very slim genre, and since then, I've watched it become a thriving community of writers and readers. All of you are to thank for this book having an audience. I'm so, so proud to be one of you.

And to North Carolina, a beautiful state with a lot of flaws and a complicated history, which made me who I am. And to everyone here who works so hard to make it better.

About Rize Press

RIZE publishes great stories and great writing across genres written by People of Color and other underrepresented groups. Our team consists of:

Lisa Diane Kastner, Founder and Executive Editor

Joelle Mitchell, Licensing and Strategy Lead

Cody Sisco, Acquisition Editor, RIZE

Benjamin White, Acquisition Editor, Running Wild

Peter A. Wright, Acquisition Editor, Running Wild

Resa Alboher, Editor

Angela Andrews, Editor

Sandra Bush, Editor

Ashley Crantas, Editor

Rebecca Dimyan, Editor

Abigail Efird, Editor

Aimee Hardy, Editor

Henry L. Herz, Editor

Cecilia Kennedy, Editor

Barbara Lockwood, Editor

AE Williams, Editor

Scott Schultz, Editor

Rod Gilley, Editor

Kelly Ottiano, Editor

Carolyn Banks, Editor

Evangeline Estropia, Product Manager

Pulp Art Studios, Cover Design

Standout Books, Interior Design

Polgarus Studios, Interior Design

Learn more about us and our stories at www.
runningwildpublishing.com

Loved this story and want more?

Follow us at
www.runningwildpublishing.com,
www.facebook.com/runningwildpress,
on Twitter @lisadkastner @RunWildBooks @RwpRIZE